THE VAMPIRE AND THE HUNTER TRILOGY: BOOK ONE

THE VAMPIRE, THE HUNTER, and the Girl

MARTIN LASTRAPES

Also by Martin Lastrapes

Inside the Outside

The Vampire, the Hunter, and the Girl

www.MartinLastrapes.com

Paper: 978-0-9857043-2-2
eBook: 978-0-9857043-3-9

Requests to publish work from this book should be sent to:
martin.lastrapes@gmail.com

Cover Design: Rowan Stocks-Moore
Back Cover/Spine Design: AuthorSupport.com
Interior Design: AuthorSupport.com
Proofreader: Rosemi Mederos
Author Photograph: Greg Lastrapes

First Edition

For Mommy and Daddy

When it is dark enough, you can see the stars.
–Ralph Waldo Emerson

For what is it to die but to stand naked in the wind
and to melt into the sun?
–Kahlil Gibran

PROLOGUE

Somewhere beneath the earth, through the dirt and below the sewers, past the roots and beyond the rocks, was an underground palace with tall marble walls and elegant paintings, fireplaces the size of bedrooms and tuxedoed servants who moved swiftly and quietly. Of the hundreds and thousands of rooms within this palace, there was one particularly big room with walls so high the light turned black before it reached the ceiling. Like every other room in the palace, it had a fireplace and elegant paintings, but, *unlike* every other room, it had three chairs lined up side by side at its center, each respectively occupied by the vampire, the hunter, and the girl.

The three of them had burlap sacks over their heads, concealing their vision. One of the palace's swift and quiet servants entered the marble room through its exceedingly tall doors, approaching the vampire, the hunter, and the girl, removing the burlap sacks from their heads. As the trio looked around, trying to figure out where they were, the servant made a swift and quiet exit. While they could now see their surroundings, they couldn't move to explore them, as their arms and legs were strapped to their respective chairs.

"What's going on?" asked the hunter.

"This feels like a dream," said the girl.

"This is no dream," said the vampire.

Their voices echoed up the tall marble walls, trailing off somewhere in the darkness. The tall doors opened again and another tuxedoed servant entered the room with such swift quietude that he seemed almost to float as he walked to the fireplace, which was burning logs the size of full-grown trees. The servant pushed a button on the marble wall beside the fireplace and, in an instant, the fire inside doubled in size, sending a wave of heat through the air.

"Excuse me," said the girl to the servant, "what's going on?"

The servant, however, ignored the girl and her question before exiting the tall marble room. Once again alone, the vampire, the hunter, and the girl sat silently, each of them equally confused as to where they were and, more importantly, why they were there together. The tall doors opened once again and a long red rug unrolled towards the trio, stopping at their feet. A couple dozen tuxedoed servants poured through the open doors, lining up shoulder to shoulder on either side of the red rug. From the darkness of the open doors, a methodical clicking of heels sounded, growing louder and louder, until a tall, handsome figure appeared in the doorway. The servants all dropped to one knee, bowing their heads as the handsome figure passed, walking down the long red rug.

This figure—who was, in fact, their captor—wore a dark suit with a red tie. His black hair was slick and shiny, combed tight over his scalp, displaying a pointed widow's peak. His skin was pale, his cheeks sharp. His lips were rosy and his teeth white, each of them perfectly straight, not a molar out of place. When the tall, handsome figure reached the end of the rug, four more of his servants entered the marble room with a large throne made of solid gold and red velvet, setting it down behind him. Without looking back, the handsome figure sat down. He looked over each of his guests—the vampire, the hunter, and the girl—smiling as he crossed his legs, setting his hands in his lap. All at once, the servants poured out of the tall marble room, shutting the doors behind them, leaving their master alone with his guests.

"Hello," he said. "Welcome to my home. I am Dracula."

PART ONE

THE VAMPIRE LOOPHOLE

CHAPTER ONE

THE VAMPIRE

Adam first sucked Olivia's blood in the sandbox of Heritage Park, stopping briefly to yank the silver crucifix from her neck as it seared a red cross into the top of his hand. Kneeled beneath the jungle gym with Olivia cradled in his arms, Adam buried his face into the nape of her neck, his fangs breaking the skin down to her throbbing carotid artery. She moaned as he entered her, blood trickling down, pooling in the shallow dip of her clavicle. Adam felt the air move as her eyelids fluttered shut. He'd been waiting for this moment for so long, to feel her blood pulsing over his lips, delicious and warm. His head spun, dizzy with satisfaction, the full moon overhead, flanked by an unmotivated flock of sparsely present stars.

Adam had watched Olivia from afar for weeks, biding his time. He knew her routine, knew her schedule. He knew when she worked at the strip club and when she worked at the bowling alley. On this night, when Adam would finally pull the trigger, Olivia was working a late shift at the bowling alley. Adam waited outside, amongst the darkness, watching as she exited through the sliding doors, finally done for the night. She walked through the mostly empty parking lot, hurrying to her car, the sweet smell of fear lifting from her pores, like the sugary perfume of a pastry shop.

As Olivia passed him in the darkness, unaware of his presence, Adam engaged his amplified vampire senses, taking her in, smelling the coffee and donuts she'd had for breakfast, the veggie burger and fries she'd had for lunch, the shot of tequila she'd had an hour earlier to help get through her shift. He could smell the hybrid odor of metal and gasoline from the pump, the offensive smell mingling with her sweet scent as she nervously ran her hand along her neck. He could smell the heavy scent of smoke in her hair and the salty layer of dried perspiration on her skin. He could hear her irritated throat, tender from yelling over loud music and drunken bowlers.

As she reached her car, he could hear the silent pulse of Olivia's cell phone vibrating in her purse, quickening the beat of her heart, exasperating her already heightened state of anxiety. He watched as she burrowed her hand through her purse, searching for her keys, cursing under her breath for not taking them out before she exited the bowling alley. Only after she was in her car, doors locked, exhaling a relieved breath inside of her illusion of safety, did Olivia check her phone to see who'd called. Pressing the phone to her ear, she listened to the voicemail. Adam listened as well, lying belly-down atop the roof of her car. "Hey, Olivia, it's Jesus. Just checking to see if you wanted to grab something to eat. Maybe we could watch a movie at my place or something. I'm going to be up for a while, so call me back when you get this. Later."

Adam gripped the edges of her roof with his fingertips, his vampire strength holding him steady, no matter how fast she drove, how hard she turned. Exiting the parking lot, Olivia cracked her window open, unwittingly giving Adam access to her delicious scent. Foothill Boulevard was practically empty, save for a few random cars. Olivia accelerated, pushing her car up to fifty miles per hour, the rush of wind pouring over Adam, blowing his hair back as they got onto the 210 Freeway. Adam would've been incapable of keeping up with Olivia's car, despite his ability to sprint faster than any of the fastest humans on earth.

Blood burned through his system like a combustion engine, so even if he were silly enough to try and chase down Olivia's car by foot, Adam would rapidly burn through the source of his amplified physical abilities. These weren't the sorts of lessons a vampire learned on their own. It was the responsibility of the vampire's maker to teach them how to exist in the world. The maker served the role of caretaker and mentor. Even when vampires were capable of taking care of themselves, they usually stayed with their maker for as long as possible. Adam's maker was a female named Cherry. "Don't take your strength for granted," Cherry told him. "A prudent vampire will never find himself desperate for blood. If you ever find that you're running low, it means you've made a series of bad decisions. If you only ever learn one thing from me, just remember that a weak vampire is a vulnerable vampire—even to humans."

Olivia exited onto Carnelian Street, which Adam was expecting, as that's how she always drove home. What he wasn't expecting, however, was for her to turn left, due north, towards Heritage Park, instead of right, due south, towards her apartment. Up to this point in his hunt, Adam knew exactly what to expect, but now, with Olivia taking an uncommon turn, he found himself feeling the excitement of the unknown, a pleasure he rarely enjoyed anymore. In his human days, Adam took for granted how much he didn't know about the world. This was especially true when he was a kid. When the adults around him knew things that he didn't know (the difference between the Congress and the Senate, for instance, or which religion was right) Adam took it as affirmation that, if you lived long enough, you'd learn a great many things.

And one of the first things Adam learned upon becoming a vampire was that immortality lasts a long, long time. He was still young for a vampire, only thirty years old (if he were still human, he'd be sixty). In terms of immortality, thirty years was a blink of the eye, a snap of the fingers. Within that first blink, Adam learned he could get by without having a job, which was nice. If he needed money, there was always a way to get it. And, when you're immortal, you have more time to save money and fewer reasons to spend it. But, while money wasn't an issue for Adam, boredom generally was.

Being immortal didn't make time move any faster—minutes were still minutes, years were years, seconds seconds—so if you couldn't figure out ways to pass the time, being a vampire would become extremely boring in a hurry. When they weren't on the lookout for human blood, passing time for vampires was much the same as passing time for humans. So, in the interest of trying to pacify his boredom, Adam did the same things he would've done if he were still human, which included bowling.

Adam had been bowling a lot more lately, though there was a long period of time—after becoming a vampire—where he hadn't bowled at all. The main reason he'd stopped was because it was at the bowling alley where Cherry turned him. Despite their eventual friendship, Adam didn't regard the memory of his turning fondly. When it came to becoming a vampire, Adam wasn't given a choice— no reasonable choice anyhow. He hated Cherry for a long time, hated her for taking away that which made him human, hated her for taking him away from his wife.

Before he was a vampire, Adam was married to a lovely woman named Emily. Poor Emily, she had no idea what happened to her husband, why he disappeared from her life. One night he went to work at the bowling alley and, without word or warning, she never saw him again. Adam never did get to say a proper goodbye to Emily. And, because of it, he held his resentment towards Cherry for a good decade or so. "Listen," Cherry told him, "one of the most important laws guiding us vampires is we can't carry on relationships with humans, regardless of the circumstances, even if the human in question used to be your wife. I know you're upset with me and I'm sorry about that, but there's nothing that can be done about it. For better or worse, the law is the law." Because she was the only vampire he knew, Adam accepted Cherry's mentorship and companionship—it would be a long while, however, before he accepted her friendship.

Vampires, for the most part, lose their connection to humanity over time. For some vampires it can be quick, almost instantaneous, while for others it may take two or three centuries. And still, for other vampires, it may take even longer than that. Adam still had many attachments to his former humanity—namely, Emily. In time, he accepted that he could never be a part of Emily's life again, but he never accepted being away from her. Nearly every day of his vampire life, Adam sat in the tree he'd once planted with Emily in their backyard. From that perch, he watched Emily through the windows of his former home, living out her mortal life one breath at a time.

For a very long time, Adam's routine as a vampire boiled down to hanging with Cherry, drinking blood at the Barbershop, and watching Emily. Cherry knew Adam watched Emily from afar and, while she didn't approve of it, she didn't bother him about it. She herself had no such connections—and hadn't for a very, very long time—but Cherry could still appreciate that Adam did and probably always would, at least until Emily died her inevitable death. When Adam wasn't spending time perched in his former tree, Cherry taught him how to hunt for blood and how to be social with other vampires. She let him live in her home and drive her car. She gave him someone to laugh with, a companion to tally the years. They grew so close that Adam could hardly remember ever hating Cherry at all.

And then one night she was gone.

He had no idea of what'd happened to her. It wasn't unusual for Adam to wake up and find Cherry gone, but, because she always came home, he learned not to worry. It was only when Cherry's absence went from days to weeks that he feared the worst. None of his vampire acquaintances knew anything about where Cherry was or what might've happened to her. When the weeks turned to months, Adam had no choice but to accept that Cherry was never coming back. He knew without question that she wouldn't have abandoned him. And while it wasn't unheard of for vampires to kill themselves,

Adam also knew Cherry wouldn't have taken her own life. She loved being a vampire far too much. As far as Adam was concerned, there was only one possible explanation.

"Vampire hunters," Cherry told him. "They're real. Very real."

"Have you ever seen one?"

"No."

"How can you be sure then?"

"I can't be sure," Cherry said. "You can't ever be sure of something you've never seen. It's about faith. I believe it. I've known too many vampires—*good* vampires—who've disappeared for no good reason. A lot of the boys at the Barbershop think it's silly talk, some sort of fairytale meant to keep vampires in line. A bogeyman. While I've never seen one with my own eyes, you can trust me when I tell you, vampire hunters are as real as the fangs beneath your lips."

"I know vampires disappear sometimes," Adam said, "but couldn't there be other reasons?"

"Mark my words," Cherry said. "If I ever disappear, know that it was a vampire hunter who took me away."

Adam never would learn what happened to her. Whether a vampire hunter killed her or she simply fell asleep under the sun, the reality was Cherry was gone and she was never coming back. Not ever. Without her around, Adam found himself to be quite lonely. And bored. Hoping only to pass the time and curb his boredom, Adam went back to the place where Cherry had turned him. The bowling alley. And it was there inside the bowling alley, sitting in the bar as he waited for a lane to open up, that Adam first laid eyes on Olivia. It would be several weeks after seeing her that first night that Adam would finally decide to strike.

Lying on the roof of her car, feeling the wind in his face, Adam thought about his prior days scoping Olivia's apartment complex and how his initial plans might have to be amended. He'd originally planned on hiding in the darkness behind the dumpster adjacent to her bedroom window. The dumpster was inside of a cinderblock shed, topless so as to give residents easy access when taking out their trash. There was room enough between the grimy steel of the dumpster and the cinderblock walls for Adam to have his way with Olivia. He'd imagined hiding in the shed, waiting for her to pass. Once she was within reach, he would snatch her. Even if there were people around, his speed and stealth, in conjunction with the night sky, would keep anybody from noticing. And of course, if that weren't good enough and there were any witnesses, there was not a human in the Inland Empire capable of disciplining him—at least, no human that Adam was yet aware of.

But, instead of her apartment complex, Olivia drove up the hill to Heritage Park, about five minutes away from where she lived. She parked on the street alongside the fenced-off walking trail. As she got out of the car, Adam slid off of the roof, quiet as a ghost, ducking beneath the windows. He maneuvered his way around the car, concealing himself from Olivia's view as she walked past, climbing over the short fence and into the park. He watched her walk along the trail, passing the sandbox and its jungle gym. When she stopped at the crest of the long grassy hill, Adam stalked behind her.

Fast.

Quiet.

He stood behind her for a moment, looking over the city down below, smelling the fear as it lifted from her pores, like she knew what was about to happen. He wrapped his arms around her body, hugging her from behind, pulling her backwards. Moving at such great speed, Olivia's hair flew forward like she was standing with her back to a turbo jet. And in a matter of seconds they were in the sandbox, beneath the jungle gym, Olivia cradled in Adam's powerful arms, his fangs piercing her virginal flesh.

CHAPTER TWO

THE HUNTER

Jesus dressed in black when he hunted, but it was not for camouflage. To camouflage yourself from a vampire was to assume that sight was the only sense they used on the prowl. Should that day come when Jesus was outmatched by a vampire and all that separated him from death were the few moments it would take for the demon monster to do its worst, it would not be because he hadn't blended himself with the night.

Everything about vampires was nocturnal, from the hours they kept to their aversion to sunlight. As evolution would have it, their eyes were made for darkness. To hide from a vampire in the middle of the night was to swim in the ocean to hide from the sharks. No, Jesus had more pragmatic reasons for wearing black while hunting vampires. Bloody reasons that would disgust a sensible person. Gory reasons that belonged in the theater of the macabre.

For them, he was death incarnate.

He was Jesus the Mexican Vampire Hunter.

Jesus Hector Guerrero had become a vampire hunter as the result of both choice and circumstance. To look at his life—from his childhood, watching professional wrestling and playing on Daniel's trampoline, to his adult years, training as a mixed martial artist and smuggling anabolic steroids—it becomes clear that his less-than-straight line into vampire hunting was one that shone with inevitability, like a hungry flame in a dark, dingy cave. But before he kneeled before the television in awe of Royce Gracie or killed his first vampire in Memorial Park, Jesus hid under his bed, shying away from the world, with nothing but a coloring book and a box of crayons to keep him company.

Jesus was a loner by nature and his mother's inability to conceive a sibling for him, despite her best and most passionate efforts with Jesus' father, ensured that he would be an only child. A creative boy with an artistic soul, Jesus loved to draw. One of his earliest memories was of being in preschool and, all of five years old, standing before a large easel with a blank canvas. For no particular reason that he could remember, Jesus decided he wanted to paint a tiger. In his mind's eye, he saw a tremendous cat with ferocious teeth and tangles of muscles beneath its orange and black stripes.

At the conclusion of about five minutes worth of painting, in which every second was a careful meditation of the patience and diligence that would one day come to define him as a vampire hunter, his canvas displayed nothing more than an indecipherable smattering of orange and black paint. Of that memory, what Jesus remembers more clearly than anything else, was the frustration that came with his inability to paint the picture he so clearly saw in his imagination. Jesus abandoned acrylic paint and adopted crayons as his medium of choice, which, of course, led to the inadvertent "disappearance" that would become the centerpiece of his mother's favorite tale.

Maria Katiana Guerrero, proud mother of the future vampire hunter, was downstairs, preparing a grilled cheese sandwich for little Jesus, while listening to *Days of Our Lives* playing in the background. It was a Wednesday afternoon and Maria had decided to keep Jesus home from preschool that day, as it was raining and she feared he might catch a cold. Maria loved being Jesus' mother and she took pride in all of her motherly duties, including—but not limited to—grilling his sandwich to a perfect golden brown, using real butter and producing her own slices from a block of Tillamook cheddar, serving it with a bowl of menudo and a chilled glass of horchata.

She avoided processed and frozen foods, buying only organic groceries, preparing all of her son's meals from scratch. Maria spent an hour or so most every Thursday evening at the 2nd Avenue Farmer's Market buying fresh fruits and vegetables for her kitchen. Despite the symbiotic relationship children often have with fast food, Jesus was, for a short period of time, raised in a world absent of Happy Meals. Whether it was preparing huevos rancheros in the morning or spending the afternoon over a pot of albóndigas for dinner, Maria never hesitated to put in the extra effort to keep her boy healthy, happy, and strong.

Whenever Maria told the story of Jesus' "disappearance"—always with a grin on her face, a nod to her audience that this was a story to be amused by—she began in the kitchen, where she slid Jesus' grilled cheese sandwich onto the plate from the cast-iron skillet before calling upstairs to him. Her call, she would tell her audience, was usually met with the sounds of Jesus bounding down the stairs, running through the hall, and leaping onto the couch like a jungle cat, where she would then place a tray with his lunch in front of him before putting on *Sesame Street*. When, on this day, Jesus' bounding steps didn't follow her call, she called for him again—and again she was met with silence.

Setting the sandwich down on the counter, Maria went upstairs, still calling for Jesus. She walked quickly through the hallway, stopping at his bedroom door, hesitating a moment before knocking, worried that behind the door was a scene not meant to be discovered by a mother's eyes. Knocking lightly, she called again for Jesus. When no answer came she opened the door. Her heart dropped. Jesus was nowhere in sight. Maria ran through the hall and down the stairs, yelling for him. She looked in the bathroom and the hall closet. She looked in the front of the house and the back, calling his name loudly, over and over again.

She picked up the phone and called her husband, Juan Miguel, wiping her streaking tears as she listened to the phone ring and ring on the other end. When he didn't answer, she threw the phone down and went back upstairs to Jesus' room. She didn't know what to do. Seized by the realization that she'd lost the only child she would ever have, Maria's body went limp with agony. She tumbled onto the floor, curling into herself. And then, with her vision blurred by tears, she saw him.

Jesus was lying beneath his bed, sound asleep, a coloring book at his head and a red crayon grasped in his tiny little fingers. Ever the mother, Maria understood the preciousness of the moment and wanted to keep it forever, so she went into her bedroom to retrieve her husband's camera and snapped a picture of her slumbering boy. At this point in her story, Maria pulled the picture out—because she always had it available—and passed it around for her audience to see. She carried that picture of her boy, proudly, lovingly, until the day of her tragic and untimely death.

ᶠᵃᵃᵃᵃᵞ

Jesus patrolled Memorial Park in the dead of night, walking under the darkened trees. He didn't patrol the park because vampires frequented the premises. In fact, in his experience, he rarely found vampires at all—generally speaking, they found him. And that's the way it had to be. Jesus learned early on in his vampire hunting endeavors that a human can't ever really hunt down a vampire. They're too fast, too strong, their instincts too ancient and wily. Jesus knew that the only way to get close enough to kill a vampire was to make himself vulnerable, to act as his own bait.

As he moved through Memorial Park, he kept his ears attuned to the silence. Walking through the small courtyard, faintly lit by the moon, Jesus wore a form-fitting, long sleeve shirt, allowing for the optimum amount of movement in the course of hand-to-hand combat; likewise, his pants were loose, allowing for a similar freedom of movement. Strapped around each of his thighs, outside of his pants, were his two primary weapons. On the left thigh was a small knife with a blade crafted from silver. On the right thigh was a red plastic water gun. Strapped to his ankle, beneath his baggy pants, was his weapon of death: a wooden stake, sharpened to a fine point.

A vampire at full strength was easily capable of overpowering most humans. Jesus, however, wasn't most humans. His muscles were strong and lean, chiseled from years of strength training and Brazilian jiu-jitsu. He supplemented his physical abilities with anabolic steroids, increasing his strength, speed, and endurance. Even with these added advantages, Jesus knew that surviving a night of vampire hunting was not guaranteed. He was well aware of the dangers he encroached upon, regularly pushing his luck like so many chips across a poker table. It wasn't a disregard for the danger that allowed him to go hunting time and time again. On the contrary, Jesus had a healthy fear of death. It kept him sharp, protecting him, never allowing him to bring his guard down, not even for a moment, because he knew a moment was all it would take.

ᵖ•••••ᵖ

Jesus' mother loved soap operas. During the day she watched American soaps—such as *All my Children* and *General Hospital*—while working around the house. In the evenings she watched telenovelas on Telemundo, such as *Dos mujeres, un camino* and *Volver a empezar.* Jesus couldn't be bothered with any of his mother's soap operas, which didn't bother Maria in the least, especially since he loved lucha libre, which was her other favorite pastime. Maria had watched lucha libre since she was a little girl, sitting at her father's feet while he drank beer and cheered on his favorite luchadores. From the time she brought him home from the hospital, Maria and Jesus watched these acrobatic men in masks and tights grappling with each other, punching and kicking, bouncing off ropes, leaping from turnbuckles, and flipping onto concrete.

A not-so-distant second behind his love of lucha libre was Jesus' love of comic books, which he also inherited from his mother. Their favorite comic book hero was Batman. Jesus loved Batman for his humanity, for his lack of superpowers. He loved that Batman lifted himself up to the level of superhero through hard work and determination, transforming his mortal shell into something extraordinary. As much as anything else, however, Jesus loved Batman for his cowl. In this way, Jesus saw Batman as an extension of lucha libre, a brave warrior who fought for justice under the anonymity of a mask.

More than once, Maria told Jesus about the significance of the luchador mask, about its roots in Mexican culture going back to the time of the Aztecs. She told him about how the intricate designs were often meant to evoke images of animals and gods and that the luchador in the mask would embody that image in his style, that it influenced the spirit of how he battled.

"Like Batman?"

Maria smiled.

"Just like Batman," she said. "As Batman, Bruce Wayne embodies the spirit of the bat. More importantly, for he and the luchadores, the mask is sacred. Most luchadores will go their entire lives without ever revealing their faces in public. Whether it's eating out at a restaurant or attending Sunday Mass, a luchador will always do it in his mask. And even when they die, many of them are buried in their mask."

"Were they hiding?"

"No, mijito," she said. "The mask was who they were. To be seen without it would be the true disguise."

As much as he loved Batman, Jesus found the luchadores to be better than any comic book superhero, because they were flesh and blood, their muscles every bit as real as their feats were improbable. His mother's favorite luchador—and, by extension, his own—was El

Santo, an iconic figure in Mexico who was not only a star in the ring but also in comic books and movies. While Jesus never got to see El Santo wrestle, Maria did show him most of the fifty-two films he starred in, including the 1969 film *Santo en el tesoro de Drácula*—or *Santo and Dracula's Treasure.* The story, which Jesus only vaguely remembered, involved El Santo inventing a time machine and using it to go back into the nineteenth century to search for Dracula's treasure, which naturally led to a duel between the two iconic figures. Many years later, after Jesus became a vampire hunter, he thought often of El Santo and the image of him fighting Dracula.

Jesus only briefly considered wearing a mask himself upon becoming a vampire hunter. While it made sense in comic books and wrestling rings, he knew a mask would only serve to make him *more* conspicuous out in public, drawing attention for all the wrong reasons and from all the wrong sources. In the end, he decided silence would be his mask. Nobody would ever know what he did—not his father, not anybody. He would hunt vampires not for praise and not for recognition. He would hunt vampires for justice.

For redemption.

For his mother.

There was a shift in the silence of Memorial Park, causing Jesus to stop. He adjusted his black gloves, pulling them tight between his fingers. A vampire was near—he could feel it. If he were right, then the only question was how this vampire would come at him. Some vampires were wild, clumsy even, in the way they threw themselves at their prey. Others liked to approach their prey from the front, politely, almost honorably, leaving themselves in full view, giving their soon-to-be victim time to appreciate what was about to happen. And then there was the smooth vampire, softly turning up from behind, offering a whispered word or two before sinking their teeth.

On this night, Jesus got the smooth vampire.

"Good evening," the vampire whispered.

He wrapped Jesus in his arms, his lips all but touching his ear. Jesus stood motionless, allowing himself to be held.

"You'll be dead soon," said the vampire. "But, not tonight. I'm going to enjoy you first. We all will."

Jesus closed his eyes, relaxing his brain, allowing his instincts to become one with the moment. The vampire gripped Jesus' hair, yanking his head back, exposing his neck. With a snarl, he exposed his fangs before attacking Jesus' neck. And, with a smile, Jesus let him.

Vampires hate garlic. It won't kill them, but it burns like acid. And despite their heightened sense of smell, vampires can't detect garlic with their olfactory system. Even if there were a clove of garlic resting beneath their nose, a vampire could close its eyes and never know it was there. Having figured this out early on, Jesus devised a few ingenious methods to use to his advantage. One of Jesus' most successful innovations was his garlic broth, which he made by simply boiling a bundle of garlic bulbs in a pot of water. Once the broth was good and strong, he funneled it into his water gun.

His other successful innovation involved taking a large bundle of garlic bulbs, removing the cloves and grilling them in a skillet, extracting all of the essential oils before crushing it all together into a fine paste. He then added a large scoop of petroleum jelly to the garlic mush, stirring it all together before pouring it into a jar where it cooled and congealed into garlic jelly. Before every hunt, Jesus applied this garlic jelly to his face and neck.

And so, at Memorial Park, upon making contact with Jesus' neck, the smooth vampire leapt back, howling like a wounded animal as he clutched his mouth with both hands. With the vampire thus stunned, Jesus pulled the water gun from his hip and shot four quick squirts in the vampire's eyes, causing him to scream, holding his face in agony. Jesus' garlic attack alone, while effective, would not be enough to kill the vampire. Vampires were resilient and, while this one was temporarily blinded, he would fully recover in a matter of minutes. And, even without sight, he was still plenty dangerous.

Jesus pulled out his silver blade, moving cautiously ahead. The vampire removed his hands from his face and held them out in front of himself, grasping at the air like a man in the dark. With his silver blade, Jesus deftly slashed each of the vampire's wrists, opening them up. As the vampire thrashed about in pain, blood pouring out, Jesus stepped in again, striking him across the neck, opening him up beneath his chin.

Like garlic, vampires were also vulnerable to silver. While they weren't impervious to being penetrated by manmade weapons, such as bullets or knives, they healed from those wounds in seconds, registering only a minimum of pain. Silver, on the other hand, caused vampires a great deal of pain, the sort that a human would feel if they touched a piece of hot metal. And, more importantly than the pain itself, silver-inflicted wounds lasted longer, taking hours to heal.

Jesus watched the vampire stumbling around in pain, holding his neck as the blood pulsed through his pale fingers. Slipping his knife back into its holster, Jesus charged the vampire, tackling him to the ground. Though he was weakened, Jesus knew the vampire would still own the advantage in strength for at least a little while longer. In order to hasten his blood loss, Jesus grappled with the vampire in the grass, defending himself with Brazilian jiu-jitsu. Within a few minutes—which, for Jesus, never ceased to feel like anything but a lifetime—the vampire was all but empty, no longer able to put up a fight.

Jesus put the vampire on his back, straddling his belly, arms pinned beneath his knees. He tore open the vampire's shirt, revealing his pale chest, colored only by the red that streaked from his neck. Jesus retrieved the wooden stake from his ankle holster and, clasping it in both hands, aimed it over the vampire's heart.

"What are you?" the vampire asked.

"For you, I am death incarnate," he said. "I am Jesus the Mexican Vampire Hunter."

He brought the stake down with all his strength, piercing it through the vampire's heart. Standing to his feet, Jesus watched the vampire melt away, flesh and blood merging into a crimson goo, seeping into the grass. All that was left behind were the vampire's clothes, soaked in red. Taking a moment to examine himself, Jesus didn't look all that worse for wear. He had two tiny puncture wounds in his neck where the vampire's fangs had briefly made contact, but they would scab over soon enough and be gone in a day or so. His clothes, however, were wet with the vampire's blood. He anticipated this, of course—expected it, really—which was why he always wore black when he hunted.

Collecting his weapons, Jesus walked back to his car, Olivia on his mind. Looking at the time, he figured she'd soon be leaving the bowling alley, so he gave her a call, letting it ring until he got her voicemail: "Hey, Olivia, it's Jesus. Just checking to see if you wanted to grab something to eat. Maybe we could watch a movie at my place or something. I'm going to be up for a while, so call me back when you get this. Later."

CHAPTER THREE

THE GIRL

In a matter of seconds, Olivia was in the sandbox, beneath the jungle gym, cradled in the powerful arms of a handsome man with pale skin and fangs beneath his lips. Her silver crucifix hung from her neck, causing him to yelp in pain as it touched his hand. Yanking it from her neck, he tossed it into the sand before pressing his lips to her flesh. She moaned as his fangs entered her, blood trickling out. With the moment finally upon her, Olivia found that it didn't hurt nearly as much as she thought it might—the anticipation was far worse than the reality.

It had all begun as such an average day, sleeping in until noon before going to the donut shop with her roommate, Elowyn. Elowyn was a stripper at Tropical Lei. Olivia also worked at Tropical Lei when she wasn't working at the Brunswick bowling alley, just down the way from Memorial Park. Elowyn hadn't slept all night and was up watching TV when Olivia got out of bed. They lived in a pleasant apartment complex adjacent to a Vons shopping center, across the street from DN Top Donuts, which was a family-owned shop that Olivia and Elowyn frequented almost daily. Soon after eating their donuts and coffee, Elowyn fell asleep, leaving Olivia to get on with her day.

Part of getting on with her day involved sitting in front of her computer with the intention of beginning her first novel. She'd been trying for weeks—unsuccessfully—to begin this novel, giving up each time when she could no longer stand the taunting presence of the blank page. Olivia had what she assumed was inspiration, as well as a chosen genre. Vampires. What she lacked was a compelling story to tell. She'd assumed all along that writing a vampire novel would come easily to her, given how much she loved watching vampire shows on TV, namely *Buffy the Vampire Slayer*. Any time she sat down to write her vampire novel, however, Olivia invariably allowed herself to be distracted with checking her email and perusing eBay, with the occasional detour into YouTube, which inevitably led her into the rabbit hole of Internet porn. But, she always forced herself back to the blank page, beginning the whole process over again.

When she finished staring at her blank page for the day, Olivia went to Brandon's Diner for lunch, eating a veggie burger and fries. She took along a Tom Robbins book to read while she ate, hoping that it might massage the beginnings of a story out of her clenched imagination. By the time Olivia got home from lunch, Elowyn was back on the couch watching TV. Olivia joined her on the couch, passing the next few hours like that until it was time to start her shift at the bowling alley. On her way to work, despite running late, she stopped to get gas; even if it meant getting chewed out by her boss, it would be worth it when she didn't have to stop for gas in the middle of the night, leaving herself vulnerable to whatever dangers might be lurking.

Olivia worked as a bartender in Brunswick's lounge. It was generally empty during the day, which was why she preferred working nights. This was a Friday night, which was always busy for Brunswick. The lanes were filled with serious and frivolous bowlers alike, from high school kids and college students to nuclear families and middle-aged bachelors. There was a Lakers game on, which was always good for business, as it attracted stragglers into the lounge, many of whom ended up buying drinks—and, more importantly, leaving tips—while waiting for a lane to open up. However much she enjoyed the money, however, Olivia wasn't a fan of the general ruckus of the bowling alley, so she began most all of her shifts with a shot of tequila.

After the Lakers game was over, the lounge remained relatively busy and the night itself turned into a profitable one for Olivia. By the time the bowling alley was ready to close, Olivia cleaned up the bar and headed out. Stepping through the sliding doors out into the cool midnight air, Olivia was overcome with dread. The parking lot was mostly empty, save for her car and a couple of others. She walked quickly through the parking lot, ignoring her instinct to run. Her cell phone pulsed her in purse, the feel of its vibration startling her. She wouldn't answer it, however, as all she wanted was to be inside of her car, doors locked. Olivia burrowed her hand through her purse, searching for her keys, cursing under her breath for not taking them out before she'd stepped through the sliding doors. Her phone stopped vibrating a few moments after she found her keys.

Only after she was safely in her car did Olivia bother to see who'd called her. It was Jesus. Despite her urge to drive away as soon as possible, she took a moment to listen to her voicemail—mostly out of guilt, since she didn't plan on calling him back anytime before sunrise: "Hey, Olivia, it's Jesus. Just checking to see if you wanted to grab something to eat. Maybe we could watch a movie at my place or something. I'm going to be up for a while, so call me back when you get this. Later."

If any other guy had called her at that time of night, Olivia would've assumed he was looking to get laid. Jesus, however, wasn't that type of guy. She appreciated that about him. She knew that if she called him back to take him up on his offer, they really would grab a bite to eat and watch a movie. If she weren't so tired, she might've actually taken him up on his offer. Instead, she started her car and drove out the parking lot, cracking her window as she did, letting the fresh air seep in. Foothill Boulevard was practically empty, save for a few random cars, so Olivia stepped on the gas pedal, accelerating to fifty miles per hour. She kept an eye out for cops, as the last thing she wanted was a speeding ticket.

With her hands on the wheel, driving from Upland back to her apartment in Rancho Cucamonga, Olivia thought about her novel. All she could see, however, was one single blank page. She'd never really suffered writer's block, not this severely anyhow. Up to that point, she'd only ever written short stories but she was pretty good at it. She'd even gotten one published. The writers she admired were novelists, and she wanted to be counted amongst them. But, for whatever reason, something about writing her first novel petrified her.

Early on in their friendship, when she'd told Elowyn she wanted to write a book, she asked Olivia what kind.

"A novel."

"I thought *all* books were novels."

"All novels are *books*," Olivia told her, "but not all books are novels."

"So when I say that I hate *novels*," Elowyn said, "what I really mean is I hate *books*?"

"Exactly."

Olivia didn't begrudge Elowyn her disdain of books, since she, herself, didn't really start reading with earnest until she was a freshman at Chaffey College. Before she'd discovered her love of books, Olivia thought she might become a screenwriter. She didn't really know much of anything about screenwriting except that she liked movies and figured it couldn't be all that hard. But from the time she was a little girl, long before she'd ever considered becoming a writer of any sort, Olivia loved watching professional wrestling with her mother. And, unbeknownst to her, the countless hours she spent watching wrestling would one day become the foundation of her storytelling sensibilities.

Olivia's mother rarely got out of bed, as she was stricken with a handful of different ailments, such as fibromyalgia and Addison's disease, forcing her into retirement when Olivia was still a child. Because she was a single mother, this meant she could be home all the time with Olivia—but, because her body betrayed her on a daily basis, she rarely left the house. When she did get herself out, it was usually for a special occasion, like back-to-school shopping or a hot fudge sundae on Olivia's birthday. Olivia didn't know any different, however, so lying in bed with her mother and watching TV for hours at a time was as normal as anything else in her world.

Every Saturday afternoon they watched *WWF Superstars of Wrestling*, and every Sunday afternoon they watched *WWF Wrestling Challenge*. Olivia loved watching the stories unfold as the wrestlers battled each other week after week, and at the end of each program, she would spend hours talking to her mother about what she imagined would happen in the coming weeks. Olivia hadn't yet learned that the storylines were written and the outcomes of the matches were predetermined, so it never occurred to her that—in those conversations she had with her mother, wondering, for example, if Mr. T could hold his own against "Rowdy" Roddy Piper or if "Jumping" Jim Brunzell was the better of the Killer Bees—she was actually using the same creative muscles that would one day serve her as a novelist.

As much as Olivia's mother loved wrestling, she hated vampires, so, after *Buffy the Vampire Slayer* premiered on the WB in 1997, Olivia was all alone in her enthusiasm. Olivia watched every episode of *Buffy* each week on the WB, and as all loyal fans did, she followed the show to UPN in 2001. As soon as box sets became available, Olivia bought every season of *Buffy*. She even bought an illegal copy of the musical episode, "Once More, with Feeling," on eBay before the Season Six box set was available.

Years after the show was off the air, Olivia came across an interview with *Buffy* creator, Joss Whedon. In the interview, Whedon talked about his inspiration for *Buffy*, how he wanted the vampires and werewolves and witches and demons to serve as metaphors and allegories for the struggles and battles teenagers face as they grow into adulthood. Olivia loved this idea and figured she'd write a screenplay about vampires. At this point in her journey, Olivia had dreams of being a screenwriter, mostly because she loved movies and hoped one day to be a part of the Academy Awards. She was relieved of her screenwriting aspirations during her first year at Chaffey College after she enrolled in a creative writing course. The class was taught by Professor Winters—first name, Arthur—and, under his tutelage, Olivia discovered she had a knack for writing prose fiction. Not long after she completed that class, Olivia decided she wanted to be a novelist. Olivia was happy that her mother got to see how excited she was about becoming a writer before she passed away a couple of years later.

She was barely twenty years old when her mother died, leaving her an orphan without any extended family. The closest thing she'd had to family, outside of her mother, was a friend in elementary school whose parents often invited her to join them in their weekend outings. That family disappeared from Olivia's life far sooner than she would've liked when the dad got a new job out of state. In the years that followed, Olivia never resented her mother for being unable to take her to Disneyland or barbecues at the park, as she knew her body simply wouldn't allow it. She only wished that life could've dealt her mother a fairer hand, a healthier one, so that Olivia could've spent more time being her little girl.

These were the thoughts passing through her mind as she pulled off the 210 Freeway, exiting Carnelian Street. For no good reason that she could think of, other than feeling a bit nostalgic for the simpler times of years past, Olivia went to Heritage Park. She parked on the street alongside the fenced-off walking trail, where she entered the park by foot. All the lights were out, but she didn't mind. She walked along the trail in the darkness, passing the sandbox that held the jungle gym and stopping at the peak of the steep grassy hill where she'd once spent a whole afternoon gliding down on ice blocks. That large stretch of green opened up at her feet like an emerald tidal wave, its dewy blades glistening beneath the moonlight.

She remembered playing soccer in her bare feet, flying her first kite, and eating charred hotdogs and pink lemonade. She missed that generous family who squeezed her into their backseat and packed a little extra food, who included her in their photos and took her to church for the first time, eventually giving her the only crucifix she would ever own. She wanted to smell the grass, feel the crunch of sand beneath her heels, slide down the slide and swing on the swing. She smiled, looking out over her city, Rancho Cucamonga, enjoying the twinkling lights of that Inland Empire suburb as they met the stars halfway, marveling at how small it all seemed when she stood on top of the world.

As she looked out over the city, an invisible force clamped around her, holding her in place while the world was yanked away. When her long black hair flew forward like she was standing with her back to a turbo jet, Olivia realized it wasn't the world being pulled away from her, but her being pulled away from the world. And in a matter of seconds she was in the sandbox, beneath the jungle gym, cradled in the powerful arms of a handsome man with pale skin and fangs beneath his lips. The last thing she saw, before closing her eyes and passing out, was the full moon overhead, flanked by an unmotivated flock of sparsely present stars.

CHAPTER FOUR

THE GIANT WOODEN FANG

When Jesus got home, he took off his bloody shoes and socks, leaving them on the porch in front of his apartment. It was after midnight and he hadn't heard back from Olivia. He hoped she was okay, that she'd safely returned home from work. If he'd known where she lived, he might've even gone to check on her, though he was relatively sure she might've found the gesture more creepy than endearing. For now, he would clean himself up and hope to hear back from her before he fell asleep.

At the foot of his bed was a hand-carved wooden trunk built by his great-grandfather who lived his whole life in Tijuana, Mexico, dying before Jesus had an opportunity to meet him. Jesus' mother received the trunk as a gift after her grandfather passed away, and so she, along with Juan Miguel and Jesus, traveled down to Tijuana to pick it up. They drove in Juan Miguel's pickup truck for nearly two hours before crossing the border. For Jesus, this was his first time going to Mexico.

They spent a few hours visiting with Maria's relatives, none of whom Jesus had ever met before. Juan Miguel played cards with a couple of old men on a flimsy folding table, while Maria drank coffee and laughed with one of the women. Jesus sat on the floor with the only other kid his age. Neither spoke the other's language, so after a few feeble attempts to communicate, they simply sat in silence in front of the television and watched cartoons. When Juan Miguel was ready to leave, a couple of the younger men helped him put the wooden trunk into the back of the pickup truck, while Jesus and Maria waited in the front seat.

Jesus remembered being parked in a long line of cars, each of them intent on entering America. As the pickup truck got closer to the front of the line, Jesus' mother looked at him very seriously and said, "There will be a man at the front who is going to ask you what country you're from. Make sure you tell him you're from America."

Jesus joked that he would instead tell the man he was from Mexico.

"No!" Maria yelled.

Jesus wasn't accustomed to such an angry tone from his mother and so he began to cry. Maria cradled his head in her arms and apologized for yelling. But, she didn't back off from the point she was trying to make.

"You can't joke like that when we get to the front of the line, mijito," she said. "If you tell them you're from Mexico, they'll keep you here. Do you understand?"

Jesus shook his head, yes.

As they waited in the line, several vendors passed by the cars on foot offering various trinkets and eats. Maria bought a bag of fresh churros—a cinnamon-and-sugar coated apology, which Jesus happily accepted. When finally they reached the front of the line, a uniformed man leaned his head into the window and asked Juan Miguel how many people he was traveling with. Upon receiving the answer, the uniformed man then asked each of them what country they were citizens of. When it was time for Jesus to reply, he felt his mother's arms tense around his body.

"I'm from America."

The uniformed man nodded before looking at Juan Miguel and asking his next question.

"What's in the trunk?"

"Nothing," Juan Miguel said. "It's empty."

The uniformed man asked to look inside, so Juan Miguel got out of the pickup truck and followed to the back. Jesus and his mother stayed inside.

"Are we in trouble?" he asked.

"No, mijito," his mother said. "They just want to make sure we're not bringing anybody from Mexico back with us."

"Why would we do that?"

"Because America is a wonderful country," she said, "and many people here would like to live there."

"Why don't they?"

"They're not allowed."

"Why not?"

"It's against the law."

"That's not a nice law."

"I agree, mijito."

"Who makes the laws?"

"Somebody more powerful than us."

When the uniformed man was satisfied with his inspection, he waved him off, letting him drive his family back into America. After arriving home, Maria and Jesus helped him carry the wooden trunk into the living room, setting it down in what everybody assumed would be a temporary spot. It sat there for many months, unused, until Jesus' mother eventually started storing blankets and sheets inside of it. After her sudden death, the trunk stayed in the same spot, untouched, holding the same set of blankets and sheets. It stayed there until Jesus was eighteen and moved out into his first and only apartment with his best friend, Daniel, taking the trunk with him. Juan Miguel seemed almost too happy to be rid of it.

While Jesus initially wanted the trunk as a memento of his mother, it later served a practical purpose, as it was ideal for housing his vampire-hunting gear. Opening the trunk, he placed his water gun, silver knife, and wooden stake inside. The trunk was already partially full with his other weapons, all of them variations of the ones he'd used earlier that evening. Removing his pants and shirt, both of which were covered with vampire blood, Jesus stuffed them into a trash bag inside the trunk.

Getting into the shower, Jesus stood beneath the hot water for nearly twenty minutes before soaping up. The crown of his head leaning against the tile wall, he watched the water at his feet swirl with streaks of red, disappearing down the drain. He washed his hair three times before he was satisfied that it was free of the vampire's blood. Even after he was sufficiently clean, he stayed in the shower for ten more minutes, a treat for his tired muscles.

After his shower, Jesus stood in front the bathroom mirror, checking the two tiny marks the vampire left on his neck. There was hardly anything to see, so he dabbed them with peroxide before leaving them be. Still naked, he examined the rest of his body for battle wounds. Relatively speaking, he was mark free. He knew from experience, however, that he'd wake up in the morning with at least a few new bruises.

Jesus slipped into a pair of flannel pajama pants, grabbed a couple of energy bars and a can of coconut water from the fridge, and sat down in front of the TV. He kept his cell phone near, hoping that Olivia might call him back. Sifting through his DVR, he found an Ultimate Fighting Championship program that he set to record while he was out vampire hunting. It was a retrospective show looking back at the early days of the UFC, spotlighting several mixed martial arts pioneers, including Jesus' all-time favorite mixed martial artist, Royce Gracie. After Maria was killed, leaving Jesus lost and heartbroken, the UFC and Royce Gracie played an imperative role in the shaping of his life.

Maria's funeral was on a rainy Wednesday morning. Jesus remembered walking under an umbrella, holding his father's hand as they entered St. Joseph's Catholic Church, the pews filled with grieving friends and family. He sat up front with his father, facing the closed casket. Jesus didn't cry at the funeral, and when well-wishers came by to give their condolences, they mistook his lack of tears for bravery, a young boy endeavoring to be a man before his time. It would've been endearing if it were true, but the truth was that Jesus didn't completely understand what was going on. His mother had been gone before, but she'd always come back. His father, too lost in his own grief, hadn't yet impressed upon Jesus the reality that his mother would not be coming home.

Jesus remembered standing beside his father in front of the closed casket at the conclusion of the service. Jesus hadn't understood that the gesture of a closed casket meant his mother's body wasn't appropriate for viewing. Juan Miguel ran the flat of his hand over the top of the glossy lid before leaning over and giving it a kiss over where he knew her lips would be. He then lifted Jesus up into his arms, telling him to give his mother a kiss. Jesus understood that his mother was in the box but didn't understand why kissing it would make a difference to her. It wasn't until Juan Miguel walked away and Jesus looked back over his father's shoulder that he finally understood what was happening. No more would she wake him up with a kiss on the forehead. No more would she insist he brush his teeth after breakfast. No more would she take him on walks through Memorial Park. No more would he fall asleep with his head on her lap. No more would she sit with him on the front porch. No more would they await the jingle of the ice cream man. No more would she tuck him in at night. No more would she read bedtime stories until the darkness came.

Jesus had no idea what caused his mother's death, only that it was sudden and tragic. His father would soon be unable to answer any of his son's questions, as any mention of Maria left Juan Miguel in a catatonic stupor. The stupors wouldn't be diagnosed until years later, so, in the mean time, Jesus learned simply to never talk about his mother in front of Juan Miguel. The closest Jesus ever got to under-standing the nature of his mother's death came a few hours after her funeral.

The house was filled with friends and family, all of them eating and chatting about matters that had nothing to do with Jesus' dead mother. Jesus moved about the house, weaving through small islands of people, many of whom took their opportunity to console him, telling him how sorry they were and how much they loved his mother. He snuck away upstairs to his bedroom, where he found his father sitting on the floor, crying like a child. He was drinking from a bottle of tequila and flipping through a photo album.

"Daddy?"

Seeing his young boy standing in the doorway, Juan Miguel waved him in. Jesus walked to his father, sitting down on his lap. Juan Miguel wrapped his boy up tight, still holding the tequila in his hand.

"Oh, mijito," he told Jesus, sobbing, "I'm so sorry."

Jesus had seen his father drink, but he'd never seen him drunk before. Not like this.

"I couldn't stop the monster."

"What monster?"

Juan Miguel drank from his bottle.

"Daddy?"

Jesus tugged on his father's sleeve.

"What monster?"

ᵖ•••ᵖ

Juan Miguel was not prepared to be a single father. While he loved Jesus dearly, the sorts of duties he now had to learn—such as preparing meals and making doctor's appointments—were all things Maria did, and he assumed she'd always be around to do them. Juan Miguel didn't see a need to pay for daycare. His boy was seven years old and, to his mind, old enough to be by himself after school. Jesus was equipped with a house key and clear directions to walk straight home from the bus stop. While Juan Miguel wasn't much of a cook—certainly not the caliber Maria was—he made a conscious effort to make Jesus home-made meals at least two or three times a week. The effort, however, was exhausting and most nights he opted for ordering pizza or simply bringing home a Happy Meal.

Jesus, who now found himself with hours and hours to fill all alone, spent a great deal of his time watching TV. During the week he enjoyed sitcoms, such as *Three's Company* and *Diff'rent Strokes*, and on the weekends he watched any wrestling program he could find. His love for lucha libre, which he'd shared with his mother, had led naturally to a love affair with the American brand of professional wrestling and its primary representative, the World Wrestling Federation.

The WWF was rapidly making its way into the American mainstream during Jesus' formative years, so every Saturday and Sunday afternoon he planted himself in front of the TV to watch the bigger-than-life figures he came to idolize. He loved all the appropriate heroes, such as Hulk Hogan and André the Giant, and he hated all of the appropriate villains, such as "Rowdy" Roddy Piper and King Kong Bundy. Jesus felt a certain kinship with the WWF's preeminent Latino star, Tito Santana, though he never quite ranked amongst his favorites. As weeks turned to months and months to years, Jesus' allegiances shifted from Hulk Hogan to "Macho Man" Randy Savage to The Ultimate Warrior to Bret "Hitman" Hart to Shawn Michaels to "Stone Cold" Steve Austin to The Rock and on and on, until the WWF began incorporating the lucha libre tradition and Jesus' loyalties shifted to stars such as Eddie Guerrero and Rey Mysterio.

When Jesus entered junior high school, his love of professional wrestling would serve to connect him with his first real friend since the death of his mother. Jesus had grown used to being alone, which, generally speaking, was fine by him, since he was a naturally shy kid and making friends didn't come easily. He was standing alone in the quads, trying to deduce the location of his first period classroom, when Daniel walked up to him. He was staring at Jesus' Hulk Hogan T-shirt, which his father had bought him for his most recent birthday.

"You know that stuff is fake, right?" Daniel said.

Oh, how Jesus hated when anybody said this to him. When it came to Santa Claus or the Tooth Fairy, people walked around on eggshells, bending over backwards at every opportunity to ensure that a child be able to enjoy their merry falsehood for as long as possible. But, when it came to professional wrestling, it seemed people were practically knocking themselves over, hoping against hope to be the first one to burst a kid's bubble. And Jesus figured out early on that nobody ever told him wrestling was "fake" in order to enhance his enjoyment of it. On the contrary, they seemed to want nothing more than the exact opposite.

"It's not fake."

"Yeah, it is," Daniel said. "They already know who's gonna win before it starts."

"It's staged," Jesus said, "but not fake. Sometimes they really get hurt."

"Maybe," Daniel said. "I just prefer watching the real thing."

"What real thing?"

"You ever heard of Royce Gracie?"

༺•••••༻

Royce Gracie was a mixed martial arts legend, best known for introducing the world to Brazilian jiu-jitsu. Traditional jiu-jitsu began in Asian culture with samurai warriors who developed it as a means of lethal hand-to-hand combat. In the 1920s, a jiu-jitsu practitioner named Mitsuyo Maeda emigrated from Japan to Brazil as part of a diplomatic mission to set up a Japanese colony. While in Brazil, Mitsuyo befriended Gastão Gracie, a local man with political connections. In exchange for helping him with his Japanese colony, Mitsuyo agreed to teach jiu-jitsu to Gastão's sons. Carlos Gracie became Mitsuyo's primary student, and he would go on to teach jiu-jitsu to his younger brother, Hélio Gracie.

Hélio was slight of frame and didn't possess much power or speed, which made his mastery of jiu-jitsu all the more astounding. He would go on to develop his own variation of jiu-jitsu in street fights and barroom brawls, which would come to be known as Brazilian jiu-jitsu, making Hélio the top sports figure in Brazil in the 1930s. When he had sons of his own, Hélio taught them Brazilian jiu-jitsu, effectively planting the seeds for what would become the most famous fighting family in the world. Hélio's most proficient and successful son was Royce Gracie.

On November 12, 1993, Royce participated in the first Ultimate Fighting Championship. Jesus had never heard of the UFC or Royce Gracie, so Daniel invited him over for a sleepover the following Friday, offering to show him the tournament on VHS. The event itself was an eight-man single elimination tournament. The objective of the tournament was to pit various fighting styles against each other to determine the best fighting style in the world. The fights were practically free of rules, as the only two things fighters couldn't do were bite or eye gauge. Lying on his belly beside Daniel, chin atop his fists, Jesus watched, dumbfounded, as Royce Gracie—a small fighter at 178 pounds—successfully defeated three separate opponents that night, winning his matches in a combined time of four minutes and fifty-nine seconds.

His first opponent was Art Jimmerson, a boxer, who tapped out almost as soon as Royce took him down to the mat. His second opponent was Ken Shamrock, a wrestler and one of the pioneers of mixed martial arts, who Royce tapped out with a rear-naked choke in less than a minute. And the man he defeated in the finals of the tournament was Gerard Gordeau, a savateur, who, as with Shamrock, Royce defeated with a rear-naked choke. Along with being the first UFC Champion and single-handedly revolutionizing the sport of mixed martial arts, Royce Gracie captured the imagination of young Jesus, inspiring him to one day become a mixed martial artist himself.

Jesus and Daniel became inseparable after that first sleepover. Daniel continued to share his love of the UFC with Jesus, while Jesus managed to instill a mild appreciation for professional wrestling in Daniel. Once the boys finished junior high and transitioned into their first year of high school, they each joined the wrestling team. Given a choice, they would've studied Brazilian jiu-jitsu, but the absence of any local dojos left wrestling as the next best option, since, at their cores, each discipline was based on grappling. Despite his new sport being something of a consolation, Jesus loved being a wrestler. Daniel, on the other hand, hated it. He found the grueling practices tortuous and the weekend tournaments tedious. So, after only one year on the team, he quit.

For Jesus, wrestling came very naturally and he flourished for the next four years, successfully growing and improving. By his sophomore year he was on the varsity team, and his junior year he was voted team captain. He loved everything about being a wrestler, from working out in the heated gym to the early morning runs he took before school. He loved the feel of his soaked-through T-shirt, heavy with sweat, hanging from his body, and the bruises he collected like badges of honor. He loved being a varsity letterman and being able to call himself a league champion, earning the title at the end of his final season on the team.

All the while, despite his status as one of Upland High School's best athletes, Jesus never felt comfortable being social or going to parties. He rarely dated, as talking to girls mostly scared him. As it was when he was a kid, when Jesus wasn't hanging out with Daniel, he was most comfortable being alone. When high school ended, he was offered a handful of wrestling scholarships to some community colleges and a few small universities; though he was happy to receive the offers, Jesus already made the decision to pursue a career as a professional mixed martial artist.

During his last two years at Upland High School, thanks to the burgeoning popularity of the UFC, a local mixed martial artist training facility called Ground and Pound opened up. Ground and Pound offered training in various styles, from Brazilian jiu-jitsu and Muay Thai to boxing and Sambo. As soon as they opened their doors, Jesus asked his father to let him join, but Juan Miguel, who wasn't overly thrilled by the idea of his only child becoming a cage fighter, insisted he finish school first. So, Jesus waited patiently, and as soon as his last day of school was complete, he signed up at Ground and Pound and immediately began his mixed martial artist training. In the end, Jesus' mixed martial arts career would only last one fight, due in large part to Daniel's death at Memorial Park.

Jesus fought his one and only professional mixed martial arts bout inside a small gymnasium in Tijuana. Despite having only trained for two months at Ground and Pound and being offered the fight on a few days notice, he pulled out a dramatic come-from-behind victory. Daniel was right there in his corner, shouting and cheering him on, before charging inside the cage after the win and lifting Jesus off the mat in a bear hug. In so many ways, the victory belonged to both of them—and Jesus knew it. His fighting future felt bright, and he wanted Daniel to be a part of it.

Two days after returning home from Tijuana, Jesus got a job at Ground and Pound as a custodian. Working in Ground and Pound meant that Jesus would have more time and access for training. To celebrate, he and Daniel went to Memorial Park in the middle of the night with a six-pack of Corona. Strolling through the park, each of them down to their last beer, Jesus and Daniel talked about the future. Daniel was in the middle of his first semester at Mt. San Antonio College with plans of majoring in kinesiology.

They talked about how, once he finished school, Daniel would be armed with enough knowledge to become Jesus' strength and conditioning coach. Daniel had no doubts that his friend would one day make it to the UFC and Jesus assured him a place in his corner when he did. Beers in hand, they daydreamed aloud about walking out of the locker room and down the aisle, entering the Octagon and taking on the best fighters in the world. Maybe he'd even become a champion some day, his hand raised in victory while UFC President Dana White put the belt around his waist. It all felt so possible, until the pale man appeared from the darkness.

He came seemingly from out of nowhere, startling Jesus and Daniel into a halt. The pale man moved like he was floating, and in a matter of seconds, he was standing in front of them.

"Good evening," said the pale man.

Jesus and Daniel said nothing.

"Boys night out?"

"What do you want?" Daniel asked.

"I want to join the fun."

Jesus tapped Daniel on the elbow and the two friends started walking away.

"You don't have to go, do you?"

The boys ignored the pale man and continued walking away.

"Well, that's a shame," he said. "You both look so delicious."

Without another word, the pale man swiftly moved behind Daniel, wrapping his arms around him and sinking his teeth into his neck. Jesus rushed in, intending to save his friend, but was easily knocked to the grass when the pale man struck him in the chest with the back of his fist. Jesus lay on the grass, trying to catch his breath, while Daniel screamed, blood soaking the collar of his T-shirt. The pale man lifted his head and smiled at Jesus, his mouth covered in Daniel's blood.

"It was nice meeting you," he said, dragging Daniel away.

Jesus got to his feet and ran after them, but he would never see his friend again.

For the second time in his young life, Jesus suffered the tragic loss of someone he loved. Daniel's was only the second funeral Jesus had ever attended. The casket was empty, as Daniel's body was never recovered. It was only Jesus' word and a futile weeklong search by the local authorities that finally convinced Daniel's parents that their only child was really and truly gone. With his better senses fogged by grief, Jesus went back to Memorial Park on the evening of Daniel's funeral. Still in the suit he wore to the service, Jesus wandered about the park, sad and drunk, shrouded with the bravery that comes with having nothing to lose, wanting nothing more than for the pale man to make another appearance.

Jesus called for him, yelling at the top of his lungs, daring the pale man to show his face. He screamed in the darkness until his voice grew hoarse, tears streaming down his cheeks. When the pale man didn't show, Jesus dropped to the grass and stared at the stars. He wanted there to be a meaning for it all, some lesson about life and the universe, some cosmic explanation for why his world seemed destined to be filled with tragedy and grief. It was then that the pale man showed his face, standing over Jesus, smiling, his feet straddling his head.

Jesus jumped up, instinctively getting into his fighting stance. The pale man stood erect, hands behind his back, head cocked to the side.

"Looking for me?"

"What'd you do with him?"

"I drank his blood."

"Where is he?"

"It doesn't matter," said the pale man. "He's all empty now."

In a burst of rage, Jesus charged him, intending to bury his shoulder in the pale man's belly, but he deftly stepped aside, causing Jesus to tumble into the grass, rolling until a tree trunk stopped his momentum. At the base of the trunk, mere inches from his face, Jesus saw a splintered chunk of tree sticking out from the roots like a giant wooden fang. The pale man watched, his hands still behind his back, as Jesus pulled himself up to his feet.

"What kind of freak are you?"

The pale man smiled.

"I thought you knew," he said. "I'm a vampire."

Jesus shook his head in disbelief.

The pale man brought his index finger to his lips as if to shush Jesus.

"I'm not supposed to tell you that," he whispered. "Then again, I do a lot of things I'm not supposed to do."

Jesus stared at the pale man, wanting to call him a liar, wanting to believe that it wasn't true. But, despite all the collective logic of his eighteen years, deep in his heart Jesus knew that the pale man was in fact a vampire.

"Are you the only one?"

"If you knew how many of us there were," the vampire said, "you'd never fall asleep again."

"Did you kill my mother?"

The vampire paused, his eyes looking up into his brain.

"I don't know," he said. "If it helps, I am about to kill you."

The vampire closed his eyes and sniffed the air.

Jesus stood up straight and, one more time, charged towards the vampire, successfully tackling him to the ground. They rolled around, struggling, and, for the briefest of moments, Jesus actually thought he was getting the best of him; but when the vampire began giggling, he knew it wasn't so. Pushing Jesus off, the vampire rose to his feet. When he opened his mouth, Jesus saw two sharp fangs appear beneath his lips. Coming at Jesus, the vampire's eyes rolled back, showing only the whites, a small map of red veins protruding from the edges.

He grabbed Jesus from behind, holding his torso like a lover. Jesus grabbed hold of the vampire's wrists and, stepping his left leg back around the vampire, he swept his feet, taking him down to the grass. Once again, they rolled around, only now Jesus was managing—if only barely—to neutralize the vampire's efforts with Brazilian jiu-jitsu, which he applied with a combination of muscle memory and adrenaline. Jesus knew he wouldn't be able to hold the vampire at bay for forever, but he refused to die without a fight. They continued rolling around the grass, until the vampire yelped and stopped moving altogether.

Jesus jumped back to his feet, ready to fight some more, when he realized the giant wooden fang had impaled the vampire, blood pulsing out of his chest in thick crimson bursts. He watched as the vampire's eyes sunk into his face, leaving two black pits in their wake. His pale skin went from white to grey to black before collapsing under its own weight, melting into a pile of crimson goo.

༺

With the UFC program still playing, Jesus fell asleep on his couch with only one energy bar eaten and the coconut water half drunk. Olivia did eventually call him back that night, but, exhausted from a long night of vampire hunting, Jesus slept through the call. The following morning, his disappointment at missing an opportunity to talk to Olivia would be offset by the voicemail she'd left for him: "Hey, it's Olivia. Sorry I missed your call. Crazy night. We'll hang out soon. Maybe this week. Goodnight."

CHAPTER FIVE

A SPECIAL KIND OF REGRET

Olivia awoke in the driver's seat of her car with the crucifix on her lap. Adam was sitting in the passenger seat, staring out at the city and its lights, relaxed and satisfied. Olivia no longer smelled of fear, her scent having tapered off soon after Adam had fed from her. She looked at the vampire, then out the window. Her vision was blurry, her head foggy. She blinked a couple of times, the city growing sharper with every snap of her lids.

"How do you feel?"

"Fine," Olivia said, "I think. I don't know. How am I supposed to feel?"

"You should feel fine," Adam said. "Tired, maybe. A little light-headed. There shouldn't be any discomfort, though. Nothing significant anyway. Except for your neck. It'll be a little sore for a few days."

Olivia brought her fingertips to where Adam's teeth had entered her, wincing at the touch. The bleeding had stopped, leaving her with two streaks of crusty blood running down her neck, disappearing into the shadows beneath her work shirt. Examining herself in the rearview mirror, Olivia wished she had a damp cloth to clean up with.

"Dab a little Neosporin on them when you get home," Adam

said, "and dress them with a couple of Band-Aids. You'll be good as new before you know it."

"There's no special vampire trick for healing them," Olivia asked, "like in *True Blood*?"

"Never seen it."

"Really?"

"I don't have cable."

"In *True Blood* the vampire blood has healing powers," Olivia said. "Sometimes a vampire will cut himself open and use the blood to heal a human's wounds."

"I hate to break it to you," Adam said, "but that's fiction. The only thing my blood will do is give you more blood to clean up. I can use it to turn you into a vampire, but, that's about it."

Olivia looked again in the rearview mirror, examining her neck.

"You think I should wear a scarf to work tomorrow?"

"To cover the bite marks?"

"Yeah," she said. "I'm wondering if a scarf would look too conspicuous."

"The holes themselves are relatively inconspicuous," Adam said. "Chances are nobody will notice. And if they do, they're not likely to assume a vampire fed on you."

Olivia picked up the crucifix on her lap and tried to put it back on, until she realized the chain was broken.

"I was going to tell you about that when you woke up," Adam said. "Sorry."

"What happened?"

Adam lifted his hand, showing Olivia the grotesque mark—bubbling and red—the crucifix had burned into his skin.

"Jesus Christ!" she said. "I didn't realize the crucifix thing was real."

"Oh, it's not," he said. "But the *silver* thing is."

"Does it hurt?"

"A little less now than it did before."

"It looks like it's moving," Olivia said, taking a closer look.

"My skin's trying to heal," Adam said, "so it probably *is* moving a little. It'll be fine in a few hours. Half a day, tops."

Adam and Olivia fell silent for a few moments, their small talk having run out of steam.

"Anyway" she said, "I held up my end of the bargain. Will you be holding up yours, or is this the part of the story where I learn never to trust a vampire?"

༺•••••༻

Olivia first saw Adam during Cosmic Bowling on a Friday night in Upland at the Brunswick bowling alley. Friday night crowds could be pretty rowdy by bowling alley standards. Olivia had grown accustomed to it over the years, which was why Adam had stood out to her so completely the first time she saw him. He was alone and serene, seemingly unfazed by the commotion around him, as if the bowling alley were completely empty. His skin was pale, unusually so, almost glowing like a mustard stain under the florescent lights. Nobody else in the bowling alley, besides Olivia, seemed to take notice of him.

She wondered if he had bowled there before. She thought that, perhaps, she'd simply neglected to notice him. He was handsome and lean, his jaw square, his hair full. He bowled with a glide in his step, as if unhindered by the laws of physics. He was clearly a good bowler. Better than good, in fact. To Olivia's eye, his technique bordered on professional. She'd watched him bowl two complete games, beginning to end, mindlessly taking orders and mixing drinks as she kept her eyes on him. He bowled a 215 and a 234 respectively, outstanding scores for anyone, let alone a loner braving the hectic, club-like atmosphere of Cosmic Bowling.

Nobody got that good without practice—and a lot of it—yet Olivia had no memory of ever seeing him. She'd been working at the bowling alley for years, so she had no doubt she would've noticed him before. It could've been that he practiced during the day, she thought, when she almost never worked. Or, maybe, he'd done most of his bowling at other allies. Olivia knew that the mystery of the handsome stranger was only interesting to her—and if her job weren't as boring as it was, she probably wouldn't have cared at all.

Olivia worked at the bowling alley two to three nights a week, spending most of her other nights tending bar at Topical Lei. She didn't have much of a social life to speak of, so a Friday and Saturday night behind the bar wasn't much of a sacrifice. If anything, tending bar on the weekends was a pleasant compromise between work and fun, as it forced her into the sort of social atmosphere she would almost never engage in on her own accord. Left to her own devices, Olivia would happily sit alone in her apartment with a stack of good books, Netflix, and a vibrator. She sometimes worried that there might be something wrong with her, because she didn't feel the same urges as so many of the people she served who went out and got drunk and woke up with regret.

Olivia started bartending when she was eighteen years old. Despite being three years below the legal drinking age, she was attractive enough for the manager to disregard her birthday. And, of course, beautiful girls were good for business, so Olivia—who didn't think of herself as beautiful, but, thanks to a lifetime of compliments and bad pickup lines, understood that others did—knew there would always be a job for her anywhere alcohol was served. Her first gig was at bikini bar in Upland. She was initially hired as a waitress during her senior year at Alta Loma High School. She'd heard the waitresses there made good money, which was true, but she soon figured out that the bartenders made better money.

So, during one of her days off, Olivia spoke to the manager about maybe tending bar and—being a man of dubious character—he agreed under one condition: Olivia had to strip for him. While she knew a whole lot of girls would've been put off by such a proposition,

Olivia was okay with it at first. From the time she was a little girl, having watched with envy as her friends lived the sort of comfortable lives that she could only dream about, Olivia had long ago learned to extend the boundaries of what she was willing to do in order to get what she wanted. But, before she showed the manager her naked body, she wanted to make one thing perfectly clear to him.

"I'm not a prostitute."

There was a thin line, in Olivia's estimation, between being a prostitute and engaging in a simple exchange of favors. The definition of that line was, on more than one occasion, the topic of discussion between Olivia and Elowyn. "If a woman stands on a street corner and a man pulls up to her in his car, negotiates a price for sex through the passenger window, then fucks her in the backseat," Olivia told her, "then that's a prostitute. However, if a woman accepts an invitation for dinner at a fancy restaurant with a man that she's not terribly attracted to and later, back at his beautiful home in the Hollywood Hills, fucks him doggy style in his Jacuzzi, then that's a simple exchange of favors."

The only problem, Olivia knew, was there were a million possible scenarios that existed between being a prostitute and a simple exchange of favors—and it wasn't always easy to tell the difference. For example, going into your manager's office and stripping your clothes off in exchange for a better paying position at work wasn't exactly clear-cut. While taking her clothes off for him was, at the very least, an erotic gesture, Olivia wouldn't let him touch her and they most definitely weren't going to have sex. But, she wasn't so naïve as to think her naked body wouldn't give him some level of sexual pleasure. And, while he wasn't giving her money in exchange, he was giving her a new job that was going to put extra money in her pocket.

In the end, Olivia knew the only difference between what she was about to do and what a prostitute did was perception. Everybody had their own measuring stick for such things and they were all subjective. Of course, nobody was going to be there besides Olivia and her boss, and even if he told anybody what she was about to do, it wouldn't be anybody of consequence—certainly nobody she was concerned about. So, when she stepped into the manager's office, closing the door behind her, gripped by a desperate need to control the perception of her role in this scenario, Olivia had only one person she needed to convince and it wasn't the man behind the desk with the creepy smile on his face.

"Whatever you say, kid."

Stripping her clothes off for the manager, she decided, didn't have to be any more sexual than removing her clothes at the doctor's office, so Olivia quickly removed her top and was about to unfasten her bra, when he stopped her.

"Slow down," the manager said. "I want to enjoy it."

Olivia slowed down, but not because she wanted him to enjoy it. She had already come this far, so she didn't see the point in letting her pride ruin the deal. She was slowly sliding her hands up her spine, letting her fingers find the hook of her bra, when he stopped her again.

"Leave your bra for now," the manager said. "Take off your pants."

Olivia sighed to herself, unbuttoning her jeans and pulling down her fly. But, just as she slipped her thumbs inside the waist, he stopped her again.

"Come around my desk," the manager said. "Stand in front of me."

"Why?"

"I want to see everything."

Olivia stepped around the desk and stood before him, waiting a beat in case he had more instructions. Leaning back in his swivel chair, his hands on his thighs, legs wide open, the manager nodded at her, a wordless command to continue. Slipping her thumbs back inside the waist of her blue jeans, Olivia pushed them down her thighs, past her knees, kicking off her flip-flops before pulling her legs completely out. She stood in front of him in her mismatched bra and panties, no makeup, her long black hair tied in a ponytail.

"Now what?"

"Surprise me."

With those two creepy words, Olivia knew that whatever power she held was now gone. Whether she first removed her bra or her panties, it would be a surprise, which meant he'd have gotten his way. And while she could still grab her clothes and storm out, it would probably have left her without a job at all, meaning she'd have suffered through all of it for nothing. So, she unhooked her bra, trying as best she could to strip away any of the gesture's inherent eroticism. Holding one arm across her chest, fingers tucked beneath her armpit, Olivia concealed her breasts from the manager's eyes, dropping her bra to the floor. With her free hand, she began removing her panties, only to be stopped once more.

"You can't cover 'em, kid."

Olivia kept her arm over her breasts, defiantly disregarding his request, hoping to make a show of her anger. All her act of defiance managed to do, however, was enhance his enjoyment. Her only recourse, she decided, was to get through this as quickly as possible, so she dropped her arm, letting him look at her naked breasts. It was the first time she'd ever bared them in front of a man before. Olivia had only been on a handful of dates in high school, and she'd only just lost her virginity a few weeks prior. The sex wasn't memorable—nor was the boy, whoever he was—and it happened so fast in the backseat of his car, she'd never even taken her top off. She wasn't even sure the boy had bothered to look between her legs before pushing himself inside her.

Olivia's breasts were smaller than she would have liked; they didn't have the size for cleavage or the weight for hang. When she stood in front of the mirror at home, examining her body, wondering if she was as sexy as so many men seemed to think she was, Olivia believed her nipples would make up for her breast size. Her nipples were nice to look at, two dollops of caramel atop her fair skin, each of them refusing to blend in like so many of the pink nipples she'd seen in the girl's locker room. Following her first sexual experience, Olivia decided she wouldn't settle again. She would wait for a man with nice hands and deep intelligence to seduce her with all the parts of himself that couldn't be seen and, when he did, he would be the first to lay eyes on her caramel dollops—so it was a special kind of regret she felt as she bared her breasts to the manager.

"Nice nips," he said.

Wanting only to keep things moving along, Olivia slid her panties down her shapely hips. From the moment she hit puberty, Olivia couldn't put one foot in front of the other without exuding sex appeal. Most of the time she wasn't even aware of it, the way her body moved when she walked, her hips seeming to have a life of their own, hypnotic in their seductive rhythm. It was, in fact, the reason why the manager had hired her in the first place. It was also why he was hesitant to put her behind the bar, where her most valuable physical assets would be less likely to help earn him money.

Olivia was now standing completely naked in front of the manager, arms at her side, completely exposed. She looked straight ahead at the wall, not wanting to see him looking at her. She waited for a signal—whatever it might be—letting her know he was done, so she could put her clothes back on. He sat up in his chair, leaning towards Olivia, startling her; opening up his bottom drawer, he pulled out a pair of transparent plastic heels, dropping them at her feet.

"Put these on, kid."

"What for?"

"For the pictures," he said, pulling out a Polaroid camera.

"I never said you could take pictures."

"If you want to be my new bartender," he said, "be a good girl."

"What're you going to do with them?"

"What do you think?"

And there it was. Their arrangement had officially devolved into an exchange of sexual gratification for personal gain, the likes of which would make Olivia—within the boundaries of her very own definition—a prostitute. In retrospect, the prostitute part didn't bother her nearly as much as being a participant in her manager's masturbatory routine. But, however upsetting the experience was becoming, she refused to let it all be for naught, so, while he loaded some film into his camera, Olivia slipped her feet into the heels. For the next ten minutes Olivia begrudgingly indulged his directions—from bending over a chair to lying across his desk.

When she returned to work the next day, the bar was vacant. With an air of indifference, as if the previous day's events hadn't happened at all, the manager told Olivia to get to work. She told him she'd never tended bar before and assumed there would be some sort of training involved. He laughed, telling her she'd have to figure it out. When she asked him what would happen if she couldn't, he said, "I guess you'll have to find a new job." Being the bright and industrious girl that she was, Olivia did figure it out—sort of. There were plenty of mistakes, of course, but they were the sorts of mistakes that a woman of great beauty can get away with.

Olivia made a promise to herself that the time she spent in her manager's office, removing her clothes and posing for dirty pictures, would be the last time she ever bartered her body in exchange for something she wanted. She held true to that promise for twelve years, until she met a vampire at the bowling alley and agreed to let him suck her blood.

CHAPTER SIX

OLIVIA AND ADAM

"Anyway" Olivia said, "I held up my end of the bargain. Will you be holding up yours, or is this the part of the story where I learn never to trust a vampire?"

Adam heard her, but only sort of. He found himself too consumed with the thought of pie to give Olivia his full attention. From the time he was a child, Adam had a sweet tooth. In high school, he'd go to Gemmels Pharmacy every morning before class and buy as much candy as he could for three dollars, using money he was supposed to spend on lunch. In elementary school his favorite holiday was Valentine's Day, because of all the candy involved; he loved collecting his Valentine cards and setting aside the bulky ones, which almost certainly would have candy waiting inside.

Adam's sweet tooth wasn't satisfied with only candy. Ice cream sundaes were high on his list, as well as milkshakes, brownies, chocolate chip cookies, and flan. Once, when there were no sweets around the house, Adam gave himself a bellyache after eating half a box of brown sugar. But, he always knew that if the world were to come to an end and he only had time to enjoy one last dessert, he would choose to have a slice of pie. Dutch apple pie was his favorite, but it wasn't the only pie he'd eat. If there were no apple pies, a lemon merengue would do or pecan or peach or chocolate cream or anything else sweet baked inside of a piecrust.

Upon being turned into a vampire, Adam was thrilled to learn that, amongst all the other things he had to give up, eating pie wasn't one of them. It wasn't just pie, either—Adam could eat anything he'd previously enjoyed as a human. And not only could he enjoy them, but, as a vampire, food tasted better on account of his amplified senses. But, no matter how much food he ate—and no matter how much he enjoyed it—he could not sustain himself on it. Human blood was the only source of sustenance that a vampire could live off of. And, as treats go, drinking blood was a far more rich and satisfying experience than eating a slice of pie could ever be. However amazing drinking blood was, however, Adam saw no reason to stop enjoying pie.

As pies went, Adam always particularly enjoyed the sort of homemade pie you could get at a local diner with a scoop of vanilla ice cream and a cup of coffee. That, for Adam, was more than just pie—it was an experience. Most diners weren't available to Adam, because they generally closed while he was still asleep. As most vampires did, Adam slept during the day to avoid sunlight. He'd never actually seen a vampire die from sunlight, but Cherry told him in no uncertain terms that it was to be avoided at all costs. "Burning flesh hurts like a mother fucker," she said, "and there's nothing about being a vampire that makes it hurt any less."

Adam, of course, had to learn the hard way, so one morning while Cherry was asleep he cracked open the front door, letting in a sliver of sunlight. He touched his fingers to the light, catching them on fire almost instantly. He slammed the door shut and slapped his hand against his pants until the fire was out, leaving him with a couple of charred digits. The commotion woke Cherry up, but all she did was laugh at him. "They'll heal in a couple of hours," she said. "I hope you learned your lesson." He did, of course. More than learning a lesson about sunlight, though, he learned that he needed to listen to everything Cherry told him.

So, as a vampire who loved eating homemade pie, Adam depended on all-night diners that were open twenty-four hours a day. Even if he went to a diner just as night fell, that, for him, would be akin to eating pie for breakfast—even as a vampire, that just didn't seem appropriate. While there were a couple of chain restaurants that fit the bill near his home in Upland, Adam's diner of choice was Corky's. Not only was Corky's a twenty-four hour diner, but they specialized in baking a whole variety of delicious pies.

"You want to get some pie?" Adam asked.

"Pardon?"

"Pie," he said. "I can hardly think of anything else at the moment."

"You can eat pie?"

"You bet I can," he said. "So, if it's all the same to you, I'd be happy to make good on my end of the bargain over a piece of pie."

They sat in Corky's at Adam's usual table in the back corner. He hardly ever looked at the menu anymore, as Corky's made fresh pies everyday and the selection was almost always different. His favorite waitress was Darlene, a sweet woman in her early forties who worked most of the overnight shifts. Adam and Darlene had developed a pleasant rapport and, as humans went, she was the closest thing he had to a friend. They hardly knew each other, of course, and the majority of their conversations were relegated to Darlene asking him what sort of pie he wanted. Still and all, it was nice to have a familiar face in his routine, since Cherry was no longer a part of his life. Darlene smiled as she approached the table.

"You brought company."

"This is Olivia."

She smiled at Darlene.

"Nice to meet you."

"Likewise."

"So," Adam said, "what's fresh?"

"We've got an apple pie that's only about an hour old," Darlene said, "but if you want to wait a few minutes, I happen to know there's a fresh pecan pie about to come out of the oven."

"Well, color me patient."

"Pecan pie it is," Darlene said. "À la mode?"

"You bet," he said, "and some coffee, too."

"And what can I get started for you, dear?"

"I'll just have some French fries," Olivia said, "and a Coke."

"You got it."

Darlene scribbled down their orders before disappearing into the kitchen. Olivia dug through her purse, pushing her phone aside, and pulling out a mechanical pencil and a Moleskine notebook. At the top of the first page—which, like every other page in her notebook, was blank, Olivia wrote, "Notes for Vampire Novel."

She looked up at Adam, pencil at the ready.

"Ready to start?"

"Sure."

In the previous weeks, as she struggled to begin her vampire novel, Olivia also struggled with the realization that she didn't know how to write about vampires in general. She constantly froze up when trying to figure out the parameters of her vampire world. Would it be like *Buffy the Vampire Slayer*, where vampires were generally known about but rarely acknowledged in mainstream society? Would it be like *True Blood* where vampires were out in the open and integrated into society? Should it be something in between? Was there a vampire template she should be honoring? Was she allowed to make up her own rules? Would people hate her if she got it wrong? Was she a terrible writer? Was her career already over before it started?

This was the reason Olivia couldn't start her novel. She inevitably locked herself up with fear and insecurity, a brutal combination for any creative type. Even when she did free herself up long enough to brainstorm some ideas, it seemed everything she thought of was either derivative of some other vampire story somebody had written or altogether boring in general. As best as she could tell, all the good ideas—as well as the bad ones—had already been done. She wasn't sure if there was a purpose for writing a vampire novel if she had nothing new to offer, yet, no matter how much she thought about it, she didn't seem to have anything new to offer. The whole enterprise of writing a vampire novel was beginning to feel hopeless and she was about to give up on it altogether, until she met Adam.

Instead of trying to imagine a vampire world, she could get genuine information straight from the source. Olivia was elated when Adam agreed to sit down for an interview, but he wanted something in return. This seemed fair enough to Olivia, until she found out what he wanted.

"I want to hunt you," Adam told her.

"You're going to kill me?"

"No," Adam said. "I just want to hunt you. And drink your blood, of course."

"Won't that kill me?"

"Not if I'm careful," Adam said, "which I will be."

"Do you actually need my permission to hunt me?"

"Technically, I'm not really allowed to hunt you at all," Adam said. "But, with your permission, I'm thinking it might sort of be okay."

"I'm not sure I understand."

"That's okay," Adam said. "Just know that I'll be very careful not to kill you."

"That's not exactly comforting."

"You don't have to say yes."

"Why do you need my permission? "

"Good question," Adam said. "If you let me hunt you, I'll give you an answer."

Olivia hesitated.

"I won't die?"

"Almost definitely."

"Will it hurt?"

"Depends on your threshold of pain," Adam said. "You will feel something, though. Not much I can do about that."

"When will it happen?"

"That's the other thing," Adam said. "I can't tell you."

"Why not?"

He looked at her, smiling.

"Right," Olivia said, "you'll tell me afterwards."

Adam nodded.

"Oh, fuck it," she said. "I'll do it."

That was the last time she saw or heard from Adam, until earlier that night when he drank her blood beneath the jungle gym at Heritage Park. And now they were sharing a booth at Corky's, Adam anticipating a fresh slice of pecan pie, while Olivia was ready to begin her research.

"What would you like to know first?"

"I don't know," Darlene said. "I assumed there might be some natural beginning point."

"There are lots of beginnings, depending on want you want to know."

"Let's start with tonight," she said. "Why'd you need my permission to hunt me?"

"Well, I didn't *need* it, per se," he said. "I simply asked for it as a courtesy. Vampires attack humans all the time, but we're not really supposed to. It's generally against the law."

"What law?"

"There are vampire laws that we're meant to follow."

"Really?"

Darlene turned up at the table with Adam's coffee and Olivia's Coke, assuring them both that their food would be out shortly. Adam smiled and waited for her to disappear back into kitchen before continuing with Olivia.

He told her that vampires were at one time primarily hunters. They foraged towns and villages, preying on humans. While it'd be easy to view vampires as monsters who wanted only to bring horror and death to humankind, Adam explained that—like any other creature—they were simply trying to survive and a vampire's core means of survival was drinking human blood. In the way that humans have evolved to desire sexual intercourse as nature's way of insuring their procreation, vampires have evolved to desire blood in the same fashion. "In fact," Adam said, "the closest approximation for a vampire's desire for blood is the human's desire for sex. The difference, of course, is blood is essential to a vampire's survival."

While it wasn't preferable, a human could reasonably live their entire life without ever having sex. Food, on the other hand, is something humans can't live without. "In human culture," Adam said, "food is routinely paired with sex. When humans go out on dates, it's almost always a night out to dinner followed by sex. There might be a movie thrown in there somewhere, but you get my point." For vampires, drinking blood served a similar function, except instead of eating a meal and *then* having sex, the meal—for all intents and purposes—*was* the sex. "So," Adam said, "a vampire feeding on blood is the rough equivalent of a human simultaneously eating a Big Mac and having an orgasm."

While humans have always hunted for sex—from prowling in dive bars to cruising dating websites—most prefer to engage in sex with the least amount of effort possible. Monogamous relationships offered something of a solution in this regard, but, as most humans figured out, monogamy was hardly a sustainable model. Prostitution was the most effective solution humans devised for satisfying their sexual needs without having to hunt. Brothels, however, were less prevalent nowadays, as most industrialized societies made them illegal. Strip clubs and massage parlors picked up much of the slack and, of course, there were always streetwalkers.

"What does any of this have to do with being a vampire?"

"Vampires," Adam said, "like humans, developed of means of getting blood without having to hunt for it. Similar to brothels, vampires have feeding posts."

"Is that as creepy as it sounds?"

"Not for vampires, no," Adam said. "Feeding posts are establishments that keep an ongoing supply of humans in captivity, so vampires can feed without hunting. Because hunting is generally against the law, feeding posts are a very important aspect of vampire culture."

"Where do the humans come from?"

"Freelance hunters bring them in."

"You just said hunting is against the law," Olivia said. "Speaking of which, you still haven't explained why you asked for my permission."

"I'm getting to that," Adam said. "Like I said, it's *generally* against the law, but it's not black and white. Vampires always need to have the *option* of hunting, just in case."

"Just in case of what?"

"Just in case there are no feeding posts available."

"Makes sense," Olivia said, scribbling down some notes. "How much does it cost to feed at a feeding post?"

"It costs nothing."

"Doesn't somebody have to run it?"

"Sure."

"And they do it for free?"

"I'm sure you're not the only human to have a hard time imagining a society where goods and services are offered for free," Adam said. "The thing is, vampires put very little value in money. We collect money but rarely find the need to spend it."

"Unless you want a slice of pie?"

"Exactly."

As if on cue, Darlene turned up again, setting down Adam's slice of pecan pie and Olivia's French fries. Adam started in on his pie right away.

"I would've assumed that eating human food would make you sick."

"Vampires can eat anything humans can eat," Adam said. "Human food simply doesn't provide any nourishment, but it still tastes good."

"Do other vampires eat pie?"

"Not to my knowledge," Adam said. "Most vampires just feed on blood."

"If human food tastes good, why wouldn't more vampires eat it?"

"One reason is that no other food source can engage our taste buds quite the way human blood can," Adam said. "It's pretty magical. I almost feel sorry for you that you'll never get to experience it. But, more than that, most vampires don't eat human food for digestive reasons."

"Vampires can't digest food?"

"We can digest food just fine," Adam said. "Most vampires simply prefer not to out of convenience. Blood doesn't need to be digested, so it's pretty ideal in all respects. We feed on it and it just sort of becomes a part of us. Human food, on the other hand, breaks down in our bodies pretty much the same as it would in yours, ultimately resulting in a bowel movement. For humans, moving your bowels is an accepted reality and, so, little time is spent reflecting on just how disgusting it is. So, to answer your question, most vampires choose not to eat human food, because they don't want to take any more shits."

"Really?"

"Given a choice," Adam said, "would you continue to shit?"

"I've never thought about it."

"Of course you haven't," Adam said. "For you, there is no choice."

"But, in *your* case," Olivia said, "you choose to shit?"

"No," Adam said, "I choose to eat pie. Shitting is just an unfortunate byproduct."

Olivia scribbled down a few notes.

"Okay," she said, "enough about that. Tell me why you asked for my permission to hunt me."

"Hunting humans scratches an ancient itch in vampires," Adam said, "satisfying a part of our nature that feeding alone can't touch. But, because it's generally against the law, most vampires simply learn to live with the desire without ever giving in to it. So, when I asked you for your permission, I was essentially trying to engage in the grey area of the law. The way I see it, if I have your permission, then it's not really hunting. It's more like roleplaying."

"Sort of a vampire loophole?"

"Sure."

"So, as long as you get permission from a human," Olivia said, "hunting them isn't considered breaking the law?"

"Hopefully," Adam said. "But, to be honest with you, I have no idea."

"How can you have no idea?"

"It's complicated," Adam said. "The thing is, for all the laws vampires adhere to, we don't actually know who makes them. We don't even know who *enforces* them. We just know that the laws have been around longer than any of us have, so it's important that we obey them."

"What happens if you don't?"

"I don't know."

"Are you serious?" Olivia said. "So, you follow a bunch of ancient laws, but you have no idea why you do it?"

"There's always stories about vampires who've broken the laws and have been punished for it."

"Punished how?"

"Nobody really knows?" Adam said. "Sometimes vampires just disappear."

"And they disappear as a punishment for breaking the law?"

"Maybe."

"So, you follow the vampire laws, because you may or may not be punished if you don't?"

"Pretty much, yeah."

"You realize that sounds crazy, right?"

"I'm sure it does," Adam said. "But, the laws also serve a practical purpose. If vampires were free to hunt humans as much as they desired, then it would only be a matter of time before we wiped out the human race. The laws are in place to keep us disciplined. As long as we stay disciplined, there will always be enough humans to feed on without ever hurting the balance of the population, insuring that vampires can go on living for eternity the way nature intended it."

"But, if humans are being hunted for feeding posts," Olivia asked, "won't there come a time when there won't be enough of us around to sustain vampires?"

"I don't think so, no," Adam said. "In fact, in the last two hundred years or so, humans have multiplied in such large numbers that vampires have actually become necessary for keeping the planet from overpopulating."

"Wouldn't vampires love it if Earth were overpopulated with humans?"

Darlene turned up at the table to check up on Adam and Olivia.

"You guys talking about the new *Twilight* movie?"

"Have you seen it?" Adam asked.

"Not yet," Darlene said. "My son can't wait to watch it, though. Next time I have a night off, I'm going to take him to the theater. Can I refill your drinks?"

"I'm good," Adam said.

"Me too," Olivia said.

Darlene smiled before leaving them alone again.

"What were we talking about?" Adam asked.

"Why vampires don't want an overpopulation of humans."

"Right," Adam said. "Vampires need humans to be alive and healthy, capable of sustaining their own population with the given availability of natural resources. Too many humans would lead to not enough resources, which would ultimately lead to chaos. Without question, vampires would enjoy a brief period of blood and debauchery, but, in time, this would prove to be unsustainable. Humans would die off on their own just as quickly as vampires could kill them."

"Yeah, but you don't know that for a certainty," Olivia said. "It's just a theory."

"That's a fair point," Adam said. "What we *do* know for a certainty is the way things are now works just fine. So, it's in everybody's best interest that the system remains as is."

"Okay," Olivia said, looking down at her notepad, "let me see if I understand this. Vampires are capable of hunting humans at will, but they don't because it's against the law."

"Right."

"And the laws vampires follow come from an unknown source."

"Yes."

"But, no vampire has ever actually seen another vampire punished for breaking the law."

"Pretty much."

"And while hunting humans is generally against the law, vampires still enjoy doing it."

"Yes."

"So, when you hunted me with my permission, you were attempting to satisfy your natural urge to hunt without breaking the law."

"Exactly."

Olivia scanned her notes, scribbling more down, while Adam finished the last of his pie.

"I have a million more things I want to ask you," she said, "but I should probably get home. Would it be possible for us to meet again like this?"

"Of course."

"Great," Olivia said. "I hope this doesn't sound offensive, but will I have to let you hunt me again?"

"Not necessarily, no," Adam said. "But, your cooperation is appreciated."

"Fair enough," Olivia said. "You need a ride home or anything?"

"I'll be fine."

Olivia got up from the table.

"Wait a minute," she said. "Do you even have a home?"

"Yes," Adam said. "I have a house in Upland."

"So many questions," Olivia said, shaking her head. "How can I get in touch with you?"

"You'll see me soon enough."

They exited Corky's together and Adam stood on the sidewalk, watching Olivia walk to her car. When she got in, locking the door behind her, she turned to Adam and waved. He smiled, waving back. He was about to start walking back to the bowling alley in Upland— a trek of about ten miles or so—when he saw Olivia take her phone out. With his hands in his pockets, Adam strolled slowly by her car, looking up at the stars so as to give Olivia the impression he was no longer paying attention to her. Whoever it was she called didn't answer, so Adam listened as she left a voicemail: "Hey, it's Olivia. Sorry I missed your call. Crazy night. We'll hang out soon. Maybe this week. Goodnight."

CHAPTER SEVEN

THE GUILLOTINE

Johnson Tribal, a local celebrity amongst the Inland Empire's mixed martial arts community, was the head trainer at Ground and Pound. He was also Jesus' only real friend. The two of them met twelve years prior, when Jesus went to Ground and Pound to begin training for what he hoped would become a professional fighting career. When he got there, Jesus knew exactly who Johnson was. His celebrity was primarily due to an unspectacular two-fight stint in the UFC, both of which Jesus had watched live on television.

Jesus worked out at Ground and Pound everyday—two or three times a day, if he could—training in Johnson's classes every chance he got. When he wasn't training, Jesus worked a part-time job at Taco Bell. The money was shit, but it was enough to pay his gym fees. He still lived with his father at the time, so he didn't have to spend money on food and housing. With the exception of the fifteen to twenty hours a week he put in at Taco Bell, Jesus was able to focus on nothing but mixed martial arts. He didn't always plan on depending on his father, however, and he swore to him that he would make it as a fighter.

"When I do," Jesus told him, "I'll repay you for everything."

"Don't be silly, mijito," his father would tell him. "Just enjoy your fighting."

Johnson didn't really have any male friends, so he and Jesus developed a friendship based mainly on how often they saw each other at Ground and Pound. Johnson even started working with Jesus one on one—partly because they'd become buddies, but also because he saw potential in him. "I think you've got a chance to do some good things in the fight game," Johnson told him. "Keep at it." Johnson's words of encouragement put Jesus over the moon, and the first person he told was Daniel. Like Jesus, Daniel knew who Johnson was, so he, more than anybody, could appreciate how exciting it was.

On a Thursday morning, soon after Jesus showed up for his first workout of the day, Johnson surprised him with a last-minute invitation to fight in a small event in Tijuana. Jesus had only been training at Ground and Pound for two months at that point and, outside of a few sparring sessions with a couple other aspiring fighters, he had no real mixed martial arts experience.

"You think I'm ready?"

"Fuck if I know," Johnson said. "Even if you're not, you'll still get paid."

"Really?"

"Yeah."

"How much?"

"Probably enough to order a pizza after the fight," Johnson said. "There's a bonus if you win, too. We might be talking extra cheese and pepperoni."

"Can my friend come along?"

"Will he pay for gas?"

"Probably."

"The more the merrier."

The weigh-ins for the fight were the following day, so Jesus, Johnson, and Daniel left first thing in the morning. Jesus was well within the limits of his weight class, which was the primary reason Johnson invited him to the event. The fighter Jesus was replacing had been stabbed the night before following a disagreement over a poker game. Because of his clout as the card's headlining fighter, the promoters agreed to let Johnson find a last-minute replacement for the stabbed fighter. Had Jesus weighed weighed either ten pounds more or ten pounds less, Johnson likely would've invited somebody else.

Jesus hadn't been to Mexico since he was a child, when he'd gone with his parents to pick up the wooden trunk. His father was happy for him, though he chose not to attend the event. As much as he supported Jesus' decision to pursue a fighting career, he didn't have the stomach to actually watch him fight. Jesus and Daniel drove with Johnson in a minivan he borrowed from Ground and Pound, reaching Tijuana in just over two hours. They went straight to the venue, which was small, about the size of a high school gymnasium. The official weigh-ins took place inside a dank and dingy locker room with mold growing in the corners and cockroaches scattering about. The actual fights weren't taking place until the following afternoon, so Johnson booked a small motel room across the border in San Diego.

"I've got to run a few errands before we head back to the motel," he said.

Johnson's errands took them first to a doctor's office, where he paid the doctor for a prescription. He then took the prescription down the street to one of the many pharmacies in Tijuana, most of which were pristine inside with white walls and glass counters, a stark contrast to the rest of the dilapidated city. The pharmacist behind the counter wore a white lab coat and spoke exceptional English. Johnson showed the man his prescription, asking for Dianbol and Winstrol, which, Jesus later learned, were forms of anabolic steroids.

Johnson began using steroids after his first fight in the UFC. The fight itself, which he'd been offered after putting together a ten-fight win streak in a series of smaller organizations, aired on basic cable, marking Johnson's television debut. Every fight fan in the Inland Empire knew about the fight—including Jesus and Daniel—and they all watched as he suffered a devastating knock out in the first round. Despite the loss, UFC matchmakers offered Johnson a second fight a few months later, this time on the undercard of a pay-per-view as a replacement for a fighter who'd injured himself in training. The fight itself would be a dark match, which meant it wouldn't actually be televised; nonetheless, it was a huge opportunity for Johnson, so he wanted to take full advantage of it.

Johnson had less than a month to prepare for the fight and, despite the short notice, he managed to win by a razor-thin split decision, which, according to many mixed martial artist pundits, could've gone either way. Johnson told Jesus and Daniel all about it back in the motel room. "I was on top of the world," he said, "until my pre-fight drug test came back." After his initial UFC loss, Johnson realized he wasn't quite good enough to excel against the caliber of fighters at the highest level, so when he got his second opportunity in the UFC he wanted to do whatever it took to give himself the best chance to win. That's when he decided to add steroids to his training regime. "I always knew there was a chance I'd get caught," he said, "but I figured it'd be worth a shot, especially if I could get a win out of it."

After the failed drug test, the UFC changed the decision, officially making it a no contest. Johnson knew there wouldn't be a third opportunity. Despite his fallout with the UFC, Johnson was still regarded as a local hero in the Inland Empire, which led to Ground and Pound offering him a job. He continued to compete in smaller venues, where drug tests were either incompetently handled or altogether nonexistent, such as the competition he took Jesus to in Tijuana. The fight purses didn't earn him enough money to make a living, so, in order to supplement them along with his salary at Ground and Pound, Johnson began selling steroids.

After picking up the steroids, Johnson took Jesus and Daniel with him to a brothel in Tijuana called Chicago Club. Jesus and Daniel were both very uncomfortable inside, but Johnson seemed right at home. There weren't many patrons inside, as it was still the middle of the day. "It doesn't really get busy in here until after dark," Johnson said. There were about six or seven women in the club, most of whom sat alone at the bar, leaned back, legs crossed, hoping to reel in a potential customer.

"Here comes my regular," Johnson said.

A young girl in a miniskirt approached their table, sitting down beside Johnson and kissing him on the cheek. He introduced her to Jesus and Daniel, though she seemed more interested in taking him away to her room. Before walking off with her, Johnson turned to Jesus and Daniel.

"Are you two going to fuck anybody?"

They each shook their heads, no.

"Suit yourself."

A couple of women approached Jesus and Daniel at their booth while they waited for Johnson. Despite not speaking English, the girls figured out relatively quickly that they weren't looking to buy sex, so they left them alone. They must've passed on the message to the rest of the girls in Chicago Club, because the only other woman who approached their booth was an elderly lady with crooked teeth and a basket of Chiclets. She smiled at them, saying something in Spanish, while setting the basket on the table. Jesus gave her five dollars and the woman beamed, giving him a handful of Chiclets before walking away.

Johnson came back about twenty minutes later, at which point they made their way back across the border into San Diego. The following afternoon, Johnson drove them back into Tijuana for the fight. Despite being spruced up for the event, the gymnasium was still dank and dreary, with creaky bleachers and dubious security. After signing in, Johnson helped Jesus warm up in the locker room. In Jesus' limited training at Ground and Pound, he'd spent the majority of his time learning Brazilian jiu-jitsu and, in that time, he'd only effectively mastered one hold.

The guillotine choke.

The lead up to the fight was brief and unceremonious, as Johnson walked Jesus up to the cage, giving him a pat on the back before sending him inside. Jesus barely remembered the referee starting the fight before he found himself on his back, staring at the rafters. The majority of the fight was a frenzied scramble, with Jesus working mostly off of instinct and his wrestling background, trying—and failing—not to get hit in the face. Using hard punches and short elbows, his opponent opened up a cut over Jesus' eye, which bled profusely for the remainder of the fight. In the third round, with Jesus' face covered in red, his opponent grew a bit overconfident and, in a moment of carelessness, found himself in Jesus' guillotine choke. Squeezing as hard as he could, Jesus held the choke until his opponent passed out, forcing the referee to stop the fight.

Johnson and Daniel celebrated with him inside the cage, hugging and high-fiving. The whole drive home, Johnson talked about how he wanted to turn Jesus into a genuine prizefighter.

"I'd train more if I could," Jesus said. "But, I have a job at Taco Bell."

"Fuck that," Johnson said. "I'll get you a job at Ground and Pound."

True to his word, Johnson got Jesus a custodial job, mostly cleaning the mats and equipment. Jesus was happy to do it, too, as it meant he'd be able to spend nearly all of his time inside Ground and Pound. His whole life seemed to be unfolding just how he hoped it would, until, two days later, he watched Daniel get killed by a vampire in Memorial Park. His motivation to be a professional mixed martial artist disappeared soon thereafter, replaced instead by an unyielding hatred of vampires.

CHAPTER EIGHT

OLIVIA AND JESUS

The majority of Jesus' friendship with Olivia took place over the phone and, despite his inviting her out the previous night, they'd never actually been on a date before. They'd only known each other for a little while, having met at Ground and Pound a few weeks prior. Jesus would've asked her out sooner, but because he was generally shy around women, he kept putting it off. If he had actually spoken to Olivia the night he called her after killing his most recent vampire, he might still have been too nervous to ask her out. When they finally spoke on the phone the next day, however, Jesus and Olivia made plans for their first date.

The two of them first met when Olivia and Elowyn, signed up for self-defense classes at Ground and Pound. The classes were Elowyn's idea. She told Olivia it was important that they knew how to protect themselves, being that they worked so many late hours at Tropical Lei. While Olivia knew it was a good idea, she also knew that Elowyn had a crush on Johnson Tribal, whom she'd met at Tropical Lei. Elowyn spent a good portion of her shift talking to Johnson, trying to seduce him into buying a private dance, so she could get him alone in the VIP room and break a few of the club's ill-enforced rules. Johnson didn't buy a dance that night, but he did give Elowyn his business card. Soon thereafter, she'd talked Olivia into signing up for self-defense classes with her.

The class, which met once a week, was built on the fundamentals of Brazilian jiu-jitsu. Despite having all but retired from professional fighting, Johnson was still the most popular trainer at Ground and Pound. Jesus, who hadn't fought professionally since his bout in Tijuana twelve years earlier, helped out with the class as Johnson's assistant. Jesus noticed Olivia almost as soon as she walked in. She and Elowyn's first night of class started with the two of them sitting on the mat with the other students, listening to Johnson's professorial pontification on the merits of Brazilian jiu-jitsu.

"If you ever find yourself in a street fight," he said, "you can bet that fight's going to end up on the ground. Most marital arts, such as Muay Thai, karate, and traditional boxing, rely on attacking your opponent with your fists, elbows, knees, or feet. But no matter how proficient you are as a striker, when the fight goes to the ground—and trust me, the fight *will* go to the ground—striking won't do you any good. But, you're not here to learn how to fight. You're here to learn how to defend yourself. And by learning the principles of Brazilian jiu-jitsu, you'll soon have the ability to defend yourself both on your feet *and* on the ground."

Jesus learned early on in their friendship that Johnson was something of a womanizer, so he wasn't surprised to learn he'd invited Elowyn to Ground and Pound with the intention of trying to fuck her. Johnson hadn't anticipated Elowyn bringing Olivia, so he let Jesus know he'd have to serve as wingman. In this case, that meant keeping Olivia occupied while Johnson made his move. While Jesus could face down a vampire in a battle to the death on an almost nightly basis, the task of keeping Olivia occupied terrified him to no end.

After a brief instruction, Johnson broke the students up into pairs. Johnson paired himself with Elowyn and Jesus with Olivia. Jesus found Olivia to be just beautiful and, frankly, he was surprised Johnson hadn't targeted her for himself. It wasn't that Jesus found

Elowyn to be unattractive, but her looks were the sort that were inspired by pop music and reality television—nothing at all like Olivia's classic natural beauty. After a very brief introduction, Olivia lay flat on her back, opening her legs, while Jesus climbed on top of her. The feeling of being between her thighs stirred something in his loins and, while it hadn't happened yet, Jesus was worried about getting sexually aroused in the middle of class.

"Do I secure my legs," Olivia asked, hooking her ankles around the small of his back, "and pull myself *into* you?"

"No, keep your legs open," Jesus said, "and hold the back of my neck. When I lift myself up, you'll feel your body lift with mine."

"Got it."

Jesus put his hands on either side of her and pushed up, inadvertently pressing his pelvis against hers.

"With your strongest leg," he said, "plant your foot into the mat."

"Okay."

"Now, plant your opposite hand in back of you."

"Okay."

"Now, with your planted leg and your hand," Jesus said, "push yourself up and away from me."

Olivia completed the drill, successfully pushing herself up and away. Unfortunately for Jesus, the friction between his and Olivia's bodies left him with a full-blown erection. Hoping to hide it from Olivia—and, really, everyone else in Ground and Pound—Jesus remained kneeled down, hunched over his thighs with his elbows planted in the mat.

"How was that?" Olivia asked.

"Terrific."

"Can I try it again?"

"That won't be necessary."

"Are you okay?"

Without saying another word, Jesus stood up and ran to the bathroom, where he stayed until the class was over. When he finally came out, he was hoping all the students would be gone, which they were—all except for Elowyn and Olivia. Johnson was chatting up Elowyn, leaving Olivia with nothing to do but stand idly by. Johnson saw Jesus come out of the bathroom and called him over. As embarrassed as Jesus was, he knew it would look strange if he didn't join them. Johnson was asking for Elowyn's phone number just as Jesus arrived.

"But, we've only just met," Elowyn said, smiling, "how do I know I can trust you?"

"Maybe you can't," Johnson said, followed by a wink. "Maybe you'd feel better if we all exchanged numbers."

"You mean me *and* Olivia would give you our numbers?"

"No, no," Johnson said. "You can give me *your* number and Olivia can give Jesus *her* number. Then we'd all be friends. How's that?"

Elowyn laughed, squeezing his arm.

"What do you think, Olivia?" she asked.

"Sure," Olivia said, shrugging.

Johnson and Elowyn went back to their one-on-one flirting, leaving Jesus and Olivia to themselves.

"Where's your phone?" Olivia asked.

"Pardon?"

"Your phone," she said, "so I can put my number in it."

Jesus handed her his cell phone.

"Should I give you mine, too?" he asked.

"That's okay," Olivia said. "I'll get it when you call me. I'm Olivia, by the way."

"I'm Jesus."

"Thanks for your help in class."

"Sure."

"Where'd you disappear to anyway?"

Before he had a chance to fumble through an explanation, Elowyn grabbed Olivia, telling her she was hungry and ready to go—and, just like that, they were gone. Jesus didn't call Olivia right away and, really, he wasn't so sure he'd be calling her at all. Part of it was nerves, but he was also half-convinced she'd only given him her number to help out Elowyn. In the passing days before the next class, Jesus became more and more convinced that Olivia wasn't ever really interested in him calling her. He even imagined she'd be grateful not to hear from him.

When she and Elowyn returned to Ground and Pound the following week, Olivia went straight for Jesus.

"What's your problem?"

"Pardon?"

"Why haven't you called me?"

Jesus didn't know what to say.

"It's been a week, you know?"

"I didn't think you wanted me to."

"When a girl gives you her number, you call her," Olivia said. "Otherwise she starts feeling all insecure and shit."

"Sorry."

"Don't apologize," Olivia said. "Just call me."

"Okay."

༼••••༽

Olivia was working a mid-shift at Tropical Lei and asked Jesus if he wouldn't mind picking her up there for their date. He assumed she'd be waiting for him outside the club, but Olivia was nowhere to be seen. He called her cell phone, and she told him she was still working but to come inside. "I'll tell the bouncer not to charge you," she said. When Jesus walked in, he saw Olivia behind the bar, so he went over to say hello.

"The next bartender is running late," Olivia said. "She should be here in a few minutes, though. Go relax on the couch and enjoy the show."

Jesus took a seat on the couch, but he felt like it might be rude to look at another woman naked before his date with Olivia. By the same token, he didn't want to offend Olivia by *not* looking, as she might take such a gesture as an indictment of her workplace. While watching a stripper do her job with Olivia a mere ten or fifteen feet away didn't exactly *feel* natural, Jesus ultimately figured it would best to *act* natural—and, in this instance, the natural action seemed to be sitting comfortably and watching the woman on stage.

So, he did.

It turned out the woman on stage was Elowyn. As soon as Jesus saw her naked breasts, he looked away from the stage. He already knew she was a stripper, but he never really thought of her as one. He'd seen her without makeup in Ground and Pound, sweating and grunting during class. They'd made small talk when Johnson was busy, and he felt like an embarrassed teenager when she asked him if he liked Olivia. He considered Elowyn to be a friend, and so it just didn't seem like he should be watching her get naked. He decided that he would avert his eyes until she finished her routine—except that turned out to be a task more difficult than he anticipated. There was just something intoxicating about seeing someone you weren't supposed to see naked get naked.

So, despite his best judgment, Jesus allowed himself to watch Elowyn strip. He just hoped Olivia didn't see him watching. As soon as that thought entered his mind, however, he started gazing around the club, away from the stage. But, try as he might, his eyes always ended up back on Elowyn's naked body. At the conclusion of her performance, Elowyn got dressed—relatively speaking—and took a seat beside Jesus on the couch.

"Care for a dance, handsome?"

Jesus didn't know what to say.

Elowyn laughed

"Just fucking with you, dude," she said. "What's up with your pal, Johnson?"

"What do you mean?"

"I haven't heard from him all week," Elowyn said. "Is he avoiding me or something?"

Jesus didn't know exactly how Johnson felt about Elowyn, but he *did* know that Johnson generally lost interest in women after he had sex with them.

"I know he's been busy training for his fight," Jesus said.

"If you hear from him, tell him to call me."

"Okay."

"Listen," Elowyn said, "Olivia would probably kill me for saying this, but she doesn't go out on a lot of dates."

"Okay."

"So, she's probably not going to fuck you," Elowyn said. "Not tonight, anyway."

"Okay."

"Just don't be a dick."

"Okay."

Olivia turned up to Jesus' great relief.

"And what are you two gossiping about?" she asked.

"I told him to smack you on the back of the head if he feels any teeth," Elowyn said, standing from the couch. "You two have fun tonight."

As Jesus stood from the couch, Olivia looped her arm around his. Elowyn poked him hard in the chest with her index finger.

"Take care of my girl, you hear?"

"I will."

"I'm not afraid to kill you."

Jesus laughed.

"I'm serious."

"Okay."

Jesus took Olivia to King's Fish House for dinner. He'd never actually eaten there before, but it seemed sort of fancy, so he hoped she might be impressed by it. The waiter came by to take their orders, collecting their menus before he left. Up until that point, Jesus had come to regard his menu as a polite distraction, but without it he was faced with the task of engaging in first-date small talk, an art form he'd never been particular adept at. Luckily for Jesus, Olivia took the initiative.

"Does our waiter look like somebody to you?" Olivia asked.

"You mean like somebody famous?"

"Yeah," she said. "I can't come up with it."

"Does he remind you of an actor?"

"No," she said, "a wrestler."

"Seriously?"

"Yeah."

"You like wrestling?"

"Is that weird?"

"No," Jesus said, "I guess I just assumed you wouldn't."

"*You* like wrestling?"

"I love it," he said. "I've been watching since I was a kid."

"Me too," Olivia said, smiling. "How about that? All this time talking on the phone and we could've been geeking out about wrestling."

Jesus was about to respond, when Olivia blurted out a name.

"'Jumping' Jim Brunzell!"

"As in one half of the Killer Bees?"

"Do you know another?"

Jesus smiled.

"Here he comes," Olivia said. "Get a good look."

The waiter came by to drop off their drinks before floating off to another table.

"Well?"

"I can totally see it," Jesus said.

"Told you."

"So, were the Killer Bees you favorite tag team?"

"They were cool," Olivia said, "but my favorite team was the British Bulldogs. You?"

"I was always a big fan of the Road Warriors."

"Well," she said, "I thought we were talking about WWF tag

teams. If we're crossing into other promotions, I'd probably say the Steiner Brothers."

"I liked them, too," Jesus said. "Speaking of other promotions, if you could only watch one, would you choose WWF or WCW?"

"That depends."

"On what?"

"What time frame should I restrict my answer to?"

"What do you mean?"

"Well, I assume you're referring to the pre-WWE days, before Vince McMahon lost his lawsuit with the World Wildlife Fund and stopped calling the company the WWF," Olivia said. "That was in 2001. So, should I base my answer on the WWF when it was called the WWF, or do you also want me to take into consideration the WWE years."

"All of the above."

"What about WCW?"

"What about it?"

"That company only became WCW after Ted Turner bought it from Jim Crockett in 1988, which, up until then, had been known as the NWA. So, do you want me to consider the NWA years or just the WCW years?"

"I hadn't given that any thought."

"I did."

Olivia's phone rang. She looked at it before pardoning herself from the table to take the call. In her absence, Jesus considered his improbably good fortune of being out on a date with a beautiful woman who loved professional wrestling.

"Good news," Olivia said, returning to the table. "Johnson finally called Elowyn."

"That's great."

"They're going out tonight," she said. "So, if you want, we can go back to my place after dinner."

"Really?"

"I've got a pretty amazing collection of wrestling videos," she said. "And you're about the only person I know who might actually appreciate it."

¡°•••°¡

Jesus was kneeled in front of a shelf in Olivia's bedroom, looking over her impressive collection of VHS tapes. She had most every major wrestling pay-per-view produced in the last twenty years, as well as numerous self-recorded episodes of everything from *WCW Saturday Night* and *Superstars of Wrestling* to *Prime Time Wrestling* and *Monday Night Raw*. She'd given Jesus the task of picking out a video for them to watch, but, so vast and amazing was her collection, he was having trouble choosing. He eventually settled on *WrestleMania IV*.

"That's actually my favorite *WrestleMania*," Olivia said.

"Sounds like I picked right, then."

Olivia smiled.

While Jesus also liked *WrestleMania IV*, the main reason he'd picked it was because it featured a fourteen-man tournament for the WWF Championship and the entire broadcast lasted for over four hours. He figured it was a good way to extend his date with Olivia. She put the tape on, and for the first hour or so, Jesus and Olivia sat together on the couch with enough space between them for a third person to fit. But, by the second round of the tournament, they moved close enough together for their thighs to touch. And by the time they'd gotten into the third round, Jesus and Olivia were holding hands, her head lying on his shoulder. Everything was perfect, until Elowyn stormed though the front door, her cheeks wet with tears.

"Your friend is a fucking dick!" she told Jesus before disappearing into her bedroom, slamming the door behind her.

CHAPTER NINE

ELOWYN

Elowyn was sitting alone on the long couch of Tropical Lei having just said goodbye to Olivia and Jesus as they headed out on their first date. She could hardly concentrate on anything other than Johnson and the looming mystery of whether or not he'd finally call her back. She was sitting with her phone in hand, contemplating if it was too soon to send Johnson another text message, when a man approached her. Elowyn snapped at him before he had a chance to say hello.

"I'm on a fucking break!"

"Sorry, I just—"

"You just what?"

The man went away without another word. Elowyn began writing a text message to Johnson, but before she could finish, another man approached her. She looked up, prepared to snap, when she saw it was Professor Winters. This was the same Professor Winters who guided Olivia towards her love of fiction writing a decade earlier, though Olivia had no idea that he was a patron of Tropical Lei—nor did she realize that he regularly visited Elowyn. Professor Winters was about the only man who Elowyn couldn't imagine yelling at and, given her sour mood, she was very happy to see him.

Elowyn first met Professor Winters two years prior when she saw him sitting in Tropical Lei like a lost puppy alone on the couch. She took a seat beside him, figuring she might sell him a lap dance, but instead they ended up having a pleasant conversation. He told her that he was a widower and he'd never been to a strip club before. He'd been married for fifty years before his wife passed away. Elowyn found him endearing and, while he left without getting a lap dance, he came back a few nights later to see her again. They talked for nearly an hour and, though he never requested a dance, Professor Winters insisted on paying Elowyn for her time. He told her about how after his wife died he didn't know how to deal with the loneliness. He figured he might meet another woman, perhaps a widower like himself, and they could keep each other company for whatever time they had left. Professor Winters never went out of his way to meet any women, however, and, truth be told, he didn't want to. "But," he told Elowyn, "even if I'm destined to live out my final years alone, I see no reason why I can't enjoy the company of a pretty young woman every now and again."

Elowyn had been feeling so gloomy about Johnson not calling her that when Professor Winters showed up she jumped from the couch and gave him a hug. She adored Professor Winters—whom she called Arthur—because he was kind and sweet and, no matter how naked she was, he never made her feel cheap or objectified. She also loved his honesty, the way he told her the most private details of his sexual life like it was no big deal. He told her about how he visited a few massage parlors and paid for happy endings. He also told her about a very nice waitress named Darlene whom he paid to have sex with in the parking lot during her breaks. While Professor Winters still enjoyed sex, he found that, at this point of his life, he was most satisfied by having a good conversation.

Professor Winters hugged her back, and Elowyn felt so comforted in his arms she nearly cried. Without having to ask, she took him back to a private room where they could be completely alone.

Elowyn helped him down onto the bed and, after making sure he was comfortable, she began taking her clothes off, slowly, just the way he liked it. Elowyn always felt special when Professor Winters looked at her, and she wished she could live every day of her life being the woman that he saw. After she was completely naked, Elowyn crawled onto the bed with Professor Winters, cuddling into his arms and resting her head on his chest. She felt so safe in his arms, and without meaning to, she began to cry.

Elowyn was consumed with the fear that she was destined to live out her life alone, never finding a man to love her as much as she wanted to love him back. She knew she was physically attractive and sexually desirable, but she just never seemed able to have a substantive relationship with a man. She never lacked for options when it came to sexual partners, but she wanted someone to be there when the sex was over. And, beyond that, she wanted someone to be there when her life was over. Someone like Professor Winters. Someone to lie by her side and hold her hand, someone to tell her that she'd done a good job and everything was going to be all right.

From the time she was fourteen, Elowyn seemed to be in a constant cycle of meeting boys, falling in love, letting them fuck her, and having her heart broken. This became the motif of her life, always giving herself over to a man in the hopes that he would repay her by staying. She had boyfriends, of course. Not every man she met was so delusional as to not want a beautiful girl like Elowyn on his arm. But even when she was in a relationship, her fear remained; because even when he was there, there was always the possibility that he would leave. And invariably, this fear would manifest itself in quiet, unspoken ways, eating its way through anything good and healthy between them like a cancer, until all that was left for him to do was fulfill the result Elowyn had feared all along.

As it was with most every boy Elowyn had ever given herself to, Johnson Tribal was handsome and well built. They'd already had sex twice and talked on the phone a few more times than that. That he'd ever called her back at all Elowyn took as a promising sign of their future together. But, she hadn't heard from him in a week, and now she was beginning to worry she'd never hear from him again. These were the thoughts that passed through her mind as she cried in Professor Winters' arms.

"What's the matter, sweetheart?"

"It's nothing," Elowyn said.

"Is it boy trouble?"

She nodded, yes.

"Who's the boy?"

"Just some guy," she said. "I thought he liked me, but I'm not so sure anymore."

"He'd be a fool if he didn't."

"Yeah, right."

"It's true," Professor Winters said. "You're beautiful and you're sweet and you've got a heart the size of the Pacific. If I weren't such an old fart, I'd try to steal you for myself."

Elowyn laughed.

"I was a handsome lad once upon a time."

"You're still handsome."

"That's kind of you to say."

"It's true."

"If only I were fifty years younger."

Elowyn smiled and Professor Winters pulled her in tighter. They lay there just like that for nearly an hour, not another word spoken between them. When it was time to go, Professor Winters sat on the edge of the bed, watching Elowyn put her clothes back on—slowly, just the way he liked it. He gave her a couple of large bills from his fold, and she gave him a kiss on the lips. When she opened her purse to put her money away, Elowyn saw a text message from Johnson waiting on her cell phone.

"It's him," she said, reading the text. "He wants to meet up after I get off."

"Perhaps this boy isn't such a fool after all."

Elowyn's shift was over, so she asked Professor Winters if he wouldn't mind walking her out to her car after she got dressed in her real world clothes.

"I'd be delighted to."

He waited for Elowyn at the club's entrance and, when she was ready, he walked her safely to her car, neither of them aware of an old and dangerous vampire named Victus watching from the darkness.

CHAPTER TEN

VICTUS

Before Victus became a vampire in the seventeenth century, he was a mercenary soldier in the Thirty Years' War. He was a violent sort who would've been at home in a more savage time, so Victus took great pleasure in pillaging small villages in Central Europe, slaughtering the men and forcing himself on the women. He should've died in 1630 after becoming ill with the bubonic plague, but a vampire named Katarina saved him. Katarina had been taking great pleasure in the war, as it allowed her to feed freely from dying men without worry of consequence. Katarina admired Victus from afar, appreciating not only his savagery but also the sheer pleasure he took in inflicting harm on his own kind. She thought it a waste that his life should end on account of a silly human ailment, so she turned Victus into a vampire.

Even as a vampire, Victus continued to participate in the Thirty Years' War, but he was no longer a mercenary for any of the participating European countries. He and Katarina simply used the war as their own personal buffet. It was an ideal environment for Victus to learn and adjust to his new abilities, as vampires were allowed to kill humans on the verge of death without fear of punishment. There were eighteen years remaining in the Thirty Years' War when

Katarina turned him, so she and Victus pillaged and fed throughout Germany until the treaties of Osnabrück and Münster that ended the war in 1648. During that time, Katarina educated Victus on the laws vampires had to follow, including the one that said vampires were allowed to hunt humans so long as they delivered them alive to a feeding post.

The two of them lived happily together in vampire bliss, hunting and feeding for nearly a century, until Katarina was killed in 1727. Between the years 1542 and 1735, a series of laws had been enacted in England, Scotland, and Ireland to punish individuals for practicing witchcraft. As a result, several men and women within those regions became hyperaware of any strange individuals whom they feared might be witches. Victus and Katarina were traveling through Scotland in 1727, taking refuge in a barn one night just before morning broke. They were asleep on a couple bales of hay when the owner of the barn—a farmer whose crops had been suffering greatly after years of prosperity—burst the doors open. He'd been convinced that his crops were suffering at the hands of witches, so when he discovered Victus and Katarina in his barn, he assumed they were the source of his misfortune.

When the Scottish farmer burst the doors open in the middle of the afternoon the sun was at its peak, spilling a wide column of sunlight onto Katarina and Victus. The scorching rays awoke the vampires immediately, causing each of them to scatter in search of darkness. Victus succeeded, crouching in the shadows of the barn's furthest corner—Katarina, however, was not so lucky. In her panic to find refuge, Katarina got trapped in the sunlight and her body became engulfed in flames. Victus was forced to watch as the farmer prodded Katarina with a pitchfork, keeping her in the sunlight. She screamed out as her flesh curled and crackled until she collapsed into a pile of black ashes. Katarina's dying scream rang in Victus' ears as he avenged her death a few moments later, braving the sunlight just long enough to bury his teeth in the farmer's neck, pulling him back into the shadows where he fed until he was empty.

Victus knew that such a feeding was against vampire law—but he was so enraged, he didn't care. If there was a punishment to come, he welcomed it. And, if it was death, all the better. He couldn't imagine living a day without Katarina, let alone an eternity. As the days, weeks, and months passed without incident, however, Victus eventually realized that no punishment would come his way. He took this to mean that his killing of the farmer was just, which, in his heart, he'd already believed to be true. Victus moved on with his life from there, walking the earth, planting himself for decades at a time in whatever spot he found satisfying, from Africa and the Middle East to New Orleans and, most recently, the Inland Empire.

Victus knew he could never find a vampire to fill his heart the way Katarina had, so he committed himself to his freelance work as a hunter. He currently resided in a small house in Rancho Cucamonga, which he'd inherited from a married couple he hunted twelve years earlier, delivering them to the Barbershop where they died a week later. After spending over two centuries alone, Victus found his next companion in the parking lot of Tropical Lei. He'd been walking along Foothill Boulevard, hunting, when her scent first caught his attention. The last time Victus had taken in such a delectable scent a few years prior, it led to one of the most delicious and satisfying feedings of his entire life.

He knew he was fortunate to cross paths with such a scent even just once, so coming across an equally delicious scent for the second time in his life convinced Victus that fate was favoring his long-suffering heart. He followed the scent to its source, leading him to the parking lot of Tropical Lei. The scent came from a woman who, to his eyes, looked more like Katarina than any woman he'd ever seen before. Victus watched as she walked to her car in the company of an old man who also had a delectable—if inferior—scent. The woman and the old man hugged, kissing briefly on the lips, and, as she got into her car, Victus heard the old man speak her name.

Elowyn.

Victus had no doubt that he could—and would—find Elowyn again. But he was still on the hunt, and, wanting to save Elowyn for another day, the old man would more than suffice. Victus shuffled on his back beneath the old man's car, grabbing onto the metal frame and pulling himself up off the asphalt, holding on as the engine revved. The old man drove for nearly twenty minutes, eventually arriving at Corky's. Victus was pleased to find that the old man had taken him to Rancho Cucamonga, as the Barbershop was only a few minutes away.

He continued hanging under the car until the old man entered Corky's, at which point he came out from beneath and took his place in the darkness. He didn't have to wait long for the old man to come out—but, to Victus' surprise, he didn't exit alone. He was with a waitress who followed the old man back to his car. The old man opened the passenger door for the waitress before getting in on the driver's side. Victus could've taken both of them quite easily, but he preferred hunting one human at a time. He found that the process was more enjoyable when he didn't have to compromise his focus.

Victus expected the car to start up, at which point he would've figured out a stealthy way to tag along. He figured out that the old man and the waitress weren't going anywhere once they began having sex inside the car. Victus watched as the waitress straddled the old man in the driver's seat, grinding over him until he was done. Then he listened as the old man talked about his dead wife. After about ten minutes, the old man walked the waitress back into Corky's, and when he came back out, he found Victus standing beside his car.

"Can I help you, son?" the old man asked.

"Yes."

"What do you need?"

"I need *her*."

"Who?" the old man asked. "Darlene?"

"No," Victus said. "The one you call Elowyn."

Victus stepped closer to the old man, sniffing the fear as it billowed from his pores like a thick fog.

"I have money, if that's what you need."

"That's not what I need."

The old man turned around, intending to run back into Corky's, but, before he could, Victus took hold of him. He tried to scream, but no sound came out. Victus pulled him back into the shadows, drinking his blood until the old man passed out. He didn't kill him, though. He carried the old man back to his car, which he used to deliver him to the Barbershop. Victus thought he might go back to Tropical Lei the following night to look for Elowyn, but, as luck would have it, he smelled her scent as he exited the Barbershop. She was in a car with a man parked at the intersection, waiting for the red light to turn green. Victus noted that it was not the same car she'd left Tropical Lei in.

Because it was the middle of the night and the street was virtually empty, nobody saw Victus climb atop the roof of the car. He held on as the light turned green and the car accelerated forward, driving for about five minutes until they reached an apartment complex. When Elowyn and the driver got out of the car, Victus followed from a stealth distance until they reached their destination. They entered an apartment, while Victus waited outside the door, listening as they ate dinner and had sex. Elowyn's glorious scent filled the apartment, pushing through the cracks of the door in the moments that followed their coitus.

"You can't be here in the morning," the man said.

"Why not?" Elowyn asked.

"Because I don't want you here in the morning."

Victus watched as Elowyn stormed naked from the apartment, holding her clothes in her arms. He'd stepped away from the door a moment before she exited, so she never knew he was there. She stopped beside a tree, putting her clothes on, before walking barefoot on the sidewalk. Victus followed behind Elowyn for the hour it took her to walk home to her apartment, never once giving her so much as a hint that she wasn't alone. He watched her put her keys into the door and storm inside, yelling as she slammed the door behind her: "Your friend is a fucking dick!" Victus could've taken Elowyn by force at any point that night before she entered her apartment. But her scent was so rich and intoxicating that he wasn't ready for it to go away, not yet anyway.

CHAPTER ELEVEN

DARLENE

arlene got up at seven in the morning, early enough to fix her son Max's breakfast and walk him to the bus stop. Her mother lived with she and Max in their two-bedroom apartment to help out since Darlene worked mostly overnight shifts waiting tables at Corky's. Despite having her mother there, Darlene still made sure she was up every weekday morning to see Max off to school, even if it meant not sleeping when she got home from Corky's just to make sure she was awake. As soon as Max was off to school, Darlene's head would hit the pillow, letting the world disappear for the rest of the morning and much of the afternoon. Without fail, her mother had a warm pot of coffee waiting for her when she woke up, and they'd sit together at the kitchen table eating pastries and chatting about all the things that didn't matter.

Darlene and her mother nearly always picked Max up together at the corner when the school bus dropped him off and, walking back home, they'd each hold his hands, Max happily in the middle. For Max, who was in the middle of second grade, this was all he knew. His mother and grandmother had always been there, raising him, each of them doing their best to make up for the father he'd never met and would never know. A big part of how she made up for Max's absent father was by trying to provide him with a comfortable life, a lot of toys, and regular visits to Disneyland. When it came to Max, Darlene would truly do anything to make him happy. Unfortunately, she wasn't able to do everything she wanted for Max on her waitress salary alone, especially since the tips weren't particularly big during the overnight shifts.

After school, Darlene made Max a snack and watched TV with him before helping with his homework. At bedtime, her mother would get Max into the bath while Darlene started getting ready for work. Once Max was put to bed, Darlene would spend a little more time with her mother, watching the news over a cup of tea, before heading out to Corky's for the night. On the night Victus killed Professor Winters, Darlene was in Corky's practically alone, except for the hostess at the register and a heavyset man with sad eyes and freckled arms. The heavyset man was a regular customer at Corky's, usually coming in during Darlene's shifts, though he barely spoke to her outside of ordering his meals. He always sat in his booth for at least an hour or so after finishing his burger and fries before leaving a generous tip and shuffling out the door.

As the heavyset man was leaving on this particular night, he crossed paths with Professor Winters who was entering Corky's. Professor Winters stood at the register, making small talk with the hostess until he caught Darlene's eye. She moved through the dining room with a smile on her face, giving Professor Winters a big hug. Darlene removed her apron and grabbed her coat from behind the counter, letting the hostess know she was taking her ten-minute break. She looped her arm with Professor Winter's and they headed outside.

The air was chilly, so they hurried the short distance to Professor Winters' car, which faced the chain-link fence that separated the parking lot from the steep drop leading to the 210 Freeway. Once they settled into his car, Darlene exchanged a few pleasantries with Professor Winters before putting her hand on his crotch. He wasn't quite hard yet, but he assured her that his little blue pill would be taking effect soon enough. While she waited, Darlene lifted her feet onto the dashboard, removing her panties from beneath her skirt. With Professor Winters watching, she slowly unbuttoned her blouse, exposing her bra for him. Reaching over, he gently fondled her breasts, removing them from her bra, letting them hang over the underwire.

Darlene was in her early-forties and found that the more time passed the less men looked at her the way Professor Winters did. She appreciated his hungry fingers, the way they devoured her breasts, her thighs, her pussy, the way his passion for her betrayed all traces of civility. Just as soon as that magic blue pill took effect, Darlene hiked her skirt up and straddled Professor Winters in the driver's seat. It was an awkward fit, but, as this wasn't their first time fucking in his car, she knew exactly how and where to plant her knees. As much as she enjoyed Professor Winters' company and was always happy to see him, they were not friends with benefits. In order to supplement her waitress income, Darlene occasionally sold sex during her breaks. Professor Winters just happened to be one of her customers.

It all started innocently enough a few years before when her ex-boyfriend—who, at the time, was her current boyfriend—would come visit her during her shifts. They'd sneak out to his car and mess around for however long they could before she had to get back to work. Darlene enjoyed fucking him and watching movies and strolling through the mall, but, more than that, she liked that he was nice to Max. He bought him toys and took him for ice cream. Sometimes when she was working, he'd visit with Max and watch Disney movies. But, he eventually cheated on Darlene, so she broke up with him. The toughest part was explaining to Max why his buddy wasn't around anymore.

The ex went to Corky's all the time after they broke up, wanting to talk to Darlene, trying to make things right, but she'd been hurt too many times by too many men and wasn't interested in giving this one another chance. Finally, after one of his many groveling attempts, he asked Darlene what it would take. Without even meaning the words she said, Darlene told him he'd have to pay her if he ever wanted to see her naked again. From there, the hypothetical negotiations began. He wanted to know how much he could do with her and for how much money. While it'd started out as a hypothetical, Darlene soon started taking the negotiations seriously. She thought about Max, about how it wasn't fair for him to suffer on account of her failed relationship, how she and the ex owed him for the collateral damage they'd both caused. That was the first night Darlene ever exchanged sex for money.

Darlene was pulling her panties back on when her ex took some cash from his wallet, handing it to her. She hesitated a moment—knowing full well she was crossing a line, weighing the regret against the opportunity to make Max happy—before taking the money. It was even easier when they did it again a few nights later. It was just sex, after all. Sex with a man who she'd already had sex with many times before, long before the idea of paying for it ever came into the fold. She was still physically attracted to him, so it wasn't like she was forcing herself to do something unpleasant. She used the extra money to buy Max toys and take him out for pizza with her mother. It was nice.

And so things went like that for a few weeks, which turned into months. It was almost like having a boyfriend again, minus the headaches. Once in a while, she even invited him back into Corky's for a piece of pie. Darlene was nearly seduced into the idea that maybe they could work things out, maybe their differences weren't all that far apart, when he asked her if she'd be interested in fucking his friend for the same price. Darlene, of course, was stunned and insulted, though the ex didn't know *why* she was insulted, as it's what she'd been doing with him. She'd assumed that he was enjoying their arrangement in the same way she was, that, while they were engaging in their own personal prostitution ring, it still felt intimate and personal. Emotions and hurt feelings aside, Darlene never forgot why she agreed to let her ex pay for sex in the first place. So, in the interest of giving Max the best life possible—and in order to supplement her waitress wages—Darlene agreed to fuck her ex-boyfriend's friend.

An hour later the friend showed up to Corky's. Darlene had met him a few times over the years and they'd even shared a few words here and there, but, really, she didn't know him all that well. The fact that she knew him at all, however, helped get her comfortable with what she was preparing to do. He wasn't exactly handsome and he could stand to exercise a little, but he was very kind—polite, even—which Darlene appreciated. Before they went outside to his car, Darlene made sure he understood the ground rules, which she was making up on the spot, letting him know what she would and wouldn't do. She also made sure to collect her payment up front before going to his car.

In the end, Darlene was surprised at how easy it was. She entirely expected to wrestle with some great moral burden before it was all over, but she simply got in the car, waited for him to put on his condom, climbed on his lap, and the whole thing was over in less than a minute. She actually had nine minutes left on her break. The very next day, she took Max to Toys "R" Us and let him pick out any toy he wanted.

The ex stopped visiting her at Corky's, but his friend continued to visit Darlene for a quick fuck every now and again. He was always polite and sometimes he gave her a little more money than she asked for, which she appreciated. Soon enough, the visits just became normal, blending in with the blur of routine, one friend turning into two and three and four—before she knew it, Darlene had a roster of regulars. Even as her supplemental enterprise grew, she only accepted new clients after one or two visits where she could vet them a bit, making sure they were safe. Months turned to years and years turned to whatever and somewhere along the way Darlene and Professor Winters crossed paths and he became a regular. Professor Winters didn't visit her as much as the others, though she wished he would. He was bright and articulate, and he had a way of engaging her in conversations that made her feel smarter than she was, which she liked.

Professor Winters was the only client Darlene didn't make wear a condom. He was sweet and old and had been married for fifty years, which, in her mind, made him as harmless as a virgin. She'd gotten her tubes tied after Max was born, so, even if Professor Winters had even one healthy sperm left in his body, it wasn't going to meet any of her eggs. The only other client she'd allowed to have unprotected sex with her was a heavyset man named Peter Tallook. It had occurred three months earlier, and at the time, Darlene was in need of the extra cash. Peter seemed harmless enough, so she considered her unprotected sex with him a safe risk. Professor Winters, she figured, was an even safer risk.

Darlene rode Professor Winters to climax before settling into the passenger seat of his car. He handed her the handkerchief from his breast pocket to clean herself with. As she wiped away the remains of his orgasm, Darlene caught Professor Winters gazing out the window, a melancholy smile on his face.

"You feeling okay?" Darlene asked.

"Yes," Professor Winters said, "I'm feeling wonderful, my dear."

"Something on your mind?"

He turned his smile to Darlene.

"You've got a sharp intuition," he said. "I was actually thinking about my wife."

Darlene smiled, not knowing how to respond.

"She's been gone for a couple of years," Professor Winters said, "but I still find myself feeling guilty, like I'm doing something behind her back."

"I'm sure she'd understand."

"I like to think so," Professor Winters said. "She and I always talked about growing old together. It's a sweet cliché that sometimes gets bandied about, but we meant it. We talked about watching our hair grow white and kissing each other's wrinkles. She joked that if I ever needed a diaper, she wouldn't be the one to change it, but I knew she'd have done anything for me—and I her. We did get to spend a few golden years together before she passed. She saw my grays turn to whites, and I met her wrinkles with my lips. And at night, we'd lie in bed and laugh like children over nothing in particular, just the pure giddiness of being together. But, while neither of us talked about it, we were always aware of the ugly truth that shadowed our blessed union. One of us had to go first. I didn't like the idea of her being alone, and I often worried about how she'd get along without me. I guess it never really occurred to me that *I'd* be the one having to live without *her*. But, to tell you the truth, I wouldn't have it any other way. I like knowing that she got to have us until the very end. She hated leaving me behind, though, and she fought it all the way to the very end. We were supposed to go simultaneously, hand in hand, in the middle of our final sleep. I told her to save me a seat in the clouds, as I would most assuredly be following right behind her. In the meantime, I don't think she'd take much exception to me making my time without her a little less lonely."

"It sounds like a beautiful life."

"It was," Professor Winters said. "It really and truly was."

CHAPTER TWELVE

A GOOD MAN IS HARD TO FIND

As an aspiring novelist, Olivia hadn't really had much of her work published. She'd had a few stories posted on various blogs, and one story, loosely based on her relationship with her mother, was published in *The Pacific Review*, but, other than that, she was virtually anonymous. She knew if she were ever going to get people's attention as a writer, she would have to publish a novel. She'd first decided to become a writer when she was eighteen years old, watching the Academy Awards with her mother.

Every year, from the time she was a little girl, Olivia and her mother lay in bed together, watching the festivities unfold, from the red carpet interviews to the elegant speeches. But, when she was eighteen, she seemed to watch the awards through a different lens. Perhaps it was because she was engulfing on the adult portion of her life and, therefore, was feeling the tug of purpose, but something about that year's ceremonies inspired Olivia—all those beautiful people, wearing those beautiful clothes, giving their beautiful speeches. She wanted to be part of it. She wanted to walk down the red carpet, take pictures, give interviews, and accept awards.

But, short of fucking every movie producer from here to the Pacific, the only way Olivia was going to get invited to the Academy Awards was to become a viable and productive cog in the film industry. And the only problem with that, in her estimation, was she had no skills that Hollywood was in need of. Curled up against her mother, head resting against her musky bosom, Olivia asked for advice.

"Well," her mother said, "you can be an actress. You're certainly pretty enough."

Olivia was too shy for acting.

"Maybe you can be one of the wardrobe people."

Olivia hated fashion.

"How about being a producer?"

Olivia had no idea what producers even did.

"You always get good marks in English," her mother said. "Perhaps you can be a writer."

With that, Olivia's writing aspirations were born. It mattered very little to her that she knew nothing about screenwriting. It also mattered very little to her that she wasn't much of a reader. The most reading she did was usually at the dentist's office before a teeth cleaning when she flipped through *Time* or *Us Weekly*. She most certainly didn't read books, but, since she intended on writing for Hollywood, she figured that wouldn't matter much at all—in fact, she thought, it might well work in her favor.

"When you think about it," she often asked her reflection in the bathroom mirror, "how hard is it really to tell a story?"

Olivia fantasized about a life of luxury in a Spanish mission style home. She couldn't remember where the fantasy came from, as she'd never been to a Spanish mission or church, though she was convinced that she was Spanish in her past life. In her fantasy, she woke up every morning in a wrought iron bed with a large, ornate filigree headboard. She'd have a tall archway entry with heavy wooden double doors and a wrought iron chandelier overhead. She would lay in bed with her mother and tell her over and over about the home she would one day own, and her mother would help decorate her fantasies, adding such details as a sunken Roman tub and a balcony overlooking the Pacific Ocean.

Unlike so many of her peers, Olivia didn't see an immediate need to go to college, especially since she was making plenty of money as a bartender at the bikini bar, but she did imagine she could benefit from taking some creative writing classes. So, after she graduated from Alta Loma High School, she enrolled—for what would turn out to be a very short stint—at Chaffey College. She registered in only one course, a screenwriting class taught by Professor Winters, which met once a week on Friday mornings. Professor Winters was an elderly man with white hair and a kind face. Olivia, who had a soft place in her heart for old men, adored Professor Winters—in large part because, during the apex of his career, he spent time as a staff writer on *The Golden Girls*.

On the first day of class, Professor Winters asked the students to introduce themselves by saying their name, what sort of books they liked to read, and who some of their favorite authors were. Olivia thought this would be a futile exercise, figuring Professor Winters would quickly find that nobody in the class enjoyed reading any more than she did. But, as one student after another introduced themselves, their favorite genres, and their favorite authors, Olivia came to the quick conclusion that she was in the minority and, essentially, out of her element. And then, before she knew it, Professor Winters was looking at her, prompting her with his raised eyebrows to introduce herself.

"My name's Olivia."

"And what do you like to read?"

"I don't really read books."

"No?"

Olivia shook her head.

"But, you want to be a screenwriter, yes?"

"Most definitely."

"Well, then," Professor Winters said, "you need to read books."

"But, books aren't movies."

"They are stories, though," he said. "And the best stories you're going to find live on bookshelves."

"Can't I just read screenplays?"

"Have you ever read a screenplay?"

"No."

"Most are garbage," Professor Winters said, "even the good ones. You won't learn anything useful from reading a screenplay. Have I mentioned yet what Bea Arthur told me on the set of *The Golden Girls*?"

"No."

"She told me nothing," he said. "You know why?"

Olivia shook her head, no.

"Because I was nobody," he said. "Just a face."

"But, you were on the writing staff, right?"

"Sure," Professor Winters said, "but so were a bunch of other faces. We ate pizza and made up stories about old ladies and cheesecake, but, at the end of the day, we were disposable. There were a million writers every bit as good as me waiting for a chance at my job. And, eventually, one of them got it."

"What happened?"

"I had the misfortune of being disposable," he said. "It was the stars who were important, not the writers. So, what's the moral of that story?"

"I don't know."

"Write a book."

"But, I want to write movies."

"Have you heard of Stephen King?"

"Yeah."

"So has Bea Arthur."

"But, this is a screenwriting class, right?"

"Unfortunately."

"You don't like screenwriting?"

"It's good money if you can get it," Professor Winters said. "But,

I prefer books. Anyway, you can't write a screenplay until you know how to tell a story. And you'll never learn how to tell a story until you start reading books."

While she didn't particularly enjoy being put on the spot on the first day of class, Olivia did enjoy the special attention Professor Winters was paying her. After class, he invited her to chat in his office.

"What do you like writing about?" he asked.

"I've never actually written anything."

"So, you don't read *or* write?"

"Yes," Olivia said, "but I *want* to write."

"What do you imagine you'll be writing about?"

"I don't know," she said. "Probably vampires."

"I'm guessing you've never read *Dracula*," Professor Winters said. "Have you seen the movie?"

Olivia shook her head, no.

"Well, aren't you a piece of work," he said, smiling. "You want to write about vampires, but you've never seen *Dracula*."

"I like *Buffy the Vampire Slayer*."

"You like Joss Whedon, then?"

"I love him!"

"He's a good writer," Professor Winters said. "His old man, Tom, got me the job on *The Golden Girls*. He was one of the head writers. We met in the sixties writing for *Captain Kangaroo*. You probably don't know *Captain Kangaroo*, but it used to be a big deal. It gave my mother something to brag about."

Olivia smiled.

"Do you know Joss, personally?" she asked.

"I met him a time or two," Professor Winters said. "I don't know him as an adult, if that's what you're asking. I bet he reads books, though."

"All right," she said, "you've made your point. What should I be reading?"

Professor Winters went to his bookshelf, retrieving a short story anthology.

"Take this home with you," he said. "Read 'A Good Man is Hard to Find' by Flannery O'Connor. I suspect you'll enjoy it."

Trusting that Professor Winters knew what he was talking about, Olivia read "A Good Man is Hard to Find" as soon as she got home. It started off kind of boring for her, as it was about a family taking a road trip. There was the grandmother, who was the main character, her son, his wife, and their four children—or was it three children? She wasn't exactly sure. The grandmother was annoying and constantly nagging her son, and just when it seemed that's what the story was going to be about, they had a car accident. Trapped on the side of the road, they're greeted with an escaped convict called The Misfit. The Misfit has his buddies murder the grandmother's family in the woods before having some sort of philosophical conversation with her. When he's done, he shoots her three times in the chest.

Olivia loved it and told Professor Winters as much. He told her to next read *The Metamorphosis* by Franz Kafka, which, as Olivia found out, was the story of a man named Gregor Samsa who woke up one morning to find he'd transformed into a giant cockroach. When Olivia loved that story as well, Professor Winters figured he had a pretty good bead on what sort of stories she liked, so he told her it was time to read a novel.

"A novel?" she said. "Really? Aren't there any other short stories I'd enjoy?"

"Sure there are," he said, "but, if you want to write movies, you're better off reading novels."

He told her to read *Skinny Legs and All* by Tom Robbins, the heroine of which was a fiercely bright, ingenious, and sexually conscious woman whom Professor Winters thought Olivia might relate to. He loaned her his very own copy from his bookshelf and Olivia loved *Skinny Legs and All* so much, she finished it in three days. For the remainder of the semester, Professor Winters introduced Olivia to all the different authors he thought she would love—from Tim O'Brien and Michael Chabon to Nick Hornby and Chuck Palahniuk—and he was right almost every single time.

After the class was over, Olivia didn't keep in touch with Professor Winters, which she regretted. She hoped that he was all right wherever he was. She liked to think he was enjoying retirement somewhere with his wife whom he always talked so lovingly about in class. She enjoyed fantasizing about Professor Winters on a cruise with his wife, lying by the pool with a margarita at his side, while he read Olivia's yet-to-be written vampire novel. In her fantasy, Professor Winters loved the book and was so very proud of Olivia, beaming to his wife about the girl he'd inspired so many years ago.

CHAPTER THIRTEEN

BAREFOOT ON THE SIDEWALK

Elowyn called Olivia from her car as she left Tropical Lei. She was so excited about Johnson texting her that she'd actually forgotten Olivia was out on her date with Jesus.

"Sorry to interrupt your date," Elowyn said, "but Johnson texted me!"

"That's great," Olivia said. "When?"

"Just a little while ago," Elowyn said. "He wants to hang out."

"Are you going to?"

"Let's just say I won't be coming home tonight."

"I get the picture."

"Anyway," Elowyn said, "I just wanted to let you know, so you wouldn't worry or anything."

"I appreciate that."

"And if your date's going well, you'll have the apartment all to yourself."

Elowyn called Johnson when she got home and was elated when he answered on the second ring. She told him she was low on gas and he had to pick her up. This, of course, wasn't true. Elowyn was just hoping to ensure she'd be spending the night at Johnson's apartment. Johnson, for his part, acted somewhat annoyed, but that didn't bother Elowyn in the least. In the end, he picked her up. She didn't mention anything to him about a sleepover but figured that, once she tuckered him out with a good few hours of fucking, he wouldn't feel like driving her home anyway.

Everything at Johnson's apartment was going exactly according to plan. They'd stopped by Taco Bell on the way there to pick up some dinner, which they ate on the couch while watching *The Ultimate Fighter*. Elowyn had acquired an appreciation for mixed martial arts on account of the self-defense classes she'd been taking with him. She'd even gone to Ground and Pound a few times to take some classes in Brazilian jiu-jitsu just because she enjoyed it so much. Grappling, it turned out, came extremely natural to her. In her fantasies, she and Johnson would be together all the time, training at the gym by day and cohabitating by night. After dinner, Johnson went to take a shower and, while he didn't invite Elowyn to join him, he didn't discourage her when she did. She didn't actually get in the shower with him, though; she simply sat on the toilet and watched him clean up, occasionally reaching in to give him a tug. After his shower, Johnson went straight to his bedroom and Elowyn followed right behind him. He lay down on his bed, lounging with his hands behind his head.

"Why don't you go ahead and get naked?" Johnson said.

"My pleasure."

Elowyn removed her clothes, slowly, which she hoped he would enjoy.

"What's the hold up?"

"Sorry."

Elowyn quickly stripped off the rest of her clothes before joining Johnson on his bed. She went down on him for a bit, happy to see that he was enjoying himself, before lying on her back in hopes that he would return the favor. He didn't. Johnson instead mounted her, clumsily pounding away for little more than a minute before finishing. Rolling onto his back, he exhaled and closed his eyes. While she hadn't come anywhere near to climaxing, Elowyn was still happy to have satisfied him.

Having excused herself to the bathroom, Elowyn sat on the toilet, pissing away the remnants of Johnson's climax, daydreaming about what they might do in the morning. She thought, perhaps, she would wake him up with a blowjob, after which they could go out to breakfast. Pancakes, eggs, coffee, perhaps a walk around the park or an afternoon at the movies. She'd ask for popcorn from the snack bar, so she could feed it to him in the dark, listening to each kernel crunch as she rested her head against his chest. She'd ask about dinner and he'd tease her about not knowing how to cook. She'd order a pizza and they'd eat it on the floor, a picnic in the living room. She wanted to spend the whole weekend naked with him, watching TV, fucking, sharing their stories as they fell in love. She truly believed it could be like that forever.

When Elowyn went back to his bedroom, she saw that Johnson wasn't there. Still naked, she walked into the living room and found him on the couch, fully dressed and watching TV. She sat beside him, resting her head on his shoulder.

"I was thinking we could get breakfast in the morning," she said.

"I've got plans."

"What kind of plans?"

"Just stuff."

"Can I tag along?"

"No."

"I can just wait for you here then."

"You can't be here in the morning."

"Why not?"

"Because I don't want you here in the morning."

"Did I do something wrong?"

"Listen," Johnson said, "you should get dressed, so I can take you home."

Elowyn stormed into his bedroom, gathering her clothes from the floor, before hurrying back through the living room.

"You want a ride or what?"

"Fuck you!"

Elowyn was already out the door and running naked through the apartment complex, stopping beside a tree to put her clothes on. She held her heels in her hand, walking barefoot on the sidewalk. The distance between Johnson's apartment and hers was fifteen minutes by car, so, by foot, it would take her an hour to get home. She didn't care. If there was danger about, she was too hurt and angry to think about it.

When she finally made it home, sweating and out of breath, Elowyn stormed though the front door. She saw Jesus sitting on the couch with Olivia, and the sight of him only reminded her of how angry she was at Johnson. "Your friend is a fucking dick!" she told Jesus before going into her bedroom, slamming the door behind her. Elowyn threw herself onto the bed, burying her face in her pillow, where she cried until Olivia came to check on her a few moments later.

CHAPTER FOURTEEN

HIS FATHER'S SILENCE

Every Wednesday night since he'd moved out twelve years earlier, Jesus went to his father's house to do laundry. In part he went because he'd never owned his own washer and dryer but also because it gave him an excuse to see his father regularly. Juan Miguel was quiet and, like his boy, something of a loner. He didn't have any friends of his own, and he'd never really dated since Jesus' mother died. His routine was generally relegated to working during the day and drinking beer in front of the TV at night. And while he never exactly said as much, Jesus knew his father looked forward to his weekly laundry visits.

Jesus still had a key to the house, so, with his laundry basket hugged against his hip, he let himself in. He found his father sitting on the couch in the living room, beer in hand, watching the news on Telemundo. Juan Miguel's eyes lit up when he saw Jesus.

"Hi, mijito," his father said, giving him a hug. "Are you hungry?"

Jesus knew that one of the primary means by which his father expressed his love was by feeding him. He almost always offered him food as soon as he walked in the door. Even when Jesus wasn't hungry, he always let his father prepare a meal for him.

"I could eat something," Jesus said. "Thank you."

"I'll make you a couple quesadillas," his father said. "I've got some fresh beans and rice, too."

"Sounds good."

"Go put your clothes in, mijtio," his father said. "I'll get your food ready."

Jesus took his laundry basket into the garage where the washer and dryer were. Amongst all his other dirty clothes was a series of bloodstained shirts and pants. He remembered being a boy and, not long after his mother died, standing beside his father in the garage as he tried to figure out how to do a load of laundry. It always seemed so easy when his mother did it. Jesus would be sitting in front of the television, and his mother would disappear into the garage with a basket of clothes. A couple of hours later they were cleaned and folded, like magic. After she died, however, Jesus and Juan Miguel figured out that there was nothing magical about doing laundry.

They were playing Hide and Seek the night they learned Maria had been killed. It was a Wednesday night and she was out of the house on a walk, which she did for exercise a few nights a week. She'd made breakfast for Jesus that morning and, when he came home from school in the afternoon, they watched cartoons together, while he colored in his coloring books. When Maria went walking later that evening, Juan Miguel assumed she was walking with her girlfriends, as she normally did. He learned later from the police that she was all alone.

Jesus ran around the living room looking for a spot to hide, while Juan Miguel counted to ten with his eyes closed and his hands over his ears. After scurrying about for the first five seconds, Jesus had the idea of hiding in the garage. It was dark in there, filled with cardboard boxes and shadows, as well as the family's two cars, which sat side by side, fitting snugly between the grim walls. Jesus climbed into an empty cardboard box beside the dryer; he barely fit inside and needed to pull his knees tight against his chest, ducking his head between his legs in order to bring the lid down.

It was hot inside the box and sweat was beginning to roll from Jesus' brow, matting his curls to the side of his head, when he heard a car pull up in front of the garage door. Two car doors opened and closed before a set of footsteps made their way to the front door. Jesus heard knocking, followed by the muffled sounds of his father speaking with two men. Soon after the conversation began, Jesus heard his father scream. He climbed out of the box as quickly as he could, wiping the sweat from his forehead as he hurried to the front door where he found his father crying in the entryway.

There were two policemen at the door, each of them looking very sympathetic. All three men saw Jesus at the same time, so Juan Miguel went to him, kneeling down and wrapping him up in his arms. He was still crying, but he couldn't yet bring himself to say anything. After the policemen left, Juan Miguel took Jesus to the neighbor's house, a place he'd never actually been before. He sat on the couch watching TV with the kind woman who lived there; she gave him cookies and milk, and he eventually fell asleep. He awoke the next morning in his own bed, having no recollection of how he got home. Juan Miguel was sitting on the edge of the bed when he woke up, and it was then that he told him his mother was gone. Because Juan Miguel used the word "gone," as opposed to "dead," Jesus was under the impression that his mother would eventually come home.

Even after the funeral, Juan Miguel simply couldn't bring himself to talk about his wife's passing—not with Jesus, not with anybody. At first it seemed that he was simply avoiding it, like it was just too difficult to accept. Not long after her funeral, Jesus asked his father a question about his mother and, instead of answering, Juan Miguel sat still and silent, looking straight ahead. Young Jesus asked his father another question, but he got no response. He shook his father's legs, trying to gain his attention, but Juan Miguel didn't respond to that either. It was as if he were in a deep sleep with his eyes open.

This happened a few more times before Jesus made the connection that his father disappeared whenever he tried to talk to him about his mother. Sometimes he would be gone for a few minutes, other times he'd be gone for a few hours. He always came back, however, and he never seemed to be aware of what had happened. When Jesus tried to explain to his father what was happening, he didn't believe him. Juan Miguel assumed Jesus was simply imagining things. But, when Jesus made the mistake of asking a question about his mother while Juan Miguel was driving, they crashed into a fire hydrant.

Soon after the car accident, Juan Miguel was diagnosed with severe depression, which was manifesting itself in catatonic stupors—a clinical syndrome of akinesis and mutism—at the mention of his wife. These catatonic stupors resulted in a profound lack of responsiveness and a seeming impairment of consciousness. For the duration of the stupor, Juan Miguel's speech and spontaneous movement were absent and he was unaffected by external stimuli. Because his stupors stemmed from depression, his doctors diagnosed them as benign. While there was an initial treatment of benzodiazepines and brief discussions regarding psychiatric treatment and electroconvulsive therapy, it became clear enough—to Jesus at least—that as long as there was no mention of his dead wife, Juan Miguel was generally free of stupors.

Jesus didn't want his father to disappear into silence ever again, so he vowed never to mention his mother around him. In a way, it was like losing her for a second time. It wasn't until Jesus got a little older, more aware of the world, that he started wondering what caused his mother's death. His father never did tell him and, because they had no close family for him to communicate with, he never found out. One afternoon when he was a teenager, Jesus convinced himself that it had been long enough, that the catatonic stupors could no longer affect his father. He asked him about his mother, wanting to know the cause of her death. And, just as it was when he was a kid, Jesus watched him disappear.

It was only after he watched Daniel killed by a vampire that Jesus remembered his father's words on the day of his mother's funeral, how he was drunk and crying as he apologized to Jesus for not being able to stop the monster. From that moment on, Jesus didn't need to hear his father say it. He knew the truth. That didn't stop Jesus from wishing things could be different, that he and his father could talk openly about what happened. He wished he could tell him that he knew a vampire killed his mother, that there was nothing they could've done, that even if they were both by her side it might well have happened all the same. As the years passed and he grew more comfortable with the truth, Jesus never—not once, not ever— begrudged his father's silence.

ᛧ•••••ᛧ

Jesus sat on the edge of the couch, leaning over the coffee table as he ate his dinner. Juan Miguel continued watching TV, beer in hand, enjoying the quiet company of his son beside him. His eyes went to Jesus' neck, which had a light bruise, like a hickey, and a pair of tiny scabs.

"Did you have another fight, mijito?"

"Yes."

"Are you hurt?"

"I'm okay."

"Did you win?"

Jesus nodded, yes.

"That's good," his father said. "I'm sorry I can't be there."

"You don't have to be sorry."

"I know," his father said, "but I am."

CHAPTER FIFTEEN

A VAMPIRE CELL

Adam and Olivia had their second meeting at Corky's a few days after their first. It was late, of course, past midnight in fact. Adam hadn't requested to hunt her and, for her part, Olivia hadn't offered. Darlene was working the overnight shift, as she often did, and was pleased to see Adam out again with Olivia. She went to the table to take their order.

"What's good tonight?" Adam asked.

"Chocolate banana cream," Darlene said.

"You like it?"

"If it had a job, I'd marry it."

"Bring us two slices, then."

"Coming right up."

Darlene disappeared into the kitchen, leaving Adam and Olivia alone in their booth. Olivia, figuring Darlene would be back sooner rather than later, made small talk before getting into her vampire questions. She found that the chatting was easier this time around, pleasant even. After Darlene dropped off their pie slices, Adam and Olivia kept chatting about nothing in particular. There were only crumbs left on their plates when Olivia finally asked her first question of the night.

"How do you turn a human?"

"Turn a human?"

"You know," Olivia said, "into a vampire."

The last part she said in a whisper, leaning over the table so only Adam could hear. Had she known that he had amplified hearing senses, she'd have realized that she could've whispered to him from across the diner and he'd still be able to hear her.

"It's not too terribly complicated," Adam said. "You have to drain them first."

"You mean their blood, right?"

"Yes," Adam said, "but, to turn them, you can't drain them all the way. You've got to leave enough inside to keep them alive. Once they're on the cusp of death, the human needs to feed on the vampire."

"What do you mean?"

"They drink the vampire's blood."

"That's necessary?"

"Oh, yes," Adam said. "They'll die otherwise."

"Does the human *bite* the vampire?"

"No," Adam said. "The vampire cuts himself open, feeding the human from the wound."

"Then what?"

"Then the human dies."

"They die? What's the point, then?"

"What I mean is they die their *human* death," Adam said. "Their eyes shut and their organs close up shop. As every human cell dies, it's replaced immediately by a vampire cell."

"How long does it take?"

"A few hours."

"Then what?"

"Then they wake up as a vampire and feed one more time from their maker."

"What's it feel like?"

"When you wake up as a vampire," Adam said, "there's still a part of you that's human working itself out of your system. This results in hallucinations."

"What kind of hallucinations?"

"Most vampires have conversations with loved ones," Adam said. "Living or dead."

"What kind of conversations?"

"Depends on the vampire," Adam said. "But, generally speaking, they have whatever conversation they need to have."

"Who did *you* see?"

"Emily."

"Who's that?"

"My wife."

"You're married?"

"I was," Adam said. "As a human."

"What happened to Emily?"

"She went on without me," Adam said. "That's what humans do."

"Is she alive?"

"Yes."

"Do you see her?"

"I'm not allowed to, remember?"

"Right," Olivia said, scribbling in her notebook. "Did you ever consider turning her?"

"Never."

"Why not?"

"She wouldn't want to be a vampire."

"How do you know?"

"I know Emily."

"How do you know when somebody wants to be turned?"

"I suppose they can ask for it," Adam said, "but most humans don't get a choice."

"How did you feel the first time you turned a human?"

"Who ever said I did?"

"Have you?"

Adam smiled before shaking his head, no.

"Really?"

"Is that so hard to believe?"

"I just figured *all* vampires did it."

"You're not totally wrong," Adam said. "A lot of them do. I just never have."

"Why not?"

"I don't know," Adam said. "Partly because I've never had a reason to, I suppose, and partly because nobody's ever asked."

"So, you would do it if you were asked?"

"Maybe," Adam said. "I wouldn't know for sure until the moment presented itself."

"Are there any laws regarding when and how a vampire can turn a human?"

"Nope," Adam said. "We're free to turn humans into vampires whenever we like. Adding members to the fold is never frowned upon."

Olivia's questions subsided for the time being as she focused her attention on filling the pages of her notebook. Adam turned his attention to Darlene, who was sitting on the other side of Corky's with the heavyset man with the sad eyes. While Adam was capable of listening to their conversation, he was just as capable of tuning them out, which, out of respect for Darlene, was exactly what he did.

PART TWO

THE MASSACRE AT THE BARBERSHOP

CHAPTER SIXTEEN

VICTUS AND ELOWYN

Elowyn sat at the bar inside Brunswick, drinking her fourth Rum and Coke and feeling sorry for herself. Olivia had watered down the last two, though Elowyn didn't seem to notice. She had the night off from Tropical Lei, but didn't feel like being home alone, where, in all likelihood, she'd find herself thinking about Johnson. She knew he was a jerk, but she couldn't stop herself from wanting to call him. Elowyn decided she was better off spending her evening in Brunswick's empty lounge with Olivia, rather than alone at home where she might do something she'd probably regret.

"You know what I want?"

"Another Rum and Coke?"

"Expedience."

"Should I pour your drinks faster?"

"No," Elowyn said. "I mean with men."

"Explain yourself."

"You know the whole sweet little courting thing you're doing with Jesus?"

"Sure," Olivia said, "I guess so."

"I don't want that anymore."

"Did you ever?"

"Yeah," Elowyn said. "I think so."

"Maybe make them wait a little longer before you fuck them."

"You know, I thought about that," Elowyn said, "but I don't think fucking them too fast is the problem."

"What's the problem then?"

"Courtship," Elowyn said. "Or whatever my idea of courtship is. That's the thing, I don't even know how it's supposed to look or feel, but I keep waiting for it like I'll know it when I see it. And when it happens, everything will be right as rain."

"So, you're done with that now?"

"Completely."

"What do you want instead?"

"Expedience."

"And how's that go?"

"I just want a handsome stranger to come up to me," Elowyn said, "tell me I'm the most beautiful creature he's ever seen, and ask me to spend the rest of my life with him."

"You're drunk."

"Not enough."

"You really think that'd be better?"

"It couldn't be worse," Elowyn said. "Every relationship I get into turns to shit."

"Why do you think that is?"

"Men are assholes."

"I'm sure there's a non-asshole out there somewhere just aching to prove you wrong."

"You're sweet."

"Thanks," Olivia said. "Want another drink?"

"Sure," Elowyn said. "More rum and less Coke, if you don't mind."

"You got it."

"How's the vampire novel coming along?"

"Still unwritten."

"I thought you said there was an exciting new development."

"There is," Olivia said. "It just hasn't made its way to the page yet."

"What's it going to be about," Elowyn asked, "besides vampires?"

"Love," Olivia said. "I think."

"I *love* when humans and vampires fall in love!"

"Me too."

"It's so fucking beautiful and tragic," Elowyn said. "Like Buffy and Angel."

"Or Buffy and Spike."

"To each her own," Elowyn said. "You know, I might actually read this book."

"Thanks."

"How does it end?"

"I have no idea," Olivia said. "I'm still trying to figure out how it starts."

"Just remember," Elowyn said, "the vampire and the human can't have a life together. That's what makes it so tragic. The vampire will live forever in his youth, and the human will grow old and die. Unless something crazy happens."

"Like what?"

"How should I know? You're the writer."

Elowyn finished her last Rum and Coke, draining it in one long gulp, before standing up from her stool.

"You leaving?"

"Yes, ma'am."

"Are you okay to drive?"

"I'm fine."

"You sure?" Olivia asked. "You can hang out a little while longer and drive home with me."

"I'm okay," Elowyn said. "Really. I'll see you at home."

Elowyn exited the bowling alley, leaving the ruckus behind the sliding doors, trying to convince herself not to do something stupid. Shuffling through her purse trying to find her cell phone, she was beginning to think she'd overreacted and perhaps Johnson wasn't such an asshole after all. Maybe she'd simply put too much pressure on him. Maybe she should just call him for a quick chat so that they could talk out whatever it was that was keeping them apart. Elowyn had her phone in hand with Johnson's number at the ready, when she was greeted by a voice from the darkness.

"Hello."

"Who's there?"

"My name is Victus."

A large, rugged man stepped out form the darkness. He had a long, thick beard and wavy hair that grew past his shoulders.

"I hope I didn't startle you," Victus said.

"Can I help you?"

He lifted his nose to the air, taking in a deep breath.

"You are intoxicating."

"I have to go."

"Please," Victus said, "don't go. I only want to tell you how beautiful you are."

"Have we met before?"

"You are an angel."

Elowyn smiled.

"You really think so?"

"I think of nothing else."

Victus leaned his face into her neck, smelling Elowyn's skin. Elowyn closed her eyes and tilted her head, letting him in. She could still feel his breath on her neck when she opened her eyes, only to find that Victus was no longer there.

He spoke to her from the darkness.

"Please excuse me."

"Where are you?"

"I won't be far."

"Promise?"

"You have my word."

¡•••••¡

Elowyn was performing onstage at Tropical Lei, stripping her clothes off as she wondered whether or not she'd ever see Victus again. Three days had passed since their first encounter and Elowyn was beginning to wonder if they had even actually met. Maybe he was just a dream, a byproduct of Rum and Coke. She thought about how she acted with him and how he seemed to say everything she wanted to hear. The thought of him was turning her on as she worked the pole.

Craving the company of a man who would embarrass himself over how much he wanted her, Elowyn decided to spend the last twenty minutes of her shift roaming Tropical Lei for a scratching post. Most of the men she tried to seduce, however, either didn't have enough money to take her to the back or simply didn't believe she was as horny as she claimed. It was a rarity that Elowyn couldn't net at least one man when she set her mind to it, so she hardly knew what to do with herself. So unbearable was the pulsing between her legs, Elowyn decided to call Johnson.

She wasn't sure if he would take her call, but, if he did, she'd tell him in no uncertain terms that she needed to get laid. Elowyn was digging through her purse as she exited Tropical Lei, looking for her phone so she could make the call that she knew would be a mistake. She'd just hit the send button when she saw Victus standing beside her car. She had the phone to her ear as Johnson said hello. Elowyn hung up without saying a word.

"You found me."

"I did."

"I'm done with work," Elowyn said. "Are you hungry?"

"Starving."

Elowyn let Victus into her car and she left Tropical Lei for the last time. She floated some ideas for food—Mexican or Indian were on her mind—but Victus offered to prepare a meal for her at his home; so taken with the gesture, as no man had ever offered to make her dinner, Elowyn decided to take him up on his offer. Victus lived in a small two-bedroom house built in 1928, which sat on edge of a steep hill overlooking Rancho Cucamonga. There were no street-lights around, so, when Elowyn turned her car off, she was swallowed up by the night. Victus exited the car, moving quickly to the driver's side to open Elowyn's door.

Entering the house, Elowyn expected Victus to hit a light switch, but he made no such move. Instead, he lit the fireplace, filling the living room with a soft orange glow. Elowyn could see that Victus' home had no forms of artificial light; in fact, he hardly had any crea-ture comforts at all, save for a couch, a bookshelf filled with litera-ture, and a tiger-skin rug in front of the fireplace. Above the fireplace was a large mirror with a rusty frame.

"You don't have a television?"

"No."

"Or a computer?"

"No."

"How do you get on the Internet?"

"I don't."

"But, how do you connect with people?"

"I go to them."

Victus took Elowyn into the backyard, where she swooned over the view.

"It's so nice up here," she said. "So peaceful."

Victus moved behind Elowyn, slipping his arms around her waist. She closed her eyes, fully embracing the feeling of her body against his. In that moment, nobody else existed in the whole wide world. Victus dipped his face in to the nape of her neck, touching his lips to her skin.

"I've opened myself up before," Elowyn said.

"Yes."

"Too many men."

Victus sniffed the air.

"Monsters," Elowyn said. "All of them."

"Yes."

Elowyn reached her arms up, lacing her fingers behind Victus' neck.

"I wish it could be like this forever."

"As you wish."

ᵖ•▲▲•ᵠ

Elowyn woke up naked on the rug beside the fireplace, groggy from a long sleep. Victus lay behind her, their bodies pressed together. Elowyn touched her fingers to her neck, feeling the tender holes where Victus had entered her. Flashes of the previous twenty-four hours were coming to her, many of them memories of excruciating pain, like her blood was boiling from the inside. She stood up from the rug to look in the mirror over the fireplace, wanting to examine the wounds on her neck. When at first she saw no reflection, Elowyn thought perhaps she was looking through a window or perhaps even a hole in the wall. But, the longer she looked at the mirror, the more she realized she could see everything else in the living room, from the bookshelf to the empty walls—everything but herself. She couldn't even see Victus when he stood up behind her, wrapping his arms around her waist.

"What's happening?"

"We'll be forever now."

"I don't understand."

"We shall never grow old."

"What did you do?"

"You know what I did."

"What are you?"

"You know what I am."

Elowyn turned to face Victus, examining his naked body, finding two puncture wounds on the inside of his thigh, just beneath his groin. Another flash of memory came to her, prompting Elowyn to touch her fingers to her mouth, feeling Victus' blood on her chin, the taste of it on her lips.

"I wasn't dreaming?"

"You weren't dreaming."

Victus' blood pumped through her veins, practically singing to her, confirming the reality of her new form.

"You're a vampire," Elowyn said.

"Yes."

"And now *I'm* a vampire."

"Yes."

"Why did you do this to me?"

"So I could have you forever."

"You want to have me forever?"

"And ever."

The memories from the previous night continued to flash into her mind as she pulled Victus' face towards her own, kissing him on the lips. She remembered standing outside, looking out over the sprawling palette of Rancho Cucamonga. She remembered closing her eyes and feeling Victus' teeth pierce her soft neck. She remembered the fear and confusion, the pain and the pleasure, the feeling of his lips on her skin, drinking her blood. She remembered her body becoming too weak to fight him off. She remembered him lifting her into his arms and carrying her inside the house, removing her clothes and leaving her to die on his tiger rug. She remembered her tired muscles and blurry vision. She remembered the emptiness of being drained. She remembered laying her head on his lap. She remembered him taking the nail of his index finger to the soft of his wrist, just above the palm, slitting it open. She remembered the slit over her mouth, blood pulsing out, the metallic taste of it on her lips. She remembered growing warm, like she were a hot air balloon, feeling as if her body was expanding from the inside, tearing at the seams. She remembered screaming, writhing in agony. She remembered Victus caressing her hair, slick with sweat, promising it was almost done. She remembered him dipping his face into the nape of her neck, slipping his fangs back in, drinking from the blood that was now a mixture of them both. She remembered him opening the soft of his wrist one more time, and she remembered feeding from it again, more willing this time, more grateful. She remembered her gums swelling and aching, burning with an intense pressure that dissipated only when two brand new fangs pierced through. She remembered Victus opening his naked legs to her, pulling her face in. She remembered biting into the meat of his thigh. She remembered the rush of blood over her lips, so warm, so alive. She remembered feeding until she fell asleep on the tiger rug beside Victus, the warmth of the fireplace as soothing as a lullaby.

Elowyn's phone rang in her purse, causing her to cover her ears.

"Why is it so loud?" she asked.

"Your senses are evolving," Victus said, "becoming sharper. It's all part of being a vampire."

"Will everything be this loud?"

"For a little while," Victus said. "You'll soon learn to control it."

Elowyn lifted her eyes to the mirror and saw her father inside of the living room. She turned around, breathless, staring at him as he stood in the doorway. He smiled at her, his arms open. Elowyn looked at Victus, confused.

"Where did you find him?" she asked.

"Whom do you see?"

"My father."

"He is with us now?"

Elowyn looked back to the doorway, where her father stood.

"He's there," she said. "Right there."

"Go," Victus said. "Speak to him."

"What do I say?"

"Whatever must be said."

Elowyn walked across the living room, her naked skin lit orange by the fireplace, stopping in front of the doorway where she believed her father was standing. She stepped into his arms, embracing him in a hug.

"Daddy."

"Elowyn."

"How did you find me?"

"I never lost you."

"It's been so long."

"I'm sorry I left you and your mother."

"I thought I'd never see you again."

"That was wrong of me."

"Mother passed."

"I know."

"I had to take care of myself."

"You did a wonderful job, sweetheart."

"Really?"

"Oh, yes," he said. "I'm so very proud of you."

"Thank you, Daddy."

Elowyn turned to Victus.

"Come here," she said. "I want you to meet my father."

Victus smiled, walking over to her.

"Daddy—"

When Elowyn turned back to her father, he was gone. The room spun and her vision blurred. Her body collapsed, but Victus caught her before she hit the floor. He carried her back to the tiger rug, laying her beside the fireplace. When she awoke a few hours later, she kissed Victus on the mouth and went to her purse, digging out a compact so she could powder her nose. Flipping it open, Elowyn looked into the small mirror only to be reminded that she no longer had a reflection. As she put the compact back in her purse, she saw a voicemail waiting for her on her cell phone. It was from Johnson: "Hey, Elowyn, you called me earlier, so I figured you wanted to hang out or something. Sorry if you can't hear me too good, I'm over at Boston's right now. Anyway, if you wanted to hang out or something, you should give me a call back."

CHAPTER SEVENTEEN

STACKS AND CYCLES

Nick Maven, an old pal of Johnson, would, in approximately twenty-four hours, become the first person to learn about Jesus' vampire-hunting alter ego. The discovery would come following a trip he and Jesus made to Tijuana to pick up steroids for Johnson. Johnson stayed behind, as he'd made plans to see Elowyn. Johnson brought Nick into Ground and Pound for a workout and to meet Jesus. Nick was visiting from out of town and had gotten in touch with his old friend, wanting to catch up and reminisce. Johnson was in the midst of training camp, preparing for his next fight. As it was with his previous few fights, this upcoming bout wasn't a particularly big deal. The fight's promoters were hoping that Johnson's UFC pedigree would help draw a crowd and, in exchange, they would look the other way when he tested positive for performance-enhancing drugs.

Of course, while Johnson had developed the dubious reputation of a fighter who doped, he decided, for reasons he couldn't quite articulate, that he would compete in his next fight without steroids, so he hadn't cycled for nearly two months. Jesus, on the other hand, was still in the midst of his most current cycle, so, before they began their training day with a five-mile run, he took his latest dose. Nick wanted to learn more about steroids, which was why Johnson invited him to work out with him and Jesus for the day.

Proper steroid use was all about stacks and cycles. Stacking was not unlike a chemistry experiment, involving the mixture of various anabolic steroids with the goal of manufacturing specific results. Jesus cycled stacks of Winstrol and Anavar, as they resulted in increased speed, strength, and agility—all traits that were ideal for vampire hunting. But, so far as Johnson knew, he used simply to stay strong and keep up with him during training. This combination was also important for Jesus, because it didn't add any significant bulk or muscle mass to his frame, which would only serve to slow him down; and, in the service of vampire hunting, Jesus needed all the speed and quickness he could muster.

"But, what if you *want* to bulk up?" Nick asked

"Then you'd stack with D-Bol," Johnson said. "It's the grandfather of anabolic steroids. That's what guys on Venice Beach were bulking up on back in the day."

"What about side effects?" Nick asked. "Shrinking testicles and whatnot."

"The side effects are real," Johnson said, "but you can minimize the risk as long as you're cycling properly."

"How long is a cycle?"

"It varies, depending on the guy and the results he's looking for," Johnson said. "Generally speaking, cycles last around one to two months with a one- to two-month break in between. The guys who don't take breaks are the ones who usually suffer the more severe side effects."

Jesus was particularly prudent when it came to his cycles, so he'd never really suffered from any side effects. For him, though, using steroids wasn't simply about increasing speed and strength; they also allowed him to increase the length of his workouts, while decreasing the time he needed for recovery. And, perhaps as important as anything else, they helped him recover faster from injuries, which, in the vampire hunting game, occurred more often than he'd like.

"Ultimately," Johnson said, "steroids aren't going to make you a better fighter. If you can't strike or grapple, steroids aren't going to teach you how. I can't walk into a major league ballpark and hit a homerun any more than some juiced-up ballplayer can get into the cage and knock me unconscious."

"And you're a fighter, too?" Nick asked Jesus.

"Not really, no."

"He could've been," Johnson said. "He had some damn good potential."

"What happened?" Nick asked.

Jesus shrugged.

"I don't know," he said. "I guess my heart wasn't in it."

"Really, it was the smart move," Johnson said. "If you're not one hundred percent committed, you can get yourself hurt. He did have one fight, though."

"How'd you do?"

"I won."

"You retired undefeated then," Nick said, smiling. "Classy."

As the three of them prepared to hit the road for a five-mile run, Jesus expressed concern that it might be a bit much for Nick. Nick, however, was a former Navy SEAL, so he was more than capable of keeping up. After he and Johnson graduated from high school, Nick joined the Army. No sooner had he completed boot camp, Nick was deployed to his first tour in Iraq. A year or so after that, he did his first tour in Afghanistan. Upon serving in multiple tours in each country, Nick decided to make a run at becoming a Navy SEAL. He graduated with Class 228, surviving BUD/S training with them, before suffering through Hell Week.

"That was the hardest thing I've ever done in my life," Nick said. "Nothing even comes close."

In order to get through Hell Week, Nick had to stay awake for days at a time, wet and sandy, freezing from the frigid temperatures of the Pacific Ocean. He endured the sort of muscle aches and pains that would have crippled a normal man, even suffering a stress fracture in his foot. While he never quit, he did think about it often, at least once a day—though, when the pain and the cold and the lack of sleep were too much to bear, it was usually more like once every five minutes. And, during some particularly rough stretches, about once a minute.

Class 228 began with one hundred fifty men and, when they were done, only twenty graduated. Nick was one of the twenty. He was a warrior, one of the elite, and on his way to becoming a Navy SEAL until everything went awry. Nick was discharged from the Navy SEALs without ever being deployed on a combat mission.

"What happened?" Jesus asked.

"I saw some things I wasn't supposed to see."

"What'd you see?"

"Nothing I'm comfortable talking about."

After the run, they spent the next few hours lifting weights and working the heavy bags before sparring in the cage. Nick, who was trained in close quarters combat, participated in some light sparring as well before letting Johnson and Jesus go full speed together. Nick sat on the mat, his back against the cage, watching in amazement at how fluid and proficient Johnson and Jesus were with their grappling skills.

Jesus put Johnson on his back with an explosive double-leg takedown. Johnson went into butterfly guard, hooking his feet beneath Jesus' midsection and wrapping his arms around his ribs, attempting to keep him from passing into half guard. Jesus, however, did eventually pass Johnson's guard before hooking him into a guillotine choke, forcing him to tap out. They sparred like that for five-minutes at a time, with one-minute breaks, each of them having moments where they got the better of the other.

After their day of training was complete, Jesus, Johnson, and Nick went to Boston's to have dinner and watch the latest UFC pay-per-view. The main event was a heavyweight championship bout featuring a former professional wrestler. Jesus was excited for the fight, as he was a fan of the wrestler. Johnson, on the other hand, considered himself a mixed martial arts purist and didn't like the idea of his sport being tainted by a "fake" fighter. Nick, for his part, didn't follow the UFC or professional wrestling, so he didn't care either way.

"So," Jesus asked Nick, "what do you do for a living?"

"Security."

"What kind of security?" Johnson asked.

"Private security."

"Like Academi?"

"What's Academi?" Jesus asked.

"It's a privately owned security service," Nick said.

"More like a corporate army," Johnson said.

"Is that who you work for?" Jesus asked.

"No," Nick said. "I work for a much smaller operation."

"Does it pay well?"

"Very."

"Well, you deserve it," Johnson said. "After going overseas to fight in couple of bullshit wars, you deserve it big time."

"I don't know that they were bullshit," Nick said. "I'm just glad I survived them."

"Trust me," Johnson said. "They were bullshit."

"There are a whole lot of details that neither one of us will ever know about those wars," Nick said. "As for my service, I was just a soldier. I wore my uniform and I followed orders."

"You had good intentions," Johnson said, "and you're brave as fuck. But, at the end of the day, you got taken advantage of by fighting in two wars that didn't need to be fought."

"Why were we there?" Jesus asked.

"Oil," Johnson said.

"You don't really think it's that simple," Nick asked, "do you?"

"I really do."

"Iraq has oil," Nick said, "but Afghanistan doesn't. So, why do you suppose we were there?"

"Minerals," Johnson said. "There are loads of untapped mineral deposits in the mountains of Afghanistan. They're worth nearly a trillion dollars."

"Where'd you hear that?"

"The fucking newspaper," Johnson said. "And *The Joe Rogan Experience.*"

"What's that?"

"It's his podcast."

"He has a podcast?" Nick said. "What's he talk about?"

"All sorts of stuff," Johnson said. "He usually has his comedian buddies on, like Brian Redban, Duncan Trussell, Ari Shaffir, and Joey Diaz."

"And that's where you heard about the U.S. government waging a war on terrorism so they could mine for minerals in Afghanistan?"

"I don't remember where exactly I heard it," Johnson said. "I'm just saying you can't be so naïve as to trust everything your government tells you. It's like that bullshit professional wrestling Jesus watches. They put on a big dramatic show with good guys and bad guys, all the while there's a handful of assholes behind the curtains determining the outcome."

"I don't really know much about all that stuff," Jesus said, "but I think it's noble to risk your life to protect others."

"So do I," Johnson said. "I just think it's a shame to have that nobility wasted on a lie."

Johnson's phone rang in his pocket. It was Elowyn. He didn't think he'd ever hear from her again, not after her outburst at his apartment. When he answered the phone, he heard her voice for just a moment before she hung up. He figured she was playing some silly chick game. He didn't want to give her the pleasure of thinking she'd gotten to him, so he didn't call her back. But, for the rest of the night, as he hung out with Jesus and Nick at Boston's, drinking beers and watching the fights, Johnson couldn't get Elowyn out of his head.

Even during the main event, as the mixed martial artist overwhelmed the professional wrestler with a first-round TKO, Johnson could hardly concentrate. During the post-fight interviews with Joe

Rogan, Johnson excused himself from the table, tucking himself away in the small hallway near the bathrooms and called Elowyn. Her phone rang and rang, until he got her voicemail. Johnson left her a message: "Hey, Elowyn, you called me earlier, so I figured you wanted to hang out or something. Sorry if you can't hear me too good, I'm over at Boston's right now. Anyway, if you wanted to hang out or something, you should give me a call back."

When Johnson got back to the table, Jesus and Nick were talking about Tijuana. The three of them were planning on driving there the following day so Johnson could pick up some steroids. Nick had never been, so he was excited to make the trip and see what it was all about.

"We should just go tonight," he said.

"That wouldn't be a great idea," Johnson said. "It's not exactly the safest place to be after dark. It's bad enough the cops out there are corrupt, but at night there's also more criminals looking for an easy mark. We'll go tomorrow during the day. It's safer that way."

༺•••••༻

Johnson was in bed, fast asleep, dreaming about Afghani minerals, when Elowyn called him back. He answered the phone, groggy, not bothering to open his eyes.

"Hello?"

"I want to see you."

"Now?"

"Yes, now."

Johnson checked his clock. It was three in the morning.

"Where are you?"

"I'll come to your apartment."

"It's late."

"I need you."

"Let's hang out tomorrow."

Elowyn was quiet.

"You still there?"

"Okay," she said. "I'll see you tomorrow."

"What time?"

"Wait for my call."

"I've got plans," Johnson said. "I might not be around."

"Please," Elowyn said. "I need you."

Johnson's opened his eyes.

"Yeah?"

"Yeah."

"How bad?"

"Very."

"Okay."

"Wait for my call."

Johnson spent the rest of the night dreaming about drilling for minerals with Elowyn.

ᵖ•••ᵖ

The following afternoon, while having a pre-trip lunch at Corky's, Johnson broke the news that Jesus and Nick would be making the trip to Tijuana without him.

"What happened?" Jesus asked.

"It's Elowyn," Johnson said. "She called me in the middle of the night talking all sexy and shit about how she needs me. She wants to meet up later, so I'm gonna hang back."

"I thought you were done with her."

"So did I," Johnson said. "You should've heard her, though."

"Should we just go tomorrow?" Nick asked.

"No, I've got customers expecting supplies tomorrow," Johnson said. "You guys would be doing me a huge solid if you went today."

"I don't mind if Jesus is still up for it," Nick said.

"I don't mind either," Jesus said.

"Well, I guess that settles that," Johnson said, handing Jesus an envelope. "There's enough there to cover what we usually get."

"Okay."

"We may as well hit the road," Jesus said. "You have your passport on you?"

"I sure do."

"Call me when you get back," Nick said. "If I'm not busy getting laid, maybe we can hang out."

"Will do. You ready, Nick?"

"You bet," he said. "Let's rock and roll."

CHAPTER EIGHTEEN

AN INVOLUNTARY PRESSURE

The drive to Tijuana was a simple trip, the majority of which was spent on Interstate 15, passing through rolling hills and dipping valleys. While they'd only just met the previous day, Jesus and Nick got along like old friends. The hills and valleys along Interstate 15 eventually gave way to golf courses and strip malls before presenting them with a sign that read "Last USA Exit." Once the border was within sight, Jesus pulled off the road into a small parking lot. After paying the attendant, he and Nick walked the rest of the way across the border, which took less than five minutes. They passed into Mexico through a one-way rotating entrance made up of horizontal bars.

Walking up a winding ramp, Jesus and Nick passed a series of merchants—selling everything from T-shirts and jewelry to marionette puppets and luchador masks—before eventually reaching the long concrete bridge that would drop them off in the bustling heart of Tijuana. Surrounding the brothels and bars, nearly invisible in plain sight, were shacks built on top of one another, dilapidated and fragile, each seemingly on the verge of collapse. The streets were poorly paved and the cars, with their strange license plates, drove as if they'd all agreed upon anarchy.

Jesus and Nick walked for twenty minutes, past barkers and prostitutes, down streets named Revolución and Constitución, before reaching the doctor's office that Johnson always used. After paying the doctor for a prescription, Jesus and Nick walked down the street to the pharmacy. As it was with most every pharmacy in Tijuana, the inside was pristine with clean white walls and clerks who spoke commendable English. Jesus and Nick were the only customers at the moment and the clerk, whom Jesus had never seen before, stood with his palms flat atop the glass counter, smiling as he listened to Jesus' order.

"You're from America, no?" the clerk asked.

"Yes," Jesus said.

"It is much cheaper here, yes?"

"It is, yes."

"You cannot buy in America," the clerk said. "That's too bad."

"I agree."

"Too many laws, yes?"

"Yes," Jesus said. "Too many."

"You look Mexican," the clerk said. "¿Hablas español?"

"No," Jesus said, "I don't speak Spanish."

The clerk smiled.

"Maybe you learn soon."

"Maybe."

As the clerk went to fill the prescription, Jesus saw him place a phone call. He pinched the phone between his ear and shoulder, leaving his hands free to prepare Jesus' order, while speaking in Spanish to whoever was on the other line. A few minutes later, he handed Jesus an unmarked paper bag with his steroids inside. As Jesus and Nick turned to leave, the clerk smiled and waved goodbye.

"Is that how it usually goes?" Nick asked.

"Pretty much," Jesus said.

They hadn't even reached the end of the block when a police car pulled up beside them. Two officers got out, calling for Jesus and Nick to stop walking.

"Is everything okay?" Jesus asked.

The first officer said something in Spanish. The second officer placed his palms on the car, demonstrating what he wanted Jesus and Nick to do.

"We're just visiting," Nick said.

The officers took Jesus and Nick forcefully by the arms, pushing them against the car and setting their hands atop the hood. The first officer frisked them, running his hands down their arms, waists, and legs, and patting their pockets before removing their wallets and passports. The second officer retrieved the unmarked paper bag, which had fallen to the street. Looking through the bag, he clicked his tongue in mock disappointment.

"I have a prescription," Jesus said.

The officer went into Jesus pockets again, pulling out the prescription. He looked at it briefly before tearing it up, letting the pieces fall to the gutter. The first officer removed all of the cash from their wallets, counting it where Jesus and Nick could see him doing it. The street they were on was desolate, nobody but the four of them.

The first officer held the stack of cash in Jesus' face.

"Where is more?" he asked.

"We don't have more."

The officer clicked his tongue, shaking his head.

"We need more," he said. "We must arrest now."

"That isn't necessary is it?" Nick asked.

"Get in," the officer said, opening the car door.

He took Nick by the arm with the intention of forcing him inside, but Nick, in a flash, tackled the officer to the street. The second officer immediately charged in to help, reaching for his gun as he did. Jesus intercepted him, dragging him to the street. It was all happening so fast that Jesus could hardly remember getting his arm around the officer's neck, putting him to sleep with a rear naked choke. Nick, after a brief struggle, also managed to leave his officer unconscious. He and Jesus gathered up their wallets and passports before running away as fast as they could back to the border.

They waited in line at Customs, looking over their shoulder every step of the way, each of them convinced they weren't going to make it back into the States. But, to their tremendous relief, Jesus and Nick made it back over without incident, running as fast as they could back to the car. As Jesus started the car, he and Nick looked at each other before bursting out into laughter.

"Holy shit," Nick said, "I can't believe that just happened!"

"Johnson's not going to believe this," Jesus said. "I don't know what I would've done if you weren't there."

"Luckily for you," Nick said, "you didn't have to find out."

Jesus took Nick back to Johnson's apartment, but he wasn't home yet, so they called his cell phone.

"Where're you at?" Jesus asked.

"I'm on my way to meet Elowyn at Beryl Park."

"Beryl Park?" Jesus said. "Why're you meeting there?"

"We're going to fuck," Johnson said, "obviously. Take Nick back to your place, and I'll pick him up when I'm finished."

Jesus updated Nick before heading back to his apartment. Nick took a seat on the couch, while Jesus went into the kitchen to fetch a couple of beers.

"Hey," Nick said, "mind if I borrow one of your shirts? Mine's a bit ragged."

"Sure," Jesus said, "I'll grab one for you."

"I'll find one."

Nick wasn't on the couch when Jesus walked back into the living. Instead, he found him in his bedroom kneeled before the wooden trunk with the lid open. Nick turned to Jesus, who was standing in the doorway, and held up a bloodstained wooden stake.

"Dude," Nick said, "what the fuck?"

Jesus' heart dropped as he tried to work out an explanation in his head. But, standing there in the doorway, he had no idea what to say.

"I can explain that."

"Yeah?" Nick said. "I bet I can, too."

"It's not what you think."

"Oh, I think it's exactly what I think."

"I'm not whatever you think I am."

"Really?"

"Yes."

"What do you think I think you are?"

"I'm not a killer."

"Aren't you though?"

Nick lifted the stake up in front of his eyes.

"You realize I know exactly what this is, right?"

"I don't think you do."

"This isn't a wooden stake?"

Jesus said nothing.

"And this isn't blood on it?"

Jesus said nothing still.

"I'll bet if I dug around a little bit more," Nick said, "I'd probably find some garlic and silver, too."

"I'm not crazy."

"No," Nick said, "you're a vampire hunter."

Jesus was speechless.

"Don't be so surprised," Nick said. "It takes one to know one."

CHAPTER NINETEEN

WAITING FOR EMILY

Adam lived in a small house in Upland that he'd inherited from his maker, Cherry, after she disappeared. The house was paid for and his use of utilities was minimal, but he paid all of his bills. He didn't use the lights—ever—but he did enjoy watching TV, so electricity was a must. He was a reader, too, so Adam had a beautiful mahogany bookshelf, which he'd also inherited from Cherry; she wasn't much of a reader herself, so she didn't mind when Adam filled it up with his own books. Over the decades, he'd filled and refilled the bookshelf multiple times. Whenever he needed to make room for his new books, Adam donated his old books to Goodwill and the Upland Public Library.

When Cherry first moved Adam into the house, she didn't have a TV. She'd been a vampire long before television was invented and so, in her own words, "I just never got caught up in the fad." She preferred going to the theater and watching movies where she could enjoy the communal experience of being a part of an audience. While Adam also enjoyed going to the theater, he just couldn't imagine living for eternity without television, so the first thing he contributed to his new home was a sixteen-inch Teletext color TV with remote control. And, a few years later, he bought a VCR so he and Cherry could watch movies at home every now and again.

As time passed, Adam updated from VCR to laserdisc to DVD and, eventually, to Blu-ray, while also getting progressively larger and flatter televisions. Unfortunately, Cherry disappeared before the latest boom in home entertainment technology, so Adam was left to watch his seventy-five-inch LED HDTV all by himself. When Adam wasn't hanging out on his couch watching TV, he was usually bowling, reading, or eating pie at Corky's. Of course, in between all of his other pastimes was the very necessary reality of feeding. As Adam told Olivia during their first meeting at Corky's, vampires weren't allowed to simply hunt for their own individual needs. Where it concerned vampires learning and understanding the laws of their community, it was incumbent upon the maker to pass along all their acquired knowledge. Cherry began teaching Adam the vampire laws almost as soon as he was fully turned.

"We have laws to follow?" Adam asked.

"Absolutely," Cherry said. "Very important laws."

"Says who?"

"Says all of us."

"All of us vampires?"

"Exactly."

"Who's in charge of the laws?"

"Nobody knows."

"Well, then, who enforces them?"

"Nobody knows that either."

"Then why do we need to follow them?"

"Because we'll get punished if we don't."

"By who?"

"Nobody knows," Cherry said. "We just know that sometimes vampires disappear and are never heard from again."

"Have you ever seen it happen?"

"Not with my own eyes, no."

"I'm sorry," Adam said, "but these laws just don't make a lot of sense to me."

"Well, listen," Cherry said, "if you want to take your chances on breaking the laws, go on ahead. But, when you disappear, don't forget that I was the one who tried to teach you right."

ᴖᴖᴖᴖ

When Adam was still human, he spent his happiest years married to Emily. She'd fallen ill in the last few years, but, when she was still healthy and able, Emily was a kindergarten teacher. And, before that, she was a student at Chaffey College, which was where she met Adam. Emily and Adam were in the same creative writing class, though, at the beginning of the course, they were perfect strangers. Adam was still at a point in his life where he entertained aspirations of being a writer. In the coming years, those aspirations would be whittled down to a vague disappointment. Part of the reason for his eventual disappointment was the reality of life and its many pits and hurdles. But, more than that, Adam simply never applied himself.

Adam never pushed himself to reach his potential, giving himself over completely—for better or worse—to the cause of personal fulfillment. When he met Emily, however, he still had high hopes for his writing future. Nothing was ruined yet, because his whole life was still ahead of him. He registered for that first creative writing class with the aspirations of one day emulating the paths of the great authors who came before him. Emily, on the other hand, took the class because it sounded fun. She had no deep or substantive interest in becoming a creative writer. She was just a girl who loved to read. She planned on majoring in English when she transferred to a university, so, as an avid reader, she thought it made sense to acquaint herself with the other side of the page.

From the very first day of class when he saw her sitting in the front row, Adam began falling in love with Emily. She had a pretty face and dainty fingers. Her hair was blonde, and she always wore sundresses. Adam wanted to talk to Emily but didn't have the nerve to approach her. As fate would have it, however, during the second week of class, Adam and Emily were paired up together to workshop each other's short stories. Emily's story was sweet, something to do with a little girl searching for her lost teddy bear. Adam thought maybe it was a parable for something deeper, but Emily, with a smile on her face, assured him her story was quite literal.

"I think it's nice," Adam said.

"Thank you."

Adam's story, by comparison, was much darker. It was about a vampire who fell in love with a human girl. The vampire knew everything about the girl: where she lived and what she liked to do after work. As he followed her, the story really became about the girl and what her life was all about, until the end when the vampire finally seized upon her, drinking the girl's blood. Adam wasn't sure if it was any good, but Emily liked it. She even wanted to read his other stories, if he had any. Class ended and they walked to the cafeteria together where he bought her a coffee and they shared a bear claw. When it was time for Emily to get to her next class, Adam asked if she had plans for the coming Saturday. He wanted to take her bowling.

"I work at Brunswick, so we can bowl for free," Adam said, "if you're interested."

Emily, who'd never bowled before, happily took him up on his offer.

Adam was twenty.

Emily was eighteen.

Two years later, they were married. Emily enjoyed cooking for Adam, and they made love often. He wrote short stories and read them to her at night while they lay in bed. Emily loved falling asleep to the sound of his voice, and Adam loved watching her sleep. Despite his heartiest efforts, Adam couldn't get any of his stories published. If it weren't for Emily, he would've stopped writing altogether, but she insisted he continue on. So, he did—at least for a little while longer. When he did finally give up on his dream, he never voiced it to Emily, though he suspected she must've known.

Upon graduating from college, Emily got her first and only job as a kindergarten teacher at Carnelian Elementary School. She worked there for nearly thirty years before her failing health forced her into an early retirement. For his part, Adam never finished college. He never exactly dropped out, so much as he stopped attending his classes, and, before he knew it, his part-time job at the bowling alley turned into a full-time job. They bought a house on Hellman Avenue in the developing city of Alta Loma, which, not too long after, was incorporated into the larger community of Rancho Cucamonga.

Every night when they went to bed, Emily asked Adam for a bedtime story. Even when he told her hadn't written anything new, she'd ask him to make something up. And so he'd make up stories about vampires and werewolves, fairies and mermaids, unicorns and castles and clouds made of cotton candy. Emily always fell asleep to the sound of his voice, her cheek nuzzled against his chest, her arm across his belly.

Adam and Emily often talked about raising a family together. However, after years of false alarms, a series of promising fertility tests, and one heartbreaking miscarriage, they eventually gave up. They still wanted a child, but they were each quietly convinced that, short of a miracle, they would never be able to make one together. Adam and Emily made love for the final time when he was thirty years old, just a few hours before Cherry turned him into a vampire. They were lying in bed together, staring at the ceiling, smiling as the warm scent of sex hung in the air, when the phone rang.

It was the bowling alley asking Adam if he could come in to work, as they were short-handed due to a couple of employees calling in sick. Emily asked him to stay and Adam really didn't want to go, but it was Saturday night and he knew how crazy the bowling alley could get. He told her he'd go in for a few hours, not even a full shift, just long enough to help out a little until things were in order. She lay in bed naked, watching him put on his work clothes, beckoning him over as he buttoned his shirt. Pulling him down by the collar, Emily kissed him on the lips. He left in such a hurry, Adam forgot to say goodbye.

The moon was overhead when Adam stepped out into the alley behind the bowling alley for a short break. It was indeed a crazy night and they definitely needed him there, so he was happy to help. Resting his head back against the bricks, Adam looked up at the moon, all full and bright, when Cherry turned up in front of him. She stared at Adam like she knew him, like they were old acquaintances. She appeared to be in her early twenties, so Adam didn't imagine they were ever schoolmates. He thought, perhaps, she was dating one of the guys in the bowling alley. Even when she spoke, Adam was half-convinced they'd met before.

"Do you believe in God?" she asked.

Adam stood up, putting his hands in his pockets.

"Do I know you?" he asked.

"Do you believe in everlasting life?"

"I've got to get back to work."

"I don't mean to bother you," Cherry said, "I'm just hungry is all."

"I can get you some food from the snack bar," Adam said. "Want a burger or something?"

"Don't go."

She put one hand on his arm, squeezing his bicep, while her other hand ran up his chest, stopping just beneath his throat.

"Are you okay?" Adam asked.

"I'm not supposed to be doing this."

There was a passion in her eyes that made Adam uncomfortable. He looked away, staring up at the moon.

"I'm married," Adam said.

Cherry only stared at him, no longer speaking.

"I've got to get back to work."

In an instant, Adam felt the force of her hand pushing him against the brick wall, knocking the wind out of him. He was dumbfounded as to how such a petite woman could be so strong. Cherry closed her eyes and lifted her nose to the sky, smiling as she sniffed the air. Adam tried to pull her hand off his chest, but she simply pressed him harder against the wall. When he tried to scream, Cherry covered his mouth.

"I'm so hungry," she said. "Just so very hungry."

Adam tried to speak, but his words were muffled beneath her palm. Still covering his mouth, she dragged him away from the back door and the one light that shone over it, into the darkness. Adam struggled all the while, bewildered at his inability to overpower the tiny woman. He screamed into her palm as Cherry sunk her teeth into his neck, feeding on Adam's blood until he was nearly dead. Sitting cross-legged against the dumpster, she lay his head on her lap and enjoyed the tingling satisfaction of his blood coursing through her body. He was cold and weak and the world around him was growing darker. Despite all the vampire stories he'd dreamt up, Adam had no idea what was happening to him.

Cherry caressed his hair as Adam cried in her lap.

"Am I dying?"

"Do you want to?"

"No."

"Would you like to live forever?"

"Yes."

"Promise?"

Adam's lids grew heavy. He closed his eyes, fully expecting to never open them again. Cherry opened Adam's mouth, placing her opened wrist atop his lips, letting her blood pour down his throat. Adam began to choke, coughing up Cherry's blood all over his shirt. She held his head down, leaving her wrist on his mouth, imploring him to stay calm and drink. He began to swallow if only to keep from choking, drinking until he passed out completely.

When he woke up, Adam found himself in a bed that wasn't his, inside of a room he'd never before seen. He felt strong and rested. It was night out and Cherry was sitting in a chair beside the window, watching Adam wake up.

"Where am I?"

"My home."

"Who are you?"

"My name is Cherry."

"I'm not dead?"

"Far from it," Cherry said. "You're a vampire now."

"Pardon me?"

"You're a vampire," Cherry said, "like me."

"I'm dreaming," Adam said. "This isn't real."

"This is very real," Cherry said. "Your body has already accepted the truth, but there's a small part of you that still feels human. While that part will likely stay with you for a long time, it's important for you to understand that you're not human. Not anymore."

Adam stood from the bed, exiting the bedroom. He went into the bathroom, running his hand along the wall until he found a light switch. When he flipped it up, nothing happened. Despite the absence of light, Adam realized he could see everything around him.

"How is this happening?"

"Amazing, isn't it?" Cherry said. "To see with human eyes is to see nothing at all."

Standing before the mirror, Adam saw he had no reflection. Cherry turned up behind him, resting her hands on his shoulders.

"You'll never see yourself again," she said.

"I really am a vampire."

"You really are."

"I'm so hungry."

"Of course you are," Cherry said. "I'll take you out to feed."

"What about Emily?"

"Who's that?"

"My wife."

"You can't see her anymore."

"What do you mean?"

"Vampires and humans can't have relationships, not like that," Cherry said. "It's one of the laws."

"But, I need to see her."

"The life you had before is over."

Adam exited the bathroom, making his way to the front door.

"This is your life now," Cherry said.

Opening the door, Adam stepped outside into the fresh air, taking in the scent of the grass and the leaves, the asphalt and the sky. He was in the middle of an old, suburban neighborhood with small houses and flickering streetlights. Cherry followed him outside, closing the door behind them. Adam walked ahead, stopping at the sidewalk as it met the road.

"Where are we?" he asked.

"Upland."

"How do I get back home?"

"This *is* your home."

"How do I get back to Emily?"

"Where is she?"

"Rancho Cucamonga."

"I can take you," Cherry said, "so long as you understand that you can never be a part of her life again."

"Take me."

"Do you understand?"

"Please."

Cherry led Adam to her car and drove him past Memorial Park, which was across the street from her house, onto Foothill Boulevard, traveling east towards Rancho Cucamonga. From Foothill, Adam was able to give Cherry directions, and within ten minutes, they were parked across the street from the home he'd shared with Emily on Hellman Avenue. Adam burst out of the car, moving faster than he realized he could, until he was standing on his front porch. He had his key in the door, when Cherry turned up behind him.

"Don't," she said.

"This is my home."

He turned the key.

"Not anymore," Cherry said.

Adam opened the door while Cherry stood by and watched. When he tried to step inside, he found he couldn't cross the threshold. He ran his fingers down the emptiness of the doorframe, pressing them forward against the resistance of the invisible space.

"We can't enter human homes," Cherry said, "not unless we're invited inside."

"But this is *my* home."

"This isn't your home," Cherry said, "and the woman inside is no longer your wife."

"Why did you do this to me?"

"You asked for it."

"I didn't want this."

"It's done."

A light from upstairs came on, filling the hallway. Emily called down from the top of the staircase, not showing her face.

"Hello?"

Without thinking, Adam tried again to step inside, only to be stopped by the same invisible force that stood between him and his former life.

"We have to go," Cherry said.

"I need to see her."

"If she sees you, she'll invite you in."

"That's what I want."

"And you'll feed on her."

"I would never do that," Adam said. "I love her."

Emily called downstairs.

"Who's there?" she asked.

Adam could hear Emily's footsteps coming down the stairs. Traveling ahead of her, floating through the air and wafting out the door, was the tantalizing scent of her fear. The smell filled Adam's nose and stirred his appetite, causing his fangs to push out from beneath his lips.

"You'll drain her until she's empty," Cherry said.

"But, I love her."

Cherry left him on the porch, retreating to her car across the street. Adam couldn't imagine not being a part of Emily's life, but, if it meant insuring her safety from his new form, then he had no choice. He started backing away from the doorway, slowly, waiting for Emily to appear, wanting one last look. He could hear her breathing in the stairway, a quiver in her throat, terrified to see what monster lay in wait for her. Adam backed away further into the darkness, watching as Emily discovered his key in the door. She stepped outside, her magnificent fragrance filling the air. Looking out into the night, Adam could've sworn Emily's eyes locked onto his.

"Adam?"

Before she took her next step, he was already in the car with Cherry. As they drove away, Adam trained his eyes on the rearview mirror, watching as Emily became smaller and smaller, until she disappeared altogether. He assumed that Cherry was taking him back to her home, but, before long, she'd pulled into a small shopping center, parking her car in front of the Barbershop.

In the weeks that followed, Adam went back to his former home—with Cherry's blessing—and, from a prudent distance, watched Emily. He watched her speak to the police and he watched her cry herself to sleep. He watched her talk to herself and he watched her sit in silence. He watched her weep beneath her veil and he watched her mourn. And finally, one night, two months removed from his disappearance, Adam watched Emily sitting on the toilet crying tears of joy as she held the white stick that told her she was going to be a mother.

CHAPTER TWENTY

AN HONORABLE MAN

Jesus and Nick sat on the couch, beers in hand, settling into the reality that they were both vampire hunters. He told Nick about his mother and how she was taken from him at a very young age at the hands of a vampire—or vampires.

"I wasn't there," Jesus said, "so I don't know how many there were."

"Did you know right away how she died?"

"No," Jesus said, "not until I was eighteen. I watched my best friend killed by a vampire in Memorial Park."

"And that's when you knew."

"Exactly."

Jesus told Nick about how he went back to Memorial Park following Daniel's funeral and called for the vampire to show himself.

"I don't know what I expected to happen," he said, "whether I was looking for a fight or I just wanted to die."

He told Nick about how he fought for his life when the vampire turned up and how, if it weren't for the splintered chunk of tree piercing the vampire's heart, he wouldn't be alive today.

"That's amazing," Nick said. "Do you even know how lucky you are to have survived?"

"I do," Jesus said. "I think about it every day."

"I'm guessing you started hunting after that?"

"Yeah," Jesus said, "pretty much."

"How long has it been?"

"About twelve years now."

"And you've never been trained?"

"No," Jesus said. "I've figured it out on my own."

"And you don't get paid?"

Jesus laughed.

"Who'd pay me?"

"You know how I told you I work for a private security company?"

"Yeah."

"Well," Nick said, "we're vampire hunters."

"You work for a vampire hunting company?!"

"It's more like a non-profit operation," Nick said. "We don't have clients or anything. We just hunt vampires."

"And you get paid?"

"Yeah," Nick said. "I have a salary and benefits. There's no Christmas party or anything, but the boss is still pretty generous. His name is George Wayne. He's the best vampire hunter there ever was. Taught me everything I know. He's older now, so he doesn't really go out into the field anymore. I have no doubt he still could though, if he wanted to."

"How'd you meet him?"

Nick met George soon after seeing his first vampire. At the time, he wasn't exactly sure what he'd seen, but he knew it was bad news. He was having a few drinks at a dive bar with another solider. They were celebrating the end of training, as each of them had graduated into the Navy SEALS. After a few hours of celebrating, Nick and his pal left the bar significantly more drunk than when they'd arrived. They were on their way back to the base when a vampire approached them from out of nowhere. Nick had no idea what he was looking at. The vampire walked right up to Nick's friend, taking him down to the ground. Nick thought he was picking a fight, so he went to help, but the vampire knocked him on his ass. As Nick got back to his feet, he saw the vampire feeding from his friend's neck. Nick started kicking the vampire in the ribs, but he didn't budge. He just kept feeding. After a minute or so, the vampire lifted Nick's friend over his shoulder and ran off, disappearing down the road.

"Did you go after them?" Jesus asked.

"No," Nick said, "I ran the other way."

"That was a smart thing to do"

"Maybe," Nick said, "but it wasn't honorable. A SEAL never leaves a man behind. But, I did. There were lots of questions about what happened after I reported my buddy missing. I didn't dare tell my superiors what I'd seen. They'd have never believed me anyway, and I figured it was a surefire way of getting kicked out. But, I did make the mistake of telling another SEAL, someone I thought I could trust."

"What'd he do?"

"He told some important men about what I'd seen," Nick said. "Before long, I was asked to report to my commanding officer. He was very straightforward with me and asked if I'd seen a vampire the night my buddy disappeared. I told him I didn't know what I saw. He asked me to describe it to him, so I told him exactly what I told you. He asked if we'd been drinking and I told him that we had. The very next day I was relieved of my duties. The official report said something about negligence and alcohol abuse, but I knew what was going on."

After his release from the SEALs, Nick settled in back home, unsure of what to do with the rest of his life. He'd begun spending his evenings at the local bar, drinking beer and watching whatever sports were playing on the TV. The bar was generally empty in the afternoon, so that's when Nick liked to be there. It was dark inside, which helped him forget about the world. And then one day George just turned up beside him at the bar. Nick never even saw him sit down.

"It's as if he were always there," he said.

George was an older man, not quite seventy, but close enough to see it coming. He had long salt and pepper hair, which he was forever combing out of his face with his fingers. He was strong and alert, leaner and healthier than most men half his age. He wasn't one who looked for fights, but he could handle himself just fine when he had to.

"The next round is on me," he told Nick. "You know if they have a kitchen in this place?"

"I don't know."

"I could sure go for a good quesadilla," George said, pronouncing it *kay-suh-dill-uh*.

Nick drank his beer, saying nothing.

"You look to me like a man trying to forget a bad day," George said.

"You can say that again."

"If I thought it'd make you feel better, I surely would."

The bartender dropped off two fresh beers. George slid a twenty across the bar.

"Keep the change, friend."

The bartender nodded his appreciation before stepping away.

"The name's George."

"Nick."

"Pleasure to meet you, Nick."

"Likewise."

"You probably wouldn't know it to look at me," George said, "but I'm a vampire hunter."

If Nick had met George a few months prior and he told him the same thing, he would've assumed he was a lunatic. He looked around to see who else might've heard what George had said, but the bar was empty. The bartender was the only other person there and he was wiping down tables on the other end of the bar, clear out of earshot.

"There's no such thing as vampires," Nick said.

George smiled, combing his fingers through his salt-and-pepper hair.

"You and I both know that's not true, friend."

Nick stood up, but George grabbed his wrist.

"You don't want to do that," Nick said.

"I'm not here to upset you," George said. "I just want to talk. Give me five minutes. If you don't like what I have to say, I'll walk right out of here and you'll never see me again."

Nick sat back down, massaging his wrist.

"You're a military man," George said.

"Yeah"

"Trained with the SEALs, no?"

"Who told you that?"

George smiled.

"That's a good question," he said, "and I don't blame you for asking. If you decide you want to get to know me, one thing you'll learn is I'm an honorable man. When I give you my word, I mean to keep it and there ain't no two ways about it. So, to answer your question, Nick, I can't tell you how I came upon that particular piece of information."

"What else do you know?"

"You were released from the SEALs for seeing a vampire."

"You know anything else?"

"Enough to have a chat over a beer, I suppose," George said. "I'd like to ask you something, Nick, and please don't hesitate to tell me if I'm out of line."

"Go ahead."

"What do you plan on doing with your life?"

"How do you mean?"

"You're done with the military," George said, "so now what?"

"Who says I'm done?"

"You think they'll take you back?"

"Maybe."

"Let's say they don't," George said. "Then what?"

"I'll find a job, I guess."

George smiled.

"That's exactly what I hoped you'd say."

ʕ•ᴥ•ʔ

"George never said how he found you?" Jesus asked.

"No," Nick said. "He really is loyal that way."

"So, what happened?"

"He moved me into his home in Las Vegas," Nick said. "He's got a great big mansion out there where he trains hunters. A lot of us used to live there. It's been a tough couple of years, though. A few guys were killed in action. A few others retired. Right now, I'm the only active vampire hunter George has on the payroll."

"Is he rich or something?"

"He's beyond rich," Nick said. "I have no idea where his money comes from, though. Nobody does. A least, nobody I ever met."

"So, you live in Las Vegas?"

"Yeah," Nick said. "Vampires love the desert, so there's always something to do."

"I had no idea vampires loved the desert."

"They love most any place with a warm climate," Nick said. "It's why New Orleans tends to be a hotbed. It's also why the Inland Empire has a steady flow. If you're hoping not to get bit, your best bet is to move to Minnesota—or Siberia, maybe."

"Is that why you're here?" Jesus asked. "Did George send you on a mission to the Inland Empire?"

"No," Nick said, "I'm just taking a short vacation. A little R&R. I wanted to get out of Vegas for a spell, so I gave Johnson a call and caught the first plane out."

"Is it just you and George in his mansion?"

"He's got a bunch of folks working for him there," Nick said, "but they don't live in the mansion. Just me, George, and Whisper."

"Who's Whisper?"

"She's a witch."

Jesus laughed.

"I'm serious," Nick said. "She's an honest-to-goodness witch."

"Witches are real?"

"Whisper's the only one I've ever met," Nick said, "but I can attest to her being real. She doesn't fly on broomsticks or anything, but she's pretty amazing with spells."

"She works for George, too?"

"Yeah," Nick said. "She's pretty normal. You'd never assume she was a witch by looking at her. She's actually kind of a hottie."

Jesus and Nick hadn't eaten since lunch, so they decided to head out to Corky's for a late meal.

CHAPTER TWENTY-ONE

THE BARBERSHOP

The Barbershop was the only vampire feeding post in Rancho Cucamonga and one of the most popular feeding posts in all of the Inland Empire. Adam was on his way to the Barbershop for a haircut and feeding before meeting Olivia for their date at Corky's later that evening. He knew there were other feeding posts in nearby cities, but Adam never felt any great desire to seek them out. And besides, not only could he feed at the Barbershop, but he could also get a nice haircut. Because vampires couldn't see their reflections, a good barber was not to be taken for granted. Adam got his haircuts exclusively from Donald, who was not only the head barber but also ran the Barbershop. He was the very first vampire Adam met after Cherry turned him when she took him to the Barbershop for his first real feeding.

A young-looking vampire named Eighteen greeted Adam at the door before leading him to Donald's barber chair. Eighteen, like Donald, had been a fixture at the Barbershop for as long as Adam could remember. Despite being several decades older than Adam, Eighteen looked like a teenager, which was how he got his name—his real name was Jose. Donald was Jose's maker, having turned him one night after finding him lying on the sidewalk outside of a bar in

San Diego, not far from the Mexican border. When Donald found him, Eighteen was holding his ribs, blood pulsing through his fingers. He'd been in a knife fight, Donald would later learn, and hadn't fared too well. He was only sixteen and, by the looks of things, he wasn't going to see his seventeenth birthday. Donald could easily have fed on him before leaving him to die—but there was just something about the boy that Donald found striking.

Eighteen was an orphan who didn't have much to call his own, but he'd fight like hell for what was his, which was exactly what he'd been doing when he got himself stabbed. He was a scrappy kid, stubborn, and he wasn't facing the prospect of death gracefully. Donald appreciated his fighting spirit, so he didn't bother asking the boy if he wanted to be turned. He simply did it. Eighteen had been grateful and loyal to Donald ever since. His only complaint was his youthful appearance. Even though he was a teenager verging on manhood, he still looked like a kid. He always figured he'd grow out of it, but once he became a vampire, his youth was sealed in for eternity. Donald couldn't change his looks, so, as a lark, he started calling him Eighteen.

Donald and Eighteen traveled all around the world together for decades before settling down in Rancho Cucamonga. Donald long had the idea of running his own feeding post, something quaint and comfortable, a place where vampires could not only feed but also hang out or just get a haircut. Eighteen supported anything Donald wanted to do, so he was happy to help out. Cherry had been one of Donald's patrons for almost as long as the Barbershop had been open, long before the night she took Adam in for his first feeding. Adam was so scared and confused that night, but Donald put him at ease almost instantly just by being kind and welcoming.

⁽ᵔᵔᵔᵔ⁾

Adam and Eighteen exchanged a few pleasant words before Donald turned up behind him, scissors in hand. Eighteen went back to the entrance, taking his seat by the door. Donald wrapped a cape over Adam's torso and looked into the mirror where neither of their reflections showed. There was only the empty chair. Not even the cape turned up in the mirror, nor any of the clothes Adam and Donald wore. It was one of those strange metaphysical principles of vampire nature—something to do with the clothing a vampire wore taking on their vampire essence. Like so many other facts relating to vampire nature, this was just another detail that no vampire could really explain. They simply knew it to be true, the same way they knew about silver and sunlight.

"The usual?" Donald asked.

"That'd be great," Adam said.

Despite being dead in the human sense of the word, vampires were—for all intents and purposes—very much alive. While they were frozen in the age in which they were turned, their bodies didn't exactly remain frozen. Amongst other things, vampires continued to grow hair, just as they did as humans. And, like humans, vampires weren't exactly immune to vanity, so many of them made an effort to keep themselves groomed. This, of course, wasn't easy without a reflection, which was why Donald never had a shortage of patrons.

He spritzed Adam's hair with a water bottle before running a comb through it. Starting in the back, he took a strand of hair between his fingers, pulling it taut and clipping the ends.

"I hope you're hungry," Donald said. "We got some new humans last night."

After trimming his hair, Donald applied shaving cream to Adam's cheeks and neck before scraping a straight razor along his skin, shaving it nice and smooth. Not every vampire used the Barbershop, of course. Plenty of vampires simply cut their own hair—blindly, as it were—while others depended on friends and partners for help. And still other vampires didn't worry about grooming at all, living out their eternities without a single care of how they looked.

Incidentally, the Barbershop existed in an actual barbershop, between a tanning salon and a pizza parlor. Donald rented the place from its human owner for overnight use. The human knew he was renting to a vampire and he also knew—because Donald told him as much—that if he ever told anyone of their arrangement, he'd find himself in chains in the back room with the other livestock. Donald and Eighteen always locked up the Barbershop before sunrise. During the daylight hours it serviced humans, all of whom were blissfully unaware of the macabre scene that existed behind the locked door in the back.

"Did you hear about the bloodbath in Claremont?" Donald asked.

"I didn't hear anything about it," Adam said. "What happened?"

"Some vampire went rogue in a feeding post out there," Donald said. "There must've been ten human corpses laying around on the floor, right out in the open."

"Who did it?"

"Who knows?" Donald said. "Some idiot vampire looking to get himself in trouble is all I can figure."

A vampire sitting in the chair beside Adam looked up from his magazine.

"I have a buddy who was there," he said. "I mean, he wasn't *there*, but he was close by. He heard there was some sort of monster feeding on vampires and the humans just got caught up in it."

"Bullshit," Donald said.

"I'm just saying that's what I heard," the vampire said. "My buddy told me that his friend told him that there was some giant naked monster twice as big as anyone else there. He said he walked right into the feeding post and started feeding on any vampire he could get his hands on."

"Sure thing, boss," Donald chuckled. "Did his name happen to be the Bogeyman?"

"I'm not saying it's true," the vampire said. "I'm not even saying I believe it. I'm just saying it's what I heard."

"Well, I heard you still believe in the Tooth Fairy and leave cookies out for Santa Claus," Donald said, getting a laugh from the other vampires.

"I don't actually believe it."

"I should hope not," Donald said. "You and I both know that the only creature strong enough to feed on a vampire is another vampire. And we also know that would never happen, because the son of a bitch would be dead."

"I know."

"Spreading rumors like that won't do you any good, boss," Donald said. "So, if I were you, I'd keep that story to myself. Tell your friend to do the same."

The vampire went back to reading his magazine, while Donald finished Adam's shave. When he was done, Adam went to the back room, which, like the rest of the Barbershop, was pitch black. Along the walls of the back room were several humans, naked and chained by their wrists and ankles. The fresher humans still had strength enough to moan and—when properly motivated—scream. But, for the most part, they sat quietly, backs against the wall, accepting their fate for what it was.

While hunting was in their blood, many vampires appreciated not having to go through the effort. They liked the freedom to live out their eternities in relative civility, socializing with their friends and stopping in for a feed at their leisure. There were many vampires, however, who were known to break the rules and take their chances hunting humans for their own gain. Many of these vampires were never heard from again, assuming they had any friends at all to note their disappearance.

The smell of fear in the back room was sweet and decadent. Because Adam was still a young vampire, only a few decades removed from being human himself, he wasn't completely immune to feeling sympathy for the enslaved humans at the Barbershop. Regardless of the sympathy he felt, however, Adam was still a vampire, which meant he had to feed on humans—there was simply no getting around it. He browsed the back room, sniffing the air, examining the men and women, many of whom were too exhausted to realize a new vampire had entered their private hell.

A few of the humans were left over from the previous week, when Adam last visited the Barbershop, but his appetite was drawn to the fresher blood of a man who'd been chained up the previous night. Adam kneeled down beside the man, offering him a quiet whisper of thanks before sinking his fangs into his neck. He drank until he was satisfied, careful not to drain the man to death, as the etiquette in the Barbershop—as with all feeding posts—was to leave the humans alive for as long as possible. With his haircut and feeding complete, Adam left the Barbershop, saying goodbye to Donald and Eighteen on his way out. His date with Olivia wasn't for another hour, so Adam would first stop by his former home to look in on Emily.

༼°°°°༽

Most every night for the past thirty years, Adam took his same place in the same perch in the same tree. He sat up at just the right level to look in on Emily inside the bedroom they'd once shared as man and wife. Adam treated his time in Emily's backyard as sacred and enjoyed getting lost in her life, but at the moment he found himself thinking about Olivia. Even though they'd just met a few weeks before, he felt himself falling for her. He knew it was a mistake, of course, a violation of vampire laws, but he couldn't help himself. As far as he knew, Olivia was only interested in him so that she could write her vampire novel, but, even if that were the case, Adam didn't mind. He was just happy to be around her.

The romantic feelings he was developing for Olivia left him with a pang of guilt in his belly, as he sat perched in the tree, watching Emily as she lay in bed with Rusty by her side. Rusty was Adam's thirty-year-old son. He'd watched him his whole life, though they'd never actually met. Adam knew that Emily told Rusty stories throughout his life about the kind man his father was. As much as it tortured Adam to see Emily and Rusty living a life without him, it also brought him joy, which was why he perched himself in that tree for the past thirty years.

Cherry never approved of Adam holding on to his human sympathies, but she gave him her blessing nonetheless. He knew Cherry saw it as a phase that he would eventually grow out of, but Adam knew that wasn't the case. On a couple of occasions, Cherry even perched herself in the tree with Adam, but she didn't see what the fuss was all about. All Cherry saw was a woman and her kid living in a two-story house—but Adam saw more than that. He saw cookies baked in the kitchen and homework done at the dinner table. He saw presents opened on birthdays and sparkling cider sipped on New Years Eve. He saw Disney cartoons and coloring books, bellyaches and thermometers, bedtime stories and goodnight kisses. He saw the life that was almost his.

Adam knew that Emily had moved on from the idea of them ever being together again and, by all logical reasoning, they hadn't been a couple for three decades, yet he couldn't shake the feeling that he was somehow being unfaithful to her by spending time with Olivia. Even now, perched in the tree and looking in on her, watching as Rusty sat on the edge of the bed and stroked Emily's hair, her eyes growing heavy and her deteriorating mind drifting off to sleep, Adam felt like an unfaithful husband. He knew his burden would've been much lighter had Emily moved on herself, but, after Adam disappeared from her life, she never took another man.

Emily devoted herself to being a mother, raising Rusty as best she could, letting him be the only man in her life. Whether her decision to remain single was out of loyalty, fear, or some unspoken reason that Adam would never learn, it didn't change the fact that he was the last man she would ever be with. Rather than make himself feel like a philandering husband any longer, Adam climbed down from the tree and left the backyard, driving to Corky's where he'd wait for Olivia.

CHAPTER TWENTY-TWO

THE NATURE OF HUMANS

O livia wasn't yet at Corky's when Adam arrived, so he took the liberty of sitting at his regular booth—which, in a way, had become *their* regular booth. It wasn't quite midnight yet, which was the time he and Olivia had agreed to meet. It was just as well, since he hadn't spent much time alone in Corky's lately. Darlene, who was working her usual overnight shift, came by the table to take his order.

"No Olivia tonight?" she asked.

"She should be on her way."

"You two are nice together."

"Thanks," Adam said, "though I don't know how *together* we are."

"Well," Darlene said, "if you're *not* already, you probably should be."

The heavyset man with the sad eyes and freckled arms was the only other patron in Corky's. After Darlene dropped off Adam's order—a slice of snickerdoodle pie à la mode—she sat with the heavyset man, smiling and chatting, putting a smile on his sad face. She even managed to get him to talk about himself, though his words were brief and hushed. Darlene touched his hand and smiled before heading back into the kitchen. For a while, Adam and the heavyset man were the only two people in the dining room until Olivia arrived, taking her seat in the booth.

"You been here long?" she asked.

"Not really."

"I would've gotten here sooner," Olivia said, "but I was trying to get a hold of my roommate, Elowyn. She had a date last night and I haven't heard from her since."

"Is that normal for her?"

"Well, it's not unprecedented," Olivia said, "but she usually calls me to let me know she's okay."

"I'm sure she's fine."

"I know you're probably right," Olivia said. "I'll just feel better when I hear from her."

Darlene dropped by their table to take Olivia's order.

"I'll have the blueberry pancake plate, please."

"You won't be disappointed," Darlene said, disappearing into the kitchen.

Adam looked at the necklace hanging from Olivia's neck.

"I see you fixed your crucifix."

"Oh, yeah," Olivia said, looking down at it. "It just needed a new chain."

"Sorry again."

"It's not a big deal."

"Can I at least pay for it?"

"Tell you what," Olivia said. "I'll let you buy my pancakes and we'll call it even."

"Deal."

They made more small talk, which led to the revelation that not only hadn't Olivia read *Dracula*, but she also hadn't seen the film starring Bela Lugosi.

"That's unconscionable," Adam said. "You can't very well write a vampire novel if you've never seen *Dracula*."

"Is that so?"

"It is," Adam said. "Luckily for you, I own it on Blu-ray."

"Are you inviting me to your home?"

"Would you be interested if I were?"

"I think I would," Olivia said, "yes."

Adam was thrilled. They worked out the details, which Olivia scribbled down in her Moleskine notebook, before turning to the pages with her vampire notes so they could proceed with the business at hand. With her pencil at the ready, she began asking questions.

"So," Olivia said, "last time we covered that there are vampire laws and that you're not allowed to hunt humans unless you take them to a feeding post."

"Right."

"Is it okay to be friends with a human?"

"No," Adam said. "Vampires aren't supposed to entertain any sort of social relationships with them. Frankly, humans shouldn't know we exist at all. It's in our best interest for you guys to assume we only exist in books and movies."

Darlene turned up at the table, setting down Olivia's blueberry pancakes.

"You two talking about books?" she asked, refilling Adam's coffee. "I love reading."

"Actually, we're talking about writing," Adam said. "Olivia here is an author. She's working on a vampire novel."

"Oh, that's exciting!" Darlene said. "I've never met an actual author before."

"I'd hardly call myself an actual author."

"You hush with that talk," Darlene said. "I'll bet you'll be the next Stephen King or something. I like romance novels myself. But, as long as you've got some folks kissing and touching in that vampire book of yours, I'll be sure to read it."

Darlene left them alone again, disappearing into the kitchen.

"Where were we?" Olivia asked.

"Humans and vampires and how we shouldn't intertwine."

"Right," Olivia said. "Go on."

"If humans knew that vampires existed," Adam said, "there'd be an all out war."

"You think so?"

"It's in the nature of humans," he said. "When humans are confronted with something they don't understand, their first instinct is to destroy it."

"In the case of vampires," Olivia said, "we probably wouldn't be all that out of line, don't you think?"

"Humans would be no more out of line for wanting to kill vampires than cows would be for wanting to kill butchers," Adam said. "The difference is cows don't have the means to put up a fight."

"Can a human actually kill a vampire?"

"Sure," Adam said, "if they know how to exploit our weaknesses."

"Has it ever happened?"

"I'm sure it has," Adam said. "It's believed there are some humans who are vampire hunters, not that I've ever seen one myself."

"Like Buffy?"

Adam laughed.

"Sure," he said.

"Although, Buffy had supernatural strength," Olivia said. "Do you think there are humans like that?"

"I doubt it," Adam said. "In any event, if there were an all out war, I've no doubt vampires would win. But, at what cost? The humans would be gone and with them would go our only food source."

"So, rather than risking famine," Olivia said, "vampires just keep themselves a secret from humans."

"Exactly."

"So, if the law is for vampires to stay away from humans socially," Olivia said, "aren't you breaking it by being here with me?"

"Yes."

"What happens if you get caught?"

Adam shrugged.

"You really don't know?" Olivia asked.

"Not a clue," Adam said. "But, I suppose if you don't hear from me after tonight, you'll know why."

"I don't know that I'm worth getting in trouble over."

"I'll be the judge of that."

Olivia smiled.

"About your book," Adam said, "do you have an idea of what it's going to be about now?"

"I think it's going to be a love story between a vampire and a girl."

"I like that idea."

"But," Olivia said, "their love will be difficult, because they're not supposed to be together."

"Obviously."

"I can use the stuff about vampires not being able to socialize with humans for dramatic tension," Olivia said. "So, when they do eventually hook up, there'll be an added element of danger."

"I think there should also be an antagonist," Adam said. "Who's the bad guy going to be?"

"If the girl is in love with the vampire," Olivia said, "then maybe the antagonist should be a vampire hunter."

"Oh, that's good," Adam said. "Maybe the hunter is on the trail of the vampire and the girl. He thinks she's in danger."

"But, she's not in danger," Olivia said, "is she?"

"No," Adam said, "she's not."

"But the hunter doesn't know that," Olivia said. "He only means to help, but in the end probably kills the vampire."

"That's so tragic," Adam said. "But, I suppose their relationship can only ever end in tragedy."

"Maybe the hunter will see how upset she is and feel guilty over what he's done," Olivia said. "He's not a bad guy, he only wanted to help. And maybe in the end it's the hunter and the girl who end up together."

"Maybe," Adam said. "But, what if the vampire kills the hunter?"

The front entrance of Corky's opened, jarring the relative silence, causing Adam and Olivia to look up. Adam noted a look of recognition on Olivia's face when she saw the two men enter.

"Jesus?" Olivia said.

She looked to Adam, then back at the two men. Fear exploded from Olivia's pores, filling the air. The smell of her was nearly overwhelming, causing Adam to grip the edge of the table. Before he knew it, the two men—one of whom Adam deduced was Jesus—were walking towards them.

CHAPTER TWENTY-THREE

DUELING FEELINGS

The parking lot in front of Corky's was mostly empty, so Jesus was able to park right in front of the entrance. As he and Nick approached the front door, he could see through the window that the dining room was nearly empty. Aside from the hostess at the register, he didn't even see anybody working inside. Stepping through the entrance, Jesus and Nick stood by the cash register, waiting for the hostess to seat them, though, clearly, they'd have their pick of anywhere they wanted to sit. There were only three people in the whole dining room, so far as Jesus could tell—a heavyset man with sad eyes sitting by himself and a man and woman on a date.

"Check out the hottie," Nick said. "You think this is their first date?"

Jesus took a closer look, his heart sinking when he realized he was looking at Olivia.

"You can sit anywhere you like," the hostess said. "Darlene will be right with you."

Jesus could hardly pay attention to what she was saying, so occupied was he by dueling feelings of embarrassment and betrayal. He knew Olivia wasn't his girlfriend, but he was certain they'd made a connection on their date. And while she didn't exactly owe him any sort of exclusive dating rights, it was still jarring to see her out with another man so soon after they'd gone out together.

"That's Olivia," Jesus said.

"You know her?"

"I'm sort of dating her."

"Looks like that guy's dating her, too," Nick said. "You know him?"

"Never seen him before," Jesus said. "We should probably go."

"Fuck that," Nick said. "If that tool's out with your girl, I don't think we should leave without saying hello."

"That's not necessary," Jesus said. "I'd rather go somewhere else."

Nick was already heading towards Adam and Olivia's booth, so, not knowing what else to do, Jesus followed him. They stood beside the table for a moment, saying nothing, just staring at Adam and Olivia.

"Can we help you?" Adam asked.

"This is my friend Jesus," Olivia said. "Jesus, this is Adam."

"Hey," Jesus said. "This is Nick."

Nick stared at Adam, not saying a word.

"Nice to meet you," Adam said.

He extended his hand and Nick shook it, giving him a good squeeze, before sitting down beside him. Jesus was the only one left standing.

"Have a seat," Olivia said, patting the space next to her.

Jesus sat down, letting their thighs touch.

"So, Olivia," Nick said, "Jesus says you two are dating."

Olivia was silent.

"I told him we had one date," Jesus said.

"How do you two know each other?" Olivia asked.

"Nick's friends with Johnson."

"Speaking of Johnson," Olivia said, "do you guys know where he's at?"

"Out with Elowyn."

"Really?" she said. "Are you sure?"

"I just talked to him a little while ago," Jesus said. "He's meeting her at Beryl Park."

"I haven't heard from Elowyn in a few days," Olivia said. "I was getting worried."

"Sounds like she's all right."

"So," Nick said, "is this like a first date or something?"

Darlene stopped by the table, handing menus to Jesus and Nick.

"Can I get you boys something to drink?"

"That's okay," Jesus said, standing from the booth, "we just came in to say hi."

"You sure?" Nick asked, looking at him.

"Yeah."

Nick stood from the booth and followed Jesus to the exit, neither of them offering a goodbye.

CHAPTER TWENTY-FOUR

THE NIGHT SKY OVERHEAD

"It's Elowyn," Johnson said. "She called me in the middle of the night talking all sexy and shit about how she needs me. She wants to meet up later, so I'm gonna hang back."

"I thought you were done with her."

"So did I," Johnson said. "You should've heard her, though."

"Should we just go tomorrow?" Nick asked.

"No, I've got customers expecting supplies tomorrow," Johnson said. "You guys would be doing me a huge solid if you went today."

"I don't mind if Jesus is still up for it," Nick said.

"I don't mind either," Jesus said.

"Well, I guess that settles that," Johnson said, handing Jesus an envelope. "There's enough there to cover what we usually get."

"Okay."

"We may as well hit the road," Jesus said. "You have your passport on you?"

"I sure do."

"Call me when you get back," Nick said. "If I'm not busy getting laid, maybe we can hang out."

"Will do. You ready, Nick?"

"You bet," he said. "Let's rock and roll."

Jesus and Nick each reached for their wallets, but Johnson stopped them.

"I'll cover lunch," he said. "Have a safe trip and I'll see you boys when you get back."

Once he was alone, Johnson checked his phone. Elowyn hadn't called yet. It was still early in the day, so there was plenty of time for her to get in touch with him, but he found that the longer he went without hearing from her, the more desperate he was to see her. After finishing his lunch, Johnson headed to Ground and Pound for a workout. He hoped a few hours of sweating in the gym would help keep his mind occupied, so he didn't drive himself crazy waiting for Elowyn's call.

Johnson was working one of the heavy bags, throwing round-house kicks. He threw every kick perfectly—pivoting on the sole of his foot, torquing his hips, snapping his kicking leg into the heavy bag—one after the other, his center of gravity never falling off balance. He'd been bullied as a kid, not long after he began fourth grade. He and his parents had moved to Rancho Cucamonga, so Johnson had to start at a new school in the middle of the year. He made a few friends early on, but, for reasons he never understood, he also made a few enemies. A couple of sixth graders pushed him around during recess, and when Johnson decided to push back, they knocked him to the ground, kicking and punching him until one of the proctors broke it up.

Johnson, who grew up loving martial arts films—especially ones that featured Jean-Claude Van Damme—begged his parents to sign him up for karate lessons. The following week he was a student in Red Dragon Karate, where, as time passed, he would spend a great deal of his childhood training and fighting, learning proper technique and discipline. The two boys who'd ganged up on Johnson were suspended for a couple of days, and when they came back to school, they had strict orders to stay away from him, so, even as he learned how to fight, he was never presented with the opportunity to exact any sort of revenge. He eventually came to understand that karate was less about combat and more about spiritual development; the sharper his skills became, the less he cared about seeking revenge.

Johnson loved competing in tournaments on the weekends, rarely walking away with anything less than a first-place ribbon. As a teenager, having already earned his black belt, Johnson began studying Muay Thai and judo before eventually getting into Brazilian jiu-jitsu. He'd been watching Pancrase, which was a mixed martial arts promotion that preceded the UFC. He knew, as he watched those men competing against one another, that he'd found his calling. From that point forward, Johnson dedicated himself to becoming a professional mixed martial artist at all costs. Even when using steroids became part of the cost, it was worth it to Johnson if it afforded him the opportunity to live his dream.

It wasn't until recently, having long since been banned from competing in the UFC for doping, that Johnson started to feel like maybe it was time he went back to basics. He'd lost himself somewhere along the way, lost faith in his abilities, and forgotten that there was a time when he didn't feel the need to cheat in order to achieve success in the cage. It's the reason why he'd decided to train for his upcoming bout clean, no steroids, nothing but hard work in the gym, day in and day out. He had no illusions that there was any sort of path for him back to the UFC or any other major promotion for that matter, but it wasn't really about that anymore. It was about competing with integrity, because it was the honorable thing to do. It was about continuing the spiritual journey he began as a timid fourth grade kid.

Johnson even got to thinking that maybe, if things went well with Elowyn tonight, he'd see about keeping her around for a while to see how it felt. He wasn't exactly looking for a relationship and, at this point of his life, he wasn't so sure he was capable of one, but, as he stood in front of that heavy bag throwing roundhouse kicks, one after the other with perfect technique, Johnson found that the thought of spending time with Elowyn sounded pretty all right. He checked his phone again, but she still hadn't called him, so he decided to hit the weights. After blasting through some bench presses and bicep curls, he sparred in the boxing ring with one of the other coaches.

It was after dark and Johnson was exhausted. He decided to do a thousand crunches on the mat before calling it a day. He was somewhere around his six-hundredth crunch when his phone finally rang. He'd kept it on the mat beside his hip, just in case she called. It was Elowyn. His hands were sweaty, so when he tried to answer the call, his phone fell from his grip. He picked it up, relieved to see he hadn't hung up on her.

"Hello?" Johnson said.

"How are you?"

"I'm good," he said. "I wasn't sure you'd call."

"Meet me at Beryl Park in an hour."

"You don't want to come to my place instead?"

"I want to play in the park," Elowyn said, "out in the open."

"All right," Johnson said, "I'll be there in an hour."

He gathered his things and drove back home where he took a long hot shower, thinking about how exciting it was going to be to have sex with Elowyn in the middle of the park. He'd never actually had public sex before, and the fact that Elowyn was the one suggesting it helped confirm in his mind that she might very well be the right girl to settle down with. He stood in front of his bathroom mirror, wiping the steam from the window with the back of his forearm, and gave himself a nice clean shave. After fixing his hair and spritzing some cologne, Johnson got dressed and headed out the door. His phone rang on his way over to Beryl Park. He thought it might be Elowyn, but it was just Jesus.

"Where're you at?" Jesus asked.

"I'm on my way to meet Elowyn at Beryl Park."

"Beryl Park?" Jesus said. "Why're you meeting there?"

"We're going to fuck," Johnson said, "obviously. Take Nick back to your place, and I'll pick him up when I'm finished."

Johnson was flooded with memories as he parked his car and stepped foot onto the grass of Beryl Park for the first time in years. Growing up in Rancho Cucamonga, Beryl Park had served as one of the cornerstones of his adolescence. When he wasn't practicing karate, he was usually at Beryl Park with his friends playing pickup basketball or flag football. Sometimes he'd demonstrate his karate moves for his friends, even teaching them some techniques. Beryl Park was where his parents watched him play his first little league baseball game and, sitting on the bench near the tennis courts, it's where he enjoyed his first kiss.

Walking through Beryl Park reminded Johnson that he hadn't been to visit his parents in a while. They still lived in the same house around the corner. They'd been married for nearly fifty years and, as their only child, he knew they worried about his lifestyle, fearing he'd wind up old and alone. The thought crossed his mind that, perhaps somewhere down the road, he might end up taking Elowyn over to meet them. This was the thought he was entertaining, wandering down the barren soccer field with the night sky overhead and the hum of traffic in the air, when, out in the distance, he could just make out the frame of Elowyn's silhouette. She moved with long, confident strides and within a few moments they were standing face to face. Her hair seemed richer in the darkness, her skin more pale.

"Hey," Johnson said, "it's nice to see you."

"I agree," Elowyn said. "This is an exciting moment for me."

"Me too."

Elowyn placed the flat of her hand against Johnson's cheek, tenderly running it down his neck before gripping his bicep. Her grip was strong, almost painful. Johnson enjoyed it at first, assuming her aggression was sexual. When he found her grip to be too painful, he took hold of her wrist, only to find he was unable to remove her hand. Taking Johnson's other arm into her free hand, Elowyn lifted him off the ground like a child, holding him there for a moment before tossing him onto the grass, knocking the wind out of him. As Johnson got himself to his feet, still trying to process what was happening, Elowyn was already standing before him.

"Did you not enjoy that?" she asked.

Johnson just looked at her, speechless.

Elowyn thrust the palm of her hand into Johnson's chest, knocking him back down onto the grass. As he lay there holding his hands over his sternum, gasping for air, Elowyn stepped over him, setting her feet on either side of his hips. With his instincts shifting into survival mode, Johnson turned over onto his hands and knees, crawling away from Elowyn as fast as he could, scrambling back to his feet in the process. Elowyn was a good ten feet away, but she closed the distance between them in what felt like a second. Johnson readied himself in his fighting stance. He'd always had a strict policy about not hitting women, but Elowyn was leaving him no choice.

They circled for a few moments before Johnson threw a punch, which Elowyn easily dodged. He threw two more, and she avoided each of them just as easily. Johnson then threw a roundhouse kick, pivoting on the ball of his foot, torquing his hips and snapping his kicking leg towards Elowyn's head, catching her flush on the temple. He watched, waiting for her to crumble to the grass, but she just stood there, smiling at him. Elowyn charged Johnson, taking him down to the ground, where—as he'd told her time and time again— most every fight would inevitably wind up.

On the ground, Johnson was able to briefly defend himself using the same Brazilian jiu-jitsu techniques he'd taught to Elowyn. She was so strong, so fast, that Johnson was unable to take control of her. She played with him on the grass, rolling and grappling, before securing Johnson's arms beneath her knees, laughing as he struggled to free himself.

"Why are you doing this?" he asked.

Elowyn looked at him with genuine surprise, no longer laughing.

"Are you serious?" she asked.

"Yes."

"You really don't know?"

"No."

Elowyn rolled off his body, setting him free.

"You hurt me," she said. "I loved you."

"I thought we were just messing around," Johnson said. "I figured you knew that."

"You're lying," she said. "You knew exactly what I felt. You just didn't care."

Johnson got back to his feet, backing away.

"Don't mistake this for mercy," Elowyn said. "I'm still going to kill you. I just want you to understand why."

Johnson turned and began to run down the soccer field, his life flashing before him with every step. He traveled at least fifty yards before he looked back and saw Elowyn was not behind him—when he looked ahead again, she was standing right in front of him. He collided into her, the impact jarring his head, causing him to wobble backwards. Elowyn punched him in the face, breaking his jaw. Johnson fell to the grass, holding his hands to his mouth, as Elowyn straddled him one more time.

"You deserve this," she said.

Elowyn opened her mouth and Johnson saw two long fangs grow from beneath her lips. He tried to scream, but, before he could make a sound, Elowyn was covering his mouth, her teeth piercing his neck, his blood pulsing over her lips. Johnson could only lie there, staring up at the night sky. All at once, the moon and the stars were eclipsed from Johnson's view as a large man whom Johnson had never seen before stood over him.

"That's enough."

Johnson assumed the man was there to help him.

"Must I stop?" Elowyn said, lifting her mouth from Johnson's neck. "He tastes so good."

"I know he does, but we need to keep him alive."

"Why?"

"So we can deliver him to the Barbershop."

CHAPTER TWENTY-FIVE

WEAPONS AND GADGETS

Jesus left Corky's with Nick, unsure of where they were heading next. He was feeling down, having seen Olivia there with Adam.

"Fuck her, man," Nick said. "You're a good dude, and if she wants to fuck around with some other asshole, let her."

"You're right," Jesus said. "I just feel sort of stupid for thinking she liked me."

"You didn't do anything wrong," Nick said. "We're all capable of being suckers when it comes to women."

"I hear that."

"If you want," Nick said, "we can do some vampire hunting tonight. I'm sure you can stand to blow off some steam."

"I'd love to," Jesus said, "but we can't just *find* a vampire to hunt."

"What do you mean?"

"I just mean it's not as easy as going out and finding one."

"Sure it is," Nick said. "How do *you* find vampires?"

"I don't," Jesus said. "I wait for them to find me."

"And that works?"

"Sometimes," Jesus said. "I can go weeks without seeing one. But, I've also killed as many as three in one night."

"Well, I've got some gadgets to help with the finding part," Nick said. "Let's swing by Johnson's place, so I can grab my gear."

"You brought hunting gear with you?"

"Sure," Nick said. "You never know when it'll come in handy."

On the way to his apartment, Nick called Johnson's cell phone, but got no answer.

"I guess he's still out with Elowyn."

"Should we just head for my place, then?"

"No," Nick said. "I know where he keeps the spare key."

Johnson's apartment was dark and empty. Jesus half-expected to hear him having sex with Elowyn when they walked in, but there was nobody there. He turned on the light in the living room and leaned against the wall, while Nick grabbed his gear from Johnson's bedroom. He came out with a duffle bag over his shoulder, heavy enough to shift his weight off balance. They shut off the lights and locked the door, placing the key back in its hiding place and headed out.

Back at Jesus' apartment, Nick set his duffle bag down on the living room floor, unzipping it.

"I don't have everything," Nick said. "The full artillery is at George's place. But, I brought along a few travel-friendly items."

Nick reached into his bag, pulling out a collar that looked like a miniature chain-linked fence, fastening it around his neck.

"It's made out of silver," he said. "If a vampire tries to sneak a bite, he'll burn the fuck out of his mouth."

"That's smart," Jesus said. "I use garlic jelly."

Jesus retrieved the jar from his wooden trunk and showed it to Nick.

"Creative," Nick said. "And it works?"

"Sure."

"They can still bite you, though."

"Yeah," Jesus said, "but it repels them pretty quickly. How exactly do you find vampires?"

Nick pulled out what looked like a can of hairspray.

"This usually does the trick of drawing them out."

"What is it?"

Nick pressed the button on top of the can, spraying a light mist in the air.

"Smell that?"

Jesus sniffed the mist as it sprinkled down.

"Not really," he said. "What should I be smelling?"

"Blood."

"That's blood?"

"It's not *exactly* blood," Nick said. "It's a blood essence spray. Like sharks, vampires can smell blood from miles away. Spray this in the air, and any vampires around will come out."

"So," Jesus said, "do you just walk around and spray it in the air?"

"Pretty much," Nick said. "I'll sometimes spray some on my clothes, too, just for safe measure."

Next, Nick pulled out a pair of thick black goggles, placing them over his eyes.

"Night vision," he said, tapping the lens with his fingernail. "I thought for sure you'd have some of these."

"For me, it's more about feel," Jesus said. "Once a vampire makes physical contact with me, I can fight him with my eyes closed. It's all about feeling their body and reacting to their movement."

"Show off."

Next, Nick pulled out what looked like an air horn.

"This gadget is priceless," he said, handing it to Jesus. "It's a high-pitched horn. You press the button on top, and it releases a sound that only dogs and vampires can hear. The sound doesn't fill the air, though, so it's most effective if you can get a straight shot right on their dome."

"Does it kill them?"

"No, not at all," Nick said, "but it'll shock the fuck out of their ears for a few seconds, which is all the time I need to shoot them in the heart."

"What do you shoot them with?"

Nick pulled a small pistol from the duffle bag.

"It's not a terribly big gun," he said, "but it's loaded with silver bullets. Believe me when I tell you, it's done the trick more than once."

"George provides all this stuff?"

"And then some," Nick said. "He's got a whole underground lab at his place with a bunch of nerdy engineers and scientists developing weapons and gadgets. Anyway, what do you say we get the fuck out of here and do some hunting?"

"Sure thing," Jesus said. "Let me throw on my gear real quick."

Jesus hurried into his room and put on his black pants and form-fitting shirt. He slipped on his gloves and strapped his wooden stake and silver knife to his ankles. He grabbed his garlic water gun, making sure it was full before slipping it into his pocket. He did everything he would normally do, except for spreading the garlic jelly on his neck. It was an honest mistake, a simple oversight really—but it was a mistake nonetheless, one he would soon be paying for.

Jesus took Nick to Memorial Park, where he'd killed his first vampire over a decade earlier. Nick was decked out in his silver collar and night vision goggles; the rest of his artillery he carried in a backpack. He took out the spray can with the blood scent, while handing Jesus the high-pitched air horn. Every few steps through the park, Nick would spray the blood scent in the air. After nearly an hour of walking around without encountering a vampire, he grew impatient.

"This place seems pretty dead."

"Yeah," Jesus said. "Some nights are better than others."

"Where should we head next?"

"There's a few parks out where Johnson lives in Rancho Cucamonga," Jesus said. "We can check those out."

"Lead the way, my friend."

They started with Beryl Park, as it was small and wouldn't take long to comb through. They moved past the tennis courts and the jungle gym, towards the first of the park's two soccer fields. As it was with Memorial Park, there was no action.

"Where else can we go?" Nick asked.

On a whim, Jesus decided to go next to Alta Loma High School. After walking through the quads and the hallways and the football field, they gave up and went across the street to Red Hill Park. It had several baseball diamonds and soccer fields, a walking track that stretched for several miles, an amphitheater, and a half-acre man-made lake that was never short on ducks. Jesus and Nick each agreed that Red Hill Park would be their last stop, as they'd been hunting for hours without any luck.

They walked past the soccer fields and the baseball diamonds, Nick spraying the blood scent every now and again. He removed his night vision goggles, letting them hang around his neck with the silver collar. It wasn't until they reached the manmade lake and its peaceful flock of ducks that Jesus and Nick finally heard something out in the distance. Nick sprayed the blood scent in the air before taking a moment to put his goggles back on, when a vampire with bleach blond hair charged forward from out of nowhere, knocking both Nick and Jesus onto the grass.

Jesus quickly got to his feet but no longer had the high-pitched air horn, as it'd been knocked from his grip when the bleach blonde vampire tackled them. Jesus saw Nick wasn't fighting back and he worried he might've been knocked unconscious, so he charged the vampire, knocking him to the grass. They grappled for a few moments, rolling about, nearly falling in the lake, until Jesus found himself beneath the vampire in a decidedly bad position.

The vampire went in fast for his neck, so Jesus braced himself for the brief prick he'd come to expect in such a scenario, fully expecting it to be followed by howling pain after the vampire's mouth touched the garlic jelly. He realized something was terribly wrong when the bleach blond vampire didn't recoil. Instead, Jesus felt his fangs sink all the way down into his neck, his lips adhering to his flesh, sucking the blood as it pulsed out. For the first time in his entire life, Jesus found himself in the terrifying and helpless position of being fed on by a vampire.

CHAPTER TWENTY-SIX

THE BROKEN BROOMSTICK

The Barbershop was bustling with well over a dozen vampires, a few of them waiting for haircuts, others in the backroom feeding, and the rest simply hanging out and socializing. Eighteen stood near the door, sweeping up hair and greeting guests as they came in. Donald, as always, was making pleasant conversation when Victus arrived. He was carrying Johnson over his shoulder, with Elowyn at his side. Victus was known as something of a brute when it came to dealing with other vampires, Donald included. For this reason, Eighteen never liked Victus and was always tempted to scrap with him. Donald, however, had told him more than once not to make trouble with Victus, so Eighteen held his broom to his chest and stepped aside, letting him through. While Donald trusted Eighteen's loyalty, he worried that his temper might still get the best of him, so he went to greet Victus personally.

"Hello," Donald said, touching his arm, "I see you've got a human for us."

"Yes," Victus said. "My new bride, Elowyn, hunted him down on her first night as a vampire."

"Very impressive," Donald said. "It's nice to meet you, Elowyn."

"Likewise," she said, smiling.

"Eighteen," Donald said, "would you take the human to the back-room, please?"

Eighteen took Johnson from Victus, carrying him like a child into the back room, where he would strip him nude, wash him down, and chain him up to the wall with the others.

"Come, Elowyn," Donald said, reaching his hand out to her, "let me show you around."

Victus slapped Donald's hand away before Elowyn could take it. Eighteen, who hadn't quite made it to the back room yet, dropped Johnson to the floor and hurried over to confront Victus.

"It's okay," Donald said. "Please take the human to the backroom."

Eighteen stood face to face with Victus, blatantly ignoring Donald's request.

"Touch him again," he told Victus, "and I'll kill you."

"Is that so?"

"Eighteen," Donald said, "please do as I asked."

Eighteen stared at Victus a moment longer, licking his lips, before picking Johnson up from the floor and taking him to the back room.

"So," Donald asked Elowyn, "how are you enjoying being a vampire so far?"

"I like it."

"It's amazing how quickly you adjust," Donald said. "I still remember my first night like it was yesterday. I didn't hunt, as my maker didn't think I'd be ready for it. And he was probably right. Look at me, I hardly like to hunt now!"

Elowyn and Donald laughed over this and, without thinking about it, his hand moved to touch her arm. It was a harmless gesture, but Victus didn't like it, so, in an instant, he had Donald by the throat. Victus was older than Donald, which made him stronger. He pinned Donald's head against a mirror, shattering it with his force. Donald held onto Victus' wrist, but there was little else he could do beyond waiting for him to let him go.

"It's okay, Victus," Elowyn said. "You don't have to hurt him."

Victus threw Donald to the floor beside the barber chair. All the other vampires were watching, but none of them cared to get into a fight with Victus.

"You do not touch her!" Victus said.

"I'm very sorry," Donald said. "I meant no disrespect."

Eighteen stormed from the backroom, charging at Victus with his broomstick, which he'd broken in half. Victus looked up, smiling as he saw Eighteen heading straight for him with the pointy end of his broken broomstick. Eighteen leapt towards him. Victus did the same, colliding with him in midair before tumbling down to the tile floor where they scrambled about like a couple of wild animals.

"Stop!" Donald cried.

Eighteen charged Victus again after they got back to their feet, still with the broken broomstick in hand. Victus grabbed his wrist before he could strike him with it and, with his free arm, he clotheslined Eighteen to the floor. Straddling Eighteen's torso, Victus pinned his throat to the tiles with one hand, picking up the broken broomstick with the other.

"Victus, please!" Donald said. "You don't have to do this. He's sorry. Tell him you're sorry, Eighteen!"

"Is he right," Victus said. "Are you sorry?"

Eighteen looked Victus in the eye before spitting in his face.

"Eighteen, no!"

Donald's plea was too late, however, as Victus drove the broken broomstick through Eighteen's heart, killing him on the floor of the Barbershop. As Victus stepped away, Donald hurried to Eighteen's side, watching as his partner of nearly a century went away. Victus stood to his feet, dropping the broomstick into the crimson puddle that was once Eighteen. The Barbershop was silent, but for Donald's wails.

"Come," Victus said, taking Elowyn's hand. "Let us go."

He exited the Barbershop, pulling Elowyn along with him like a child.

CHAPTER TWENTY-SEVEN

THE BLEACH BLOND VAMPIRE

Jesus screamed as he felt his blood pulsing into the vampire's mouth. With every passing moment he became more and more convinced that this was how it all would end. He was so helpless in the vampire's powerful arms, like a child in the grip of an angry adult. He could hear Nick gathering himself somewhere in the darkness, but he feared it would be too late. He could feel his life slowly draining away, one pulse at a time—when, all at once, the vampire released him before collapsing to the grass.

Jesus touched his hand to where the vampire's fangs had entered him, the blood streaming out in rivulets through his fingers. The pain was searing, but—all things considered—bearable. With a bit of an effort, Jesus stood to his feet, still holding his neck. Nick appeared by his side, each of them looking down at the bleach blond vampire curled up in the fetal position. Jesus saw that Nick was holding the high-pitched air horn.

"I guess that horn really works," Jesus said.

"Well, it does," Nick said, "but I didn't use it on this guy."

Jesus looked back down at the vampire.

"How'd you get him off me?"

"I didn't," Nick said. "He just sort of dropped off on his own."

He looked at Jesus' neck.

"The bastard fed on you?"

"I'll be all right."

Nick kicked the vampire as hard as he could in the ribs, feeling a couple of bones crack against the force of his boot. The vampire yelped in pain, wrapping his arms around his waist. They watched the vampire gather himself to his hands and knees, crawling about the grass, trying and failing like a weary prizefighter to stand to his feet. Nick put the horn right up against the vampire's ear and pressed the button. The vampire kept crawling, oblivious to the high-pitched sound it was making.

"Is it broken?" Jesus asked.

"No," Nick said, "it's brand new."

Again, they looked down at the vampire.

"I don't understand what happened to him," Jesus said. "He was so strong before."

"I'll get some answers out of him."

Nick straddled the vampire's chest and grabbed him by the collar, punching him in the face over and over again. With each punch, the vampire yelped, seemingly on the verge of tears. He gripped Nick by the arms, trying and failing to push him off.

"Are you even a fucking vampire?" Nick asked.

The vampire nodded, yes. Nick punched him again, this time feeling the vampire's orbital bone collapse beneath his fist. A strand of the vampire's bleach blond hair soaked in red as it adhered to the gash Nick opened up on his cheek. Sobbing in pain, the vampire begged for mercy.

"Please," he said, "no more."

"Doesn't work that way," Nick said.

"What are you?" the vampire asked, coughing up blood.

"We're vampire hunters," Nick said, "which sucks for you, being that you're a vampire and all."

The vampire turned his head, spitting blood onto the grass.

"I wasn't going to kill him," he said.

"Fuck you, you weren't going to kill him," Nick said.

He punched him again, flattening his nose. The vampire sobbed even harder, blood gushing from his nostrils and mouth. He could barely speak.

"I'm a hunter, too," he said.

"What are you talking about?" Nick asked.

"I'll tell you," the vampire said, "but please stop hurting me."

"Talk."

"I hunt humans and deliver them to the Barbershop."

"What's the Barbershop?"

"It's where we feed."

"Vampires?"

"Yes," the vampire said. "It's a feeding post."

"And you're the deliveryman?"

The vampire nodded.

Nick looked at Jesus.

"I don't know," Jesus said. "I think he might be delirious or something."

"I know exactly what I'm saying," the vampire said. "Go to the Barbershop. Go now. There are vampires there."

"Where is it?"

"Archibald and Foothill," the vampire said. "Go and ask for Victus."

"What's Victus going to do for us?"

The vampire smiled, his wounds healing right before Nick's eyes. The crushed bone in his orbital formed back into place, like a flat soccer ball filling with air.

"Victus will make you wish you were never born."

In a hiccup of strength, the vampire bucked Nick off his chest, throwing him into the grass. He leapt onto Nick's back, fangs bared. Before he could do anything, however, Jesus slashed the vampire's neck with his silver knife. The vampire fell to the grass, clutching his throat, blood pulsing through his pale fingers. Nick got back up to his feet and stood over the vampire, pulling out his pistol and shooting a silver bullet into his heart. The sound of the gun's blast rang in Jesus' ears as he watched the vampire melt away, leaving nothing behind except his bloody clothes.

"I don't know what happened," Nick said. "He was so weak, then, out of nowhere, he was so fucking strong."

"You think he was faking it?"

"No, not at all," Nick said. "I think he was totally helpless right up until about five second ago."

"What's it mean?"

"Your guess is as good as mine," Nick said. "The good news is he's dead. The better news is we know where to find more of them."

Jesus and Nick drove around for nearly twenty minutes before finding the Barbershop. There was a gas station on the corner and a pizza parlor next door—all of it so normal, so benign. Jesus pulled his car into a parking spot in front. It was well past closing time, so the lights were turned out; interestingly enough, however, the door was wide open. Nick rolled down his window and sprayed the air with the blood scent. No vampires came out. He sprayed some more, but still nothing happened.

"This place seems dead," Nick said.

"Yeah," Jesus said, "but why's the door open?"

"Let's find out?"

Nick got out of the car and Jesus followed him. They approached the entrance of the Barbershop cautiously. As they got a closer look, they realized the door wasn't simply open—it had been knocked off its hinges. The glass panes were shattered and the metal frame was bent out of shape.

Jesus and Nick stood on either side of the entrance, pressing their backs to the wall. Nick put his night vision goggles on and signaled for Jesus to stay put. Nick turned his head and looked inside the Barbershop.

"Jesus Christ!"

"What is it?"

Nick stepped inside without answering. Jesus followed him in, moving carefully through the darkness, glass crunching beneath his feet.

"What's going on?" Jesus said. "I can't see anything."

"It's a massacre in here."

"What do you mean?"

Nick found a light switch on the wall and flipped it on, illuminating the macabre scene for Jesus. There were dead bodies everywhere. Blood was splattered on the mirrors and spilled on the floor. All the bodies were human, including that of Donald who lay lifeless on the floor, his head torn nearly off. If Jesus or Nick had any idea that Donald had previously been a vampire, the sight of him would've piqued their interest. But, since they didn't know him, he was just an anonymous corpse amongst the dead.

Nick was more than halfway through the Barbershop, heading for the back with his gun in hand. Jesus followed behind him, careful not to step on any of the bodies; he also tried not to step in any of the blood, but that proved much more difficult. They found the door to the backroom, which was already ajar. Nick pushed it open. It was dark inside, but there was enough light from outside to show several more human bodies, naked and chained to the wall.

"This is where they fed," Nick said. "The vampire was telling us the truth."

The people weren't moving. Nick crouched down to get a closer look at one and saw he was dead.

"His throat's slit," Nick said.

"What about the others?"

Nick examined them all, one after the other, and each of them had their throats slit. Jesus walked behind him, following closely as his eyes adjusted to the darkness. Nick stopped suddenly.

"Fuck!" he said. "No, no, no! Fuck me, no!"

"What is it?"

"It's Johnson," Nick said. "They killed Johnson."

Nick crouched down, touching his finger to Johnson's neck, checking for the pulse he knew wasn't there. His throat was slit like the others, blood washing down his chest. Nick retrieved a flashlight from his backpack, handing it to Jesus. He turned it on and crouched down beside Nick, looking over his dead friend. Johnson's skin was pale and riddled with fang wounds, his head hanging awkwardly to the side. His wrists were shackled and chained to the wall. Nick stroked Johnson's hair, while Jesus tried to yank one of the chains from the wall.

"We need to get out of here," Nick said. "At some point the authorities are going to show up, and we don't need to be here when they do."

"What about Johnson?"

"There's nothing we can do for him now."

"We can't just leave him here."

"We don't have a choice."

Jesus knew Nick was right. They each took a moment to say goodbye to their friend before hurrying out of the Barbershop and heading back to Jesus' apartment.

CHAPTER TWENTY-EIGHT

LET THE RIGHT ONE IN

Olivia didn't make friends easily growing up. Because her mother spent the majority of her time in bed, Olivia had few opportunities to get out of the house. But, when she was in the sixth grade, she befriended a boy on the playground who was wearing a Hulk Hogan T-shirt. The boy's name was Timothy, and they met while waiting in line to play tetherball. Olivia asked him about his T-shirt, wanting to know where he got it. She'd never seen WWF clothing in a store before. Timothy told her his parents bought it for him out of a WWF catalogue. Olivia had no idea such a thing existed and so she asked more questions and Timothy had more answers, and before she knew it, they'd spent the rest of recess talking about professional wrestling.

During the weeks and months that followed, Olivia and Timothy became the best of friends and talked on the phone nearly every night. His mother was always delighted to hear Olivia's voice before giving him the phone. One particular Saturday, Timothy's family was having a picnic at Heritage Park and they invited Olivia to join them. Olivia's mom was happy to let her go, and she even got herself out of bed just long enough to say hello to Timothy and his parents when they arrived to pick Olivia up. Olivia couldn't remember having so much fun, running in the grass and playing catch, flipping burgers with Timothy's dad and folding up the blankets with Timothy's mother.

Timothy and Olivia had such a great time that his parents invited her to have a slumber party that night. When they took her home, Timothy's mother talked with Olivia's mother, making sure it was okay, before helping pack an overnight bag. Olivia didn't have a suitcase, since she'd never traveled before, so they emptied her school bag and put her clothes it. She and Timothy were particularly excited to stay up that night because *Saturday Night's Main Event* was airing on NBC. Usually, the only wrestling anyone got to see on TV was on Saturday and Sunday afternoons, so to have a wrestling program on in prime time during their slumber party was an extra special treat for Timothy and Olivia.

The following morning, Timothy's mom made chocolate chip pancakes. Everybody sat around the dining room table together while she served breakfast before eventually joining them. Timothy's family was Catholic, so after breakfast he had to take a shower to get ready for Mass. He told Olivia that after church his family got donuts in the recreation hall, which sounded delightful to her. She asked if she could join them, so Timothy asked his mom. She, in turn, called Olivia's mother to make sure it was okay.

Timothy's family attended St. Peter and St. Paul's Catholic Parish. Olivia had never been to such a big place before, nor had she ever been amongst so many people all at once. She found it to be a pleasant experience, especially the communal nature of the proceedings. She enjoyed the sitting and the kneeling, singing along with the choir and holding hands during the Lord's Prayer. When Timothy's family got in line for communion, they let Olivia stand in line with them; while most everyone else got a wafer from the priest, Olivia got a brief blessing and the priest's hand on her head. As much as anything else that morning, Olivia was fascinated by the statue of Jesus on the cross, which hung in front of a stained glass window above the pulpit.

Olivia couldn't wait to go back the following Sunday and not just because she got to pick two donuts at the recreational hall after Mass (though that was one of the primary highlights of the morning). She had no idea what the priest was talking about during Mass, and she had no real grasp on what religion even was. What she loved was the comradery, the pleasant and smiling faces, the tangible sense of community that existed amongst the parishioners.

Olivia's mother was an atheist, though she never told this to Timothy's mother. She had no qualms with religion or the people who practiced their chosen faith; she just wasn't interested in it herself. While she didn't believe in God, she never forced her beliefs on Olivia. In fact, she never talked to Olivia about God at all, which was why her experience at church was so fascinating. Not only didn't her mother take issue with Olivia attending Mass with Timothy's family, she was grateful that her daughter had befriended such a kind and generous family. Olivia's mother always felt guilty for not being able to do more with her, so she was happy to know she was enjoying herself outside of the house.

The following Sunday, Timothy's family picked Olivia up on the way to church and she enjoyed the whole experience just as much as she had the previous weekend. During the Mass when the donation basket was passed around, Timothy's dad gave Olivia a dollar so she could drop it in. She had no idea why she was doing it, but she liked taking part in the ritual. After Mass, they went to the movies and had pizza, and when she went home, she spent the rest of that Sunday telling her mother all about it.

During the week, Olivia and Timothy never really talked about church. They sometimes talked about what donuts they were going to eat afterwards or how strange it was that they let kids sip from the communion wine, but they never had any discussions about Catholicism or faith because neither of them had any real grasp on it. For Timothy, going to church was like going to school or eating vegetables—it was just a thing his parents made him do. And for Olivia, it was just one more activity to do with Timothy and his family, like having a picnic at the park or going to Disneyland.

Timothy's mother felt especially privileged to have introduced Olivia to the church and was grateful that her mother allowed her to join her family in their faith. So, when Timothy's father accepted a new job in Seattle, marking an end to Olivia and Timothy's magical friendship, his mother was primarily concerned for Olivia and her continued relationship with the Catholic Church. She hoped Olivia would continue attending Mass even after they were gone, so the night before their family moved away, she gave Olivia the only crucifix she would ever own. It was beautiful and silver and Olivia loved it.

She wore the crucifix for years and years after they were gone, long after she and Timothy stopped writing letters, eventually losing touch altogether. She wore it long after time blurred so many of her memories, when she could no longer remember what Timothy looked like, and she wondered if she'd recognize him as a grown man. She took tremendous care of her crucifix, never letting anything happen to it, until the night Adam fed from her beneath the jungle gym at Heritage Park and he tore it from her neck—but, even then, he only broke the chain, leaving the crucifix unharmed. She wore it every Sunday when she went to church at St. Peter and St. Paul's, where she continued to attend Mass, even after she decided that, like her mother, she was an atheist.

There was no epiphany that preceded her atheism. Olivia simply never bought into the idea of an omniscient God who watched over her. She still enjoyed going to church, but she enjoyed it the way a child enjoyed Christmas after they'd learned Santa Claus wasn't real. She enjoyed reading books by Christopher Hitchens and Sam Harris, but she had no interest in ever having a philosophical argument with anybody over the existence of God. Like her mother, she never had strong feelings about it. She was certain that God didn't exist, but she didn't begrudge anyone who believed otherwise. She also accepted that there was the possibility she might be wrong, but she never lost any sleep over it. If Hell were the punishment for being wrong, Olivia figured she'd be in good company.

Despite her atheism, she still enjoyed sitting in the pews of the church, embracing the community and good nature of the parishioners. And when her mother passed away, Olivia took comfort in the church's charitable efforts that allowed her to have a proper funeral that she otherwise wouldn't have been able to afford. Sometimes she would even go to church during the week in the middle of the day when it was all but empty so that she could sit in the quiet and the solitude, reflecting on her life and what she was doing with it.

This was exactly where she found herself the day after Jesus walked in on her and Adam at Corky's. Kneeling on the padded bar, silver crucifix in hand, eyes closed, Olivia couldn't stop seeing the hurt and disappointment on Jesus' face. She wanted to explain to him what was going on, except she could hardly explain it to herself. Adam was handsome and interesting, and she really enjoyed spending time with him in spite of the whole vampire quandary. But, Jesus was also handsome and interesting and fun to be with—and, more importantly, he wasn't a vampire, so there was no quandary to consider.

As much as she liked them both, what made things so difficult for her was that they were completely different, practically opposites. They each satisfied some part of her that the other couldn't touch, so breaking things off with either one of them meant diluting her personal fulfillment—and, while she knew it was completely self-serving, Olivia didn't want it to come to that. But, she wasn't the sort of girl who knew how to date casually, juggling two guys at a time. This was exactly the sort of situation that she needed Elowyn for, but she still hadn't heard a peep from her.

In the grand scheme of things, Olivia hadn't done anything wrong and she knew this to be true, but it didn't stop her from feeling like she owed Jesus an apology—or, at the very least, an explanation. He wasn't her boyfriend, after all, so she was obviously free to see whomever she liked, but, until that night, she hadn't really thought of Adam as a prospective boyfriend, so it never occurred to her that she might be doing anything that could potentially hurt Jesus. Of course, even if she had thought of Adam as boyfriend material, he'd made it pretty clear that the whole vampire thing made him unavailable. Then again, he'd invited her over to his house to watch *Dracula*, so maybe he wasn't entirely unavailable.

In a way, Olivia felt like she wanted to apologize to Jesus for wanting to spend time with Adam. She and Jesus, despite talking for several weeks, had only been on one date together. But, in her experience—limited as it was—it was probably the best date she'd ever been on. It was the sort of first date that carried with it the unspoken promise of future dates and perhaps even more than that. As much as she wanted future dates with Jesus, Olivia couldn't shake the feeling that, at some point, she would inevitably find herself wanting to apologize to Adam for the same thing, even though he was only ever meant to be a source of research for her novel—the very novel that she had written not one word of. Not yet, anyway.

She would write something eventually, but, for now, she told herself, she simply wanted to gather research and let the story incubate in her subconscious. And if she were actually doing any other research, then maybe she could look herself in the mirror without feeling like a liar, but the truth was that her favorite part of doing research with Adam was spending time with him. While Olivia was thirty years old, an age that for many implies a certain level of emotional maturity, she was once a young girl who loved *Buffy the Vampire Slayer*—and you'd be hard pressed to find any girl who came into puberty while watching *Buffy* that didn't harbor some intense fantasies about falling in love with a vampire.

Regardless of how much she loved *Buffy* and despite the countless masturbatory fantasies she'd entertained over the years—involving herself, a handsome vampire, and a candlelit bubble bath—Olivia thought Adam was a nutcase the first time he told her that he was a vampire. He didn't bring it up until they'd spoken a few times at the bowling alley, casually building a friendly rapport. More than once in their conversations, the topic of her unwritten novel had come up and Adam, after telling her that he too was once an aspiring author, took interest. Olivia found it nice to have somebody interested in her creative ideas, and so she appreciated Adam's attention.

She never thought it was strange that he didn't drink at the bar. He just sat there, usually watching TV when he wasn't chatting with her or waiting for a lane to open. Nor did it strike her as peculiar that he only ever bowled at night, usually after midnight. She wondered if he'd ever been in the bar before or if his first visit there was also the first time she laid eyes on him. Olivia was leaning on the bar at the time, elbows planted, reading *Let the Right One In* by John Ajvide Lindqvist. She didn't hear Adam come in nor did she hear him sit down, and if he hadn't spoken to her, she might not have known he was there at all.

"Good book?"

Olivia looked up, startled.

"Yeah," she said. "Sorry. What can I get for you?"

"Nothing, thanks," Adam said. "Just waiting for a lane. Mind if I wait here?"

"Not at all," Olivia said. "Mind if I read?"

"Not at all," Adam said. "What's it about?"

"It's a vampire novel."

"You don't say?"

"It's sort of a sweet pre-teen romance between a boy and a girl, except the girl is a vampire," Olivia said. "She's many centuries older than the boy, but physically they look the same age."

"So," Adam, "they look the same, but they're different."

"Yeah," Olivia said. "And she probably has all sorts of worldly experience that the boy could never relate to, but their relationship is still sweet and she still has very childlike qualities."

"I wonder how that would work in real life."

"You mean if vampires were real?"

"Yes."

"In the case of the little boy and the vampire girl," Olivia said, "he would eventually grow old and gray, while she remained in the same form. That's got to be awkward on a million different levels."

Adam laughed.

"You're probably right," he said. "Sounds like you've given this some thought."

"Oh, I love vampires."

"That's good to know."

And that was their first encounter. The next night he came back and sat at the bar again. Olivia was reading a different book this time, *The Los Angeles Diaries* by James Brown.

"Hi again."

"Hello."

"You already finished last night's book?"

"No," Olivia said. "I usually read more than one book at a time."

"Really?" Adam said. "You don't find it difficult spreading out your attention like that?"

"Not in this case, no" she said. "The books are very different, each one offering me something the other can't."

"What's this one about?"

"It's a memoir," Olivia said. "It's about this guy, James Brown, who's trying to balance his life as an alcoholic and a drug addict, while also being a novelist and college professor."

"Is this the singer, James Brown?"

"No," Olivia said, "not him. This James Brown grew up for a time in San Jose before his mom relocated him and his brother and sister to Los Angeles after serving a prison sentence."

"What was she in prison for?"

"Something to do with taxes and setting an apartment building on fire," Olivia said. "The fire led to the death of an old woman, but his mom was never officially connected to it."

"That sounds interesting."

"It is."

"And it's a true story?"

"Yeah," Olivia said. "Sometimes truth is stranger than fiction."

"I couldn't agree with you more," Adam said. "So, what does this book offer you that the vampire book doesn't?"

"It's more grounded in reality," Olivia said, "more human."

Each night Olivia worked, she hoped to see Adam again—and Adam, for his part, never disappointed. One night Olivia brought a Moleskine notebook to work and, when the bar was empty, she stared at the empty pages, pencil in hand, trying to think of something to write.

"What're you working on?"

"A novel."

"Really?" Adam said. "That's great."

"Thanks."

"What's it about?"

"Vampires."

"I'm intrigued," Adam said. "What's the story?"

"That's the thing," Olivia said. "I don't have a story to tell. Not yet, anyway. I was hoping something would just come to me, but it's proving not to be quite that easy."

"Is this your first novel?"

"Yes."

"Well, there's your problem," Adam said. "The first novel is tough, because it represents your first introduction to the literary universe. You want to make a good first impression, so you're trying to make it perfect. The only problem is, no matter how much you worry over it, it's never going to be perfect. Once you get comfortable with that idea, the writing should start to come to you much more easily."

"Are you a writer or something?"

"In another life," Adam said. "Anyway, I actually know a lot about vampires, so, if you think I can help, feel free to ask."

"I wouldn't take you for a vampire guy."

"Technically, I'm a vampire *and* a guy."

Olivia laughed, figuring he was making a joke. Adam wasn't laughing, however.

"You think you're a vampire?"

"It's not a thought," Adam said. "It's a fact."

Olivia turned to look at the mirror behind the bar.

"I can see your reflection," she said. "Vampires don't have reflections."

"*You* can see my reflection," Adam said, "but *I* can't."

"Likely story."

"It's the truth."

"What about garlic?"

"What about it?"

"Does it hurt?"

"Very much, yes."

"Care to prove it?"

"How?"

"I can grab some garlic bread from the snack bar."

Adam hesitated.

"That's what I thought," she said.

"If I let you hurt me with garlic," Adam said, "would you be satisfied that I'm telling you the truth?"

"Sure."

"Go get your garlic bread."

"Yeah?"

"Hurry," Adam said, "before I change my mind."

Olivia disappeared through a side door into the snack bar and reappeared a few minutes later with a basket of garlic bread.

"It's mostly butter," she said, "but there's garlic in there."

"I'm sure it'll do the trick."

Adam lay the palm of his hand flat on top of the bar, splaying his fingers out.

"Stamp the bread on top of my hand."

"That's it?"

"That's it."

"And then what?"

"And then it'll hurt."

"How'll I know you're not faking it?"

"You'll see."

Olivia, still convinced Adam was full of it, took the biggest piece of garlic bread from the basket and stamped it on top of his hand, causing him to scream. He yanked his hand from the bar, cradling it against his belly.

"That was pretty convincing," Olivia said. "You an actor or something?"

Adam slowly reached his shaking hand back onto the bar, laying it flat, palm down. The skin on top of his hand was bright red, curdled and bubbling. The sight of it caused Olivia to pass out, but Adam reached over the bar and caught her before she fell to the floor. Carrying her over to the couch inside the bar's lounge, he laid her down. When she woke up ten minutes later, Adam was gone. Olivia thought she'd never see him again.

When Adam did finally turn up again, it wasn't in the bar, but in the bowling alley's parking lot. He was standing by Olivia's car, hands in his pockets, waiting for her to come out. The sight of him was both terrifying and exciting.

"Where've you been?" she asked.

"I wasn't sure if you wanted to see me."

"Are you really a vampire?"

"Yes."

"Really?"

"You saw what the garlic did to me."

"For all I know you have a garlic allergy."

"What would convince you?"

"Let me see your fangs."

Adam curled his top lip without hesitation, revealing two fangs. Olivia clutched her hand to her chest, slowly stepping backwards.

"Please don't be scared of me," Adam said. "I'm not looking to hurt you."

"What are you?"

"You know what I am."

"Are you going to drink my blood?"

"Funny you should ask," Adam said. "I'd actually like to help you with your vampire novel, offering you a very unique and intimate insight. In return, I was just hoping you might let me hunt you."

"Hunt me?"

"Yeah."

"What for?"

"Well, ultimately blood," Adam said, "but that's only part of it. The hunting is what I'm most interested in."

"Why would you need to hunt me?" Olivia asked. "I'm right here."

"Yes, I know," Adam said. "What I mean is I'd like to hunt you at some point in the future when you won't know it's happening. If you say yes, I'll answer questions you have about vampires."

"Why would you need me to say yes?" Olivia asked. "Can't you do whatever you want?"

"That's a great example of a question that I'll answer if you say yes."

"How would it work?"

"After tonight, you won't see me for a little while," Adam said. "I won't tell you how long. I want you to feel apprehension, a little fear."

"That's kind of creepy."

"I agree," Adam said. "Will you do it?"

"Even if I say no, what's to stop you from hunting me anyway?"

"You can trust me."

"How can I trust you?" Olivia said. "We barely know each other."

"You've got to have faith."

"What if I say no?"

"Then you'll never see me again."

Silence.

"Okay."

"Yes?"

"Yes."

And that was that. Everything that happened after came and went in something of a blur. Interlaced within that blur was Olivia's blossoming romance with Jesus. She could see now—looking back on the last few weeks of her life—that Adam probably had feelings for her all along. And, if she were being honest with herself, she could see that she felt something for him, too, from the moment they first met. Not that her feelings for Adam made what she felt with Jesus any less real. But, of course, that was the problem.

And so, now here she was, sitting in the back pew of St. Peter and St. Paul's, silver crucifix in hand, trying desperately to figure out what the solution to all of this was—and, as was usually her experience, the answer wasn't coming to her. In all reality, Olivia was far too emotionally inexperienced to deal with this situation. She had no idea what she was going to say or, worse yet, what he would say to her, but, in the end Olivia decided, while looking up at the statue of Jesus, that she needed to call Jesus.

CHAPTER TWENTY-NINE

THE SHADOW OF TRAGEDY

Nick went back to Las Vegas the morning after vampire hunting with Jesus. He'd talked to George over the phone, letting him know he'd come across some interesting developments, though he didn't actually give him the specific details. George didn't like talking shop over the phone. He preferred dealing with vampire matters face to face, even when the news was good. While Nick could've rented a car and driven back to Las Vegas the very night they'd discovered Johnson dead at the Barbershop, Jesus persuaded him to take advantage of a good night's sleep.

Partly, Jesus was just being thoughtful, wanting to make sure his friend was safe, but mostly he just didn't feel like being alone. He dropped Nick off at the Ontario Airport the following day; George had a plane ticket waiting for him. With Nick gone, Jesus found himself alone in his apartment dealing with the inescapable reality of grief. Once again, he was left to suffer the death of a loved one at the hands of a vampire. Jesus couldn't help but wonder if maybe he was cursed, destined to live his life in the shadow of tragedy until his dying day. Feeling lost and alone, Jesus wished he could talk to somebody, but, given the circumstances, the only person he could reasonably talk to was on his way to Las Vegas.

And then Olivia called.

"Hello?"

"Hi," Olivia said. "What're you up to?"

"Just hanging around my apartment," Jesus said. "Nick went back to Las Vegas this morning."

"Where's Johnson?"

Silence.

"Jesus?"

"Johnson's dead."

"Oh my God! What happened?!"

"I don't know exactly," Jesus said. "Looks like he got mixed up in the wrong crowd."

"Do you think Elowyn was involved, too?"

"I doubt it."

"But, I still haven't heard from her."

"I'm sure she's fine," Jesus said. "Honestly."

"I'm sorry," Olivia said. "*I* should be the one comforting *you*."

"Don't worry about it."

"Do you need anything?"

"Some company might be nice."

"Of course," Olivia said. "Want me to come over?"

"I'll come by your place," Jesus said. "I'd rather get out of here for a little while."

"I'm actually at church right now," Olivia said. "If you like, you can meet me here. It's peaceful, you know?"

"That sounds nice," Jesus said. "Which church?"

"St. Peter and St. Paul's."

Jesus took a shower, cleaning off the previous night's hunting residue, before meeting Olivia at St. Peter and St. Paul's. She was sitting on a bench out front, beside the large wooden doors leading into the church. She smiled when she saw him walking up the stairs, meeting him halfway and giving him a hug. She took his hand and led him into the church, which was still empty except for the two-man band rehearsing up front.

"It's okay for us to be here?" Jesus asked.

"Of course it is," Olivia said. "That's why the doors are open."

She led him to the back pew and sat down with him, still holding his hand. For what felt like a very long time, neither of them spoke. Jesus looked up at the statue of Jesus and the stained glass behind it. He looked at the paintings on the wall and the throne-like seat up front. He looked at the wooden beams overhead and the piano in the corner. He looked at Olivia's hand in his own before noticing her eyes on his neck. He'd cleaned up the bite wound the night before, dressing it with a Band-Aid.

"What happened?"

Olivia touched her fingers to the Band-Aid.

"I cut myself shaving."

She leaned in, kissing Jesus' neck.

"There," Olivia said, laying her head on his shoulder. "All better."

Jesus smiled.

"I'm sorry about Johnson."

"Me too."

"When I called you, I wanted to apologize about what happened at Corky's," Olivia said. "But, you probably don't care about that right now."

Jesus shrugged, unsure of what to say.

"Adam is a friend of mine," Olivia said. "I hope you're not mad. God, look at me trying to make myself feel better. I'm sorry."

"It's okay."

"Is there anything I can do?"

"Sitting here is nice."

"Okay."

"I didn't know you were Catholic."

"I'm not," Olivia said. "I just like coming here."

"Are you religious?"

"Not really," she said. "You?"

"I was baptized as Catholic," Jesus said, "but I'm not very religious, either. My mom was. She used to take me to church every Sunday before she died."

"You were still a kid, right?"

Reaching into his pocket, Jesus pulled out his wallet. Opening it up, he took out a photograph and handed it to Olivia. The colors were fading, and it was nearly white in the seams where it had been folded. In the photograph was an adolescent version of Jesus asleep under his bed with a crayon in his hand and a coloring book beneath his cheek.

"Is this you?"

"Yeah."

"My goodness," Olivia said, "you were adorable. Your hair was so curly."

"My mother took that picture," Jesus said. "She'd been looking for me around the house. She thought I'd gone missing. When she found me, she took the picture."

"That's sweet."

"That picture was taken less than a year before she died," Jesus said. "She's the only reason I believe in God anymore. The *only* reason. I need there to be a God because I need there to be a Heaven, and I need my mother to be there so when I die I'll see her again. I have to believe that, because if it weren't true I don't know how I'd go on living."

Olivia handed the photograph back to Jesus.

He refolded it, putting it back in his wallet.

"I hope you see her again," Olivia said. "I truly do."

CHARRED AND FLAKY

Adam sat perched in the tree of his former backyard watching as Rusty put Emily to bed. She'd aged beautifully, salt and pepper hair, fine creases radiating from her eyes. Adam hated that he would never know what it would've been like to grow old with her, to see his hair change and his skin wrinkle. Emily was suffering from early-onset Alzheimer's, which she'd been diagnosed with five years earlier. Adam knew her health had been worsening in the last few months. Rusty was home with her almost constantly, making meals, helping her in the shower, watching TV, and reading from her favorite books. Sometimes Emily's eyes were clear and she spoke as if nothing was wrong, while other days she cried like a scared child, unaware of where she was or what was happening.

It was difficult for Adam to watch. On many occasions he'd left the backyard to go home before sunrise, overwhelmed with feelings of helplessness and grief, heartbroken that he'd never be able to tell her that he was sorry, that he'd always love her, that he would miss her when she was gone. What eventually put his heart at ease was watching Rusty take care of her. He was truly an angel, caring for his mother with all the attention and kindness that Adam would certainly have given her had fate not seen fit to separate them. Emily was a tremendous mother, which was why,

Adam knew, Rusty was so selfless and generous in how he cared for her.

Rusty was a freelance writer, which was why he was able to spend so much time at home with Emily. He was by no means wealthy from his work, but he made a living at it. Adam only ever saw him leave the house once or twice a week, usually to spend a few hours at Starbucks or the library or most anyplace where he could get lost in his thoughts. Whenever Rusty took breaks like this, he left Emily in the care of a personal nurse. While Rusty checked in on his mother while he was gone, Adam always took it upon himself to keep an especially close eye on things. Thankfully, Emily received exceptionally good care from her nurse.

Some nights when Rusty left the house, Adam followed him, getting in the car he'd inherited from Cherry and tailing his son to wherever he was going. One particular night Adam found himself strolling behind Rusty at Victoria Gardens, keeping a safe enough distance from him so as not to be conspicuous. Adam followed him through Borders, where they browsed books in a few of the same aisles, and the Apple Store where they perused the latest gizmos and gadgets. They sat in the food court, where Rusty ate Chinese food and Adam ate a mediocre slice of apple pie.

On this night, however, Rusty stayed home with Emily. Even after she was soundly tucked into bed, eyes closed, her mind soothed by the pleasant winds of sleep, Rusty stayed by her side, sitting in a nearby chair and surfing the Internet on his laptop. Not long after Emily fell asleep, he himself nodded off, the pale glow of his computer illuminating his face, reflecting off of his glasses. Adam continued to sit in the tree watching them, smiling, wondering what life might've been like had he not been turned, wondering what it would've felt like to be a father. He thought about the final conversation he had with Emily and how it was painfully mundane, as neither of them knew it would be the last time.

For Adam, he liked to pretend the last real conversation he had with Emily was the hallucination he had of her shortly after he was turned. It was a few hours after Cherry had taken him to his former house and, later, to the Barbershop for his first official feeding. Just before sunrise, he'd gone to bed on Cherry's couch—it would be at least a few months before he was comfortable enough to share the bed with her. All of her windows were securely sealed with foil and duct tape to keep out the sunlight. Adam woke up from a deep sleep and saw Emily standing at his feet in the same white nightgown she'd worn on their wedding night.

"Hello."

"Emily?"

"Yes, my love?"

"You look so beautiful."

"Your eyes always did make me feel special."

"How did you find me?"

"I simply came here."

"But, how did you find *here*?"

"I followed my heart."

"I can't see you anymore."

"I know."

"I'm sorry for that."

"Don't be," she said. "You didn't choose this path, but it's yours now. Travel it safely and wisely."

"I'll always love you."

"And I you."

Emily began backing away from the couch, smiling at Adam as she did. He got up to follow her, walking through the living room towards the front door.

"Adam?"

He turned his head to the hallway, finding Cherry leaning against the wall.

"Yes?"

"Who do you see?"

"It's Emily," Adam said. "She found me."

But when he turned back towards the front door, Emily was gone.

"She was here," Adam said. "She spoke to me."

"Go back to sleep."

Adam opened the front door and a rush of sunlight poured in, engulfing him, lighting his flesh on fire. Cherry hurried over, slamming the door shut, catching a few rays of sunlight for her trouble. Adam rolled around on the floor, screaming in pain as his flesh burned. Cherry grabbed Adam's blanket from the couch, throwing it on top of him. When the fire was out, most of Adam's skin was charred and flaky, like a burnt tree. Cherry laid his head in her lap, stroking his hair as he cried, assuring him that it all would be better soon. In time, all of his wounds would be healed.

༼•▪▪•༽

After watching Emily and Rusty sleep for an hour, Adam climbed down from the tree and left the backyard. The night was young and he didn't quite know what to do with himself, so he headed over to the Barbershop. When he got there, however, he was shocked to find its doors boarded up and not a vampire in sight. Because Adam didn't have any other vampire acquaintances and therefore couldn't ask anybody what'd happened, he decided to make his next stop Olivia's apartment.

Adam wouldn't actually try to visit with Olivia, since she wasn't expecting him—and, on top of that, she didn't know that he knew where she lived. Sometimes at night he would just go to her apartment and watch her through the window—or, if the blinds were closed, he'd sit on the porch and listen to whatever she was doing. He knew Olivia had a roommate, and he also knew her roommate hadn't been around for a few days because the apartment had been pretty quiet as of late. When Adam got there the blinds were closed, so he stood beside the front door and listened. He heard Olivia talking with Jesus on the couch, setting off a wave of jealousy in his belly.

Adam knew he shouldn't be worried, since he and Olivia had a date coming up to watch *Dracula* at his place—but he didn't like to think of her spending time with somebody else. And, while he knew he had no right to be upset, he couldn't help himself. Along with his feelings of jealously, Adam was also feeling pretty juvenile at the moment and so he decided it would make him feel better to interrupt Olivia and Jesus' evening. He knocked on the door and ran away into the darkness, watching as Olivia opened it and looked around. The sight of her put a smile on his face, until Jesus turned up behind her.

"Kids," Olivia said.

"Probably," Jesus said.

They went back inside, closing the door. Adam was tempted to knock again but decided against it. With nowhere else to go, he got back into his car and drove home.

CHAPTER THIRTY-ONE

GOOD GUY VERSUS BAD GUY

Olivia and Jesus spent the rest of the day together, first eating lunch and then catching a movie, before settling in at her place to watch wrestling videos. She wasn't sure if she was supposed to say anything more about Johnson, so, unless Jesus brought him up, she didn't say anything at all. She felt weird about the whole thing, because she never really liked Johnson all that much; in particular, she didn't like how he treated Elowyn. But, he was still a person and, despite his poor dating etiquette, he didn't deserve to die.

Jesus was understandably upset with the loss of his friend, so Olivia was happy to keep him in good spirits. It was the sort of role that a girlfriend might play—and the irony wasn't lost on her. She found that it actually felt sort of natural, making it easy to imagine a future as Jesus' girlfriend. She figured it would be similar to what they were doing right at that moment: sitting on the couch, holding hands, and watching wrestling.

Olivia had offered to put *WrestleMania IV* back on, as that's what they were watching at the end of their first date before Elowyn burst through the door in tears. Jesus, however, requested *WrestleMania VI*, featuring Hulk Hogan and The Ultimate Warrior wrestling each other for the WWF Championship. It was a landmark match in the history of professional wrestling, as it was the first time that two perceived good guys were competing in the main event of *Wrestle-Mania*, a departure from the more common good guy versus bad guy paradigm.

"I remember being so nervous about that match when I was a kid," Jesus said. "I grew up loving Hulk Hogan, but then The Ultimate Warrior came along and he was so cool and exciting."

"I know," Olivia said. "I remember watching it with my mom. I had no idea how to choose. I wanted them both to win."

"That's what made it so exciting," Jesus said. "In the end, you knew one of them *had* to lose. There was no way around it."

Just then, there was a knock at the door, but when Olivia went to open it, there was nobody there. Jesus stepped behind her, looking out past the porch and into the dimly lit parking lot of her apartment complex.

"Kids."

"Probably."

They sat on the couch again, their hands linking up very naturally, and continued watching *WrestleMania VI*, when, a few minutes later, there was another knock on the door.

"Probably the same kids again," Olivia said, getting up.

When she opened the door, however, there were no prankster kids waiting on the other side but rather her missing roommate with a large, brooding man she'd never before seen.

"Elowyn!" she said. "Where've you been?"

"I've fallen in love."

Olivia smiled, stepping back from the doorway, expecting Elowyn and her friend to enter, but neither of them moved.

"Who's your friend?"

"My name is Victus."

Jesus stood up from the couch and stood beside Olivia.

"Pleasure to meet you," she said. "This is Jesus."

Victus nodded.

Jesus said nothing.

"I was so worried about you," Olivia said.

"I'm okay," Elowyn said. "I'm better than okay. I've never felt so good in my entire life."

"Are you going to invite us in?" Victus asked.

Before Olivia could respond, Jesus slammed the door on them.

"What're you doing?!"

Olivia went to open the door, but Jesus stepped in front of her.

"I can't let you do that."

"Why?"

"I can't tell you why," Jesus said, "but you're going to have to trust me."

"Well, right this second, I don't trust you," Olivia said. "Please step out of the way."

"Olivia," Jesus said, "I'm trying to protect you."

"From my *friend*?"

"Mainly from *her* friend."

"We just met him!"

"I don't trust him."

"I swear to God," Olivia said, "if you don't move out of the way right this second, I'm going to have to ask you to leave."

"I'll step out of the way," Jesus said, "but please don't invite them in right away."

"Why not?"

"Please," Jesus said. "I just want to get a better feeling for who this guy is."

"Fine."

Jesus moved away from the door, letting Olivia open it. Victus and Elowyn, however, were nowhere to be seen.

"Well, that's just great," Olivia said. "They're gone."

"That might not be a bad thing."

"At this rate, I have no idea when I'll ever see her again."

Jesus was silent.

"Should we sit back down?" he asked.

"No," Olivia said, "I think you'd better go."

"Olivia—"

"Please."

Jesus exited the apartment, turning to say something. Olivia didn't want to hear it, so she closed the door before he could speak.

CHAPTER THIRTY-TWO

SHADOW OF DEATH

After killing Eighteen in the Barbershop, Victus fully anticipated Elowyn would be taken with his show of power and dominance, but instead she seemed almost disappointed in him. As they exited, Victus worried that he may have offended his new bride.

"What's the matter?"

"Did you have to kill him?"

"He attacked me."

"He was so young, though."

"He only looked young," Victus said. "He was old enough to know better than to engage me in battle."

"Is this something I'll have to get used to?"

"Fighting?"

"Killing."

"It's rare," Victus said, "I can promise you that."

"Is there any law against vampires killing each other?"

"It's frowned upon," Victus said, "but there are no laws against it. If two vampires want to settle their differences in a battle to the death, they are free to do so."

"Have you ever fed on a vampire?"

"Never," Victus said. "Vampires are to *never* feed on one another."

"So, killing isn't against the law, but feeding is?"

"It has nothing to do with laws," Victus said. "Feeding on vampire blood is lethal and will assuredly end in death."

A young vampire with bleach blond hair exited the Barbershop, catching up with Victus and Elowyn. When she saw him, Elowyn feared he was seeking vengeance for Eighteen's death.

"Victus," he said, "that was a great battle!"

"Yes, it was."

Victus took Elowyn's hand and turned to walk away. Before they could leave, the bleach blond vampire asked them to wait.

"What do you need?" Victus asked.

"I want to hunt."

"Then hunt."

"No," said the bleach blond vampire, "I want to hunt with *you*."

"We've already hunted tonight," Victus said. "You saw my prey."

"I want to learn from you."

"I'm done hunting for the night," Victus said. "I'm going to spend the rest of this evening enjoying the company of my bride. Go out and hunt yourself. Bring back a human and prove to me you're worthy of my time."

"I will, Victus," he said, "I will!"

The bleach blond vampire turned and ran the other way, while Victus and Elowyn began their walk back home. She held Victus' arm, resting her cheek against his broad shoulder as they walked down Foothill Boulevard. She watched the cars drive by, each of them containing humans who had no idea just how fragile their lives were, how easily their fates could be decided by a species they didn't even know existed. She was quickly getting used to the idea that she would live forever, physically locked into the prime of her youth, no longer needing to fear the ever present shadow of death.

"Victus," she said, "I'd like to see my friend Olivia."

"You can't."

"Why not?"

"You're a vampire now," Victus said. "It's against the law to socialize with humans."

"You mean I can *never* see her again?"

"Yes."

"Not *ever*?"

"That's correct."

"But, I didn't get to say goodbye," Elowyn said. "That's not fair."

"These are the laws we must abide."

Elowyn stopped walking, letting go of his arm.

"But, it's not *fair!*"

"It is the law, Elowyn."

"I didn't know I'd never see her again," Elowyn said. "I would've said goodbye."

"You will learn to accept it."

"I will never accept this," she said, "and I will never forgive you for taking her from me."

"Okay, okay," Victus said. "I'll take you to see your friend, but only to say goodbye."

"You will?"

"Yes."

Elowyn threw her arms around him.

"Oh, thank you, Victus!" she said. "Thank you, thank you, thank you!"

When they arrived at her former apartment, Elowyn knocked on the door. There was no answer right away, so she knocked again. Pressing his ear to the door, Victus listened for any stirring inside the apartment.

"She's not here," he said.

"Can we wait for her?"

"No."

"But, you said!"

"We'll come back tomorrow."

"Do you promise?"

"I do."

Victus and Elowyn walked home, spending the rest of the night sitting by the fireplace, curled into each other atop the tiger-skin rug. They slept together on the floor all throughout the day, passing their slumbering hours while the sun shone overhead and humans went about their day. As dusk fell and the sun went back into its nightly hiding, Victus opened his eyes and looked down at Elowyn, pleased to see her in his arms. He watched her sleep for hours before she finally woke up. He gave Elowyn a kiss, welcoming her to a new night.

She was ready to go see Olivia, but Victus convinced her that they would be better off feeding first. Olivia thought this meant they would hunt, but Victus said they would simply visit the Barbershop before going to Olivia's apartment. When they arrived at the Barbershop, Victus and Elowyn saw the front door boarded shut. He ran his fingertips along the wood, searching for a natural opening, but there was none. He pressed his ear to the wood, but there was nothing.

"Is this normal?" Elowyn asked.

"No," Victus said, "not at all."

"Will they be back?"

"I don't know."

"How will we eat?"

"There are other feeding posts."

"What if they're closed as well?"

"Then we'll do what we must," Victus said. "For now, let's go say goodbye to your friend."

Victus and Elowyn walked to Olivia's apartment from the Barbershop, arriving to see her living room light on through the front window. Elowyn raced up the stairs, anxious to see her friend. Victus followed behind her.

"Remember," he said. "This is goodbye."

"I understand."

"And it must be brief," Victus said. "When the door opens, you will not be able to walk through. Vampires can enter a human's home by invitation only."

"Okay."

"One more thing," he said. "If you find you can't control yourself and decide to feed on your friend, you may have to turn her into a vampire."

"Why?"

"The only other option within the law would be to take her to a feeding post," Victus said, "and the nearest feeding post is not very close by foot. If she died at our feet, we would risk great punishment. So, you see, to keep from breaking the law you'd have to turn her."

"But, that's only if I feed on her, right?"

"Yes."

"Then I won't," Elowyn said. "Can I knock now?"

"Go on."

Elowyn knocked, and after a brief moment, she could hear Olivia's bare feet padding across the carpet. The door opened.

"Elowyn!" Olivia said. "Where've you been?"

"I've fallen in love."

Olivia smiled, stepping back from the doorway.

"Who's your friend?"

"My name is Victus."

Jesus appeared behind Olivia, looking Victus and Elowyn up and down.

"Pleasure to meet you," Olivia said. "This is Jesus."

Victus nodded, but Jesus didn't respond.

"I was so worried about you," Olivia said.

"I'm okay," Elowyn said. "I'm better than okay. I've never felt so good in my entire life."

"Are you going to invite us in?" Victus asked.

Jesus slammed the door on them before Olivia could respond. Elowyn was going to knock again, but Victus stopped her.

"Listen to them," he said, pointing at the door. "They're having a disagreement."

Elowyn put her ear to the door and heard Jesus trying to explain himself to Olivia.

"I can't let you do that," Jesus said.

"Why?"

"I can't tell you why," Jesus said, "but you're going to have to trust me."

Elowyn looked at Victus.

"He doesn't want to let us in."

"No, he doesn't."

"Do you think he knows we're vampires?"

"I don't know," Victus said, "but we'll find out."

Victus took Elowyn's hand and led her down the stairs, into the parking lot in front of Olivia's apartment. They walked past a streetlamp, concealing themselves in the darkness, watching Olivia's door. The door opened again and Jesus exited. They watched as Olivia closed the door on him. Jesus stood there for a few moments before walking down the stairs into the parking lot. Victus and Elowyn came out from the darkness, stepping into his path. Jesus' fear filled the air with a sugary sweet aroma that stirred Elowyn's appetite. Victus stepped forward, looking down at the Band-Aid on Jesus' neck.

"You know what we are, don't you?"

"I don't know what you mean."

"Silly human," Victus said, "you can't fool me."

He tore the Band-Aid from Jesus' neck, revealing his bite wound.

"You've been attacked," Victus said, "yet you're still alive. Fascinating."

Jesus looked at Elowyn.

"Keep your eyes on me," Victus said. "Is the vampire who did this to you still alive?"

Jesus began moving backward, slowly, not speaking.

"Going somewhere?"

Jesus turned and ran as fast as he could. Elowyn started to run after him, but Victus stopped her.

"He'll get away," she said.

"No," Victus said, "he won't. We'll let him run, allow his heart to pump his blood at an exceedingly high rate. The longer we let him go, the more intense his fear will become, making him all the more delicious."

"But, we can't feed on him," Elowyn said. "It's against the law."

"Once a human knows of the existence of vampires," Victus said, "it is our duty to either turn him or kill him."

"Which will we do?"

"Kill him."

CHAPTER THIRTY-THREE

THE OTHER OPTION

Jesus and Olivia had spent the day together—having lunch and catching a movie—before ending up at her apartment, sitting on the couch and watching *WrestleMania VI*. It was a pretty perfect day, which left Jesus feeling conflicted, as he didn't feel like he were allowed to be enjoying himself so soon after Johnson's death. It was nice to feel happy though, so he decided to enjoy it for as long as he could because, in his experience, there was always another shoe just waiting to drop. Jesus and Olivia talked about the classic match between Hulk Hogan and The Ultimate Warrior.

"I remember watching it with my mom," Olivia said. "I had no idea how to choose. I wanted them both to win."

"That's what made it so exciting," Jesus said. "In the end, you knew one of them *had* to lose. There was no way around it."

There was a knock at the door, but when Olivia went to open it there was nobody on the other side. Jesus stepped behind her, looking out past the porch and into the dimly lit parking lot of her apartment complex.

"Kids."

"Probably."

Olivia closed the door and they sat back down on the couch, holding hands and watching *WrestleMania VI*. Perhaps because Jesus had death on his mind, he couldn't stop himself from noting which of the wrestlers who performed in *WrestleMania VI* were dead, many of them having died while they were still active in their careers. "Ravishing" Rick Rude, The Big Boss Man, Earthquake, Dino Bravo, Bad News Brown, Randy "Macho Man" Savage, Miss Elizabeth, Sensational Sherri, "Mr. Perfect" Curt Hennig, and André the Giant. So many professional wrestlers died young and Jesus knew that a lot of it resulted from steroid abuse—a fact that was not lost on him, considering his own use of steroids.

Jesus doped with the knowledge that he was walking a tightrope, taking his life into his own hands. He'd done his research and asked all the important questions. He knew the potential short-term risks, such as testicular atrophy, gynecomastia, and high blood pressure. He was also aware of the potential long-term risks, such as liver failure, cardiovascular problems, and neurological issues. Regardless of the potential consequences, Jesus never wavered on the choices he'd made; if it meant saving somebody else from the heartaches he'd endured, then it was worth it.

There was another knock on the door, so Olivia got up to answer it.

"Elowyn!" she said. "Where've you been?"

"I've fallen in love."

Jesus watched, noticing Elowyn and her friend hadn't made a move to enter.

"Who's your friend?"

"My name is Victus."

Jesus recognized that name. It was the same name the bleach blond vampire had given him at Red Hill Park. He got up from the couch and stood beside Olivia, taking a look at Victus up close.

"Pleasure to meet you," Olivia said. "This is Jesus."

Victus nodded.

Jesus said nothing.

"I was so worried about you," Olivia said.

"I'm okay," Elowyn said. "I'm better than okay. I've never felt so good in my entire life."

Jesus looked them both up and down, noting their pale skin and their dark eyes. There wasn't much else he could observe, short of throwing a piece of garlic at them. He didn't need to do that, however, to suspect they were both vampires. He only wished there was some way he could find out for sure.

"Are you going to invite us in?" Victus asked.

And there it was. Jesus couldn't let Olivia invite them in. He had none of his weapons on him, which meant he couldn't protect her. His only option was to shut the door before Olivia could say anything, which was exactly what he did.

"What're you doing?!"

Jesus stepped in front of her as she went for the door.

"I can't let you do that."

"Why?"

"I can't tell you why," Jesus said, "but you're going to have to trust me."

Jesus knew Olivia was angry with him, but he knew she'd think he was crazy if he tried to tell her Victus and Elowyn were vampires.

"I can't tell you why," Jesus said, "but you're going to have to trust me."

"Well, right this second, I don't trust you," Olivia said. "Please step out of the way."

"Olivia," Jesus said, "I'm trying to protect you."

"From my *friend*?"

"Mainly from *her* friend."

"We just met him!"

"I don't trust him."

"I swear to God," Olivia said, "if you don't move out of the way right this second, I'm going to have to ask you to leave."

At this point, Jesus' only options were to keep Olivia trapped in her apartment against her will until sunrise or step away from the door and let her open it. The first option made the most sense to him, but he knew there was no way he'd be able to explain it to Olivia. The other option, however, meant making them both vulnerable to a potential vampire attack.

"I'll step out of the way," Jesus said, "but please don't invite them in right away."

"Why not?"

"Please," Jesus said. "I just want to get a better feeling for who this guy is."

"Fine."

Jesus reluctantly moved away from the door, letting Olivia open it. Victus and Elowyn, however, were nowhere to be seen.

"Well, that's just great," Olivia said. "They're gone."

"That might not be a bad thing."

"At this rate, I have no idea when I'll ever see her again."

Jesus wished he could tell her more.

"Should we sit back down?"

"No," Olivia said, "I think you'd better go."

"Olivia—"

"Please."

Jesus hated leaving her like this, but if he didn't want to upset her any more than she already was, he didn't have much choice. He stepped outside, turning to face Olivia and say goodbye, but before he could say anything, she closed the door on him. With his hands tucked in his pockets, Jesus walked into the parking lot towards his car. It was so dark out that he almost didn't notice Victus and Elowyn step into his path. His heart pounded as the two vampires sniffed the air. Victus took a step forward, standing right in front of Jesus, looking at the Band-Aid on his neck.

"You know what we are, don't you?"

CHAPTER THIRTY-FOUR

OVERSIZED BODY PARTS

Jesus ran as fast as he could, out of the parking lot and onto 19th Street, his heart racing as he turned the corner up Carnelian Avenue, past the Vons shopping center and towards Beryl Park. He looked behind him and saw Victus and Elowyn on his trail. Jesus continued running, cursing himself for not carrying any weapons on him, as he turned into Beryl Park, hoping to give himself an advantage amongst the trees and equipment. Looking over his shoulder, Jesus saw Victus and Elowyn were still behind him, moving fast. Jesus knew he wouldn't be able to run at full speed much longer, as his legs were burning and his cardio was fading. He was so exhausted that, even if he decided to face Victus and Elowyn, he wouldn't have enough energy to put up a decent fight—and just as that thought entered his mind, Jesus realized that's probably exactly what they wanted.

If they were going to fight, Jesus decided he'd best do it now before his energy was completely tapped. He stopped running and turned around to face the vampires. Charging full steam ahead, Victus tackled Jesus in the middle of the soccer field. He rolled right up to his feet, while Jesus was too exhausted to get up. He simply lay there, staring up as Victus and Elowyn stood over him, two towering visions of death. Jesus always believed the day would come when he'd meet his end at the hands of a vampire, but he always figured it would come in battle and not as a helpless human unable to protect himself. He thought about Olivia and the future they might've had together. He thought about his father and all the Wednesdays he would have to spend alone. He thought about his mother and hoped that, when this was all over, he'd finally get to see her again. With his death upon him, Jesus sat up, took a deep breath, and looked his executioners in the eyes.

And then, before death came, a large figure appeared through the darkness, approaching Victus and Elowyn from behind. He was a good two or three heads taller than Victus, with shoulders as broad as a refrigerator. He was naked and pale with a bald head and cartoonishly big muscles. He had scars the size of battle ropes laced around his body like he'd been fused together from a series of oversized body parts. With hands the size of hubcaps, he grabbed Elowyn and lifted her into the air. His mouth opened wide, baring two huge fangs, which he plunged deep into her neck.

It all happened so fast that Victus only realized what was going on when he heard Elowyn scream. Jesus sat in the grass, exhausted, as he watched Victus charge at the monster. When Victus attempted to tackle him, the monster swatted him with the back of his hand, sending him ten feet back. Even as he swatted Victus, the monster continued feeding on Elowyn. She held onto his large wrists, kicking and struggling, blood gushing from her neck in thick crimson pulses. Jesus had never seen such a thing before, and he could only assume that the monster was some sort of vampire.

Victus got up from the grass and charged again at the large vampire, this time burying his shoulder into his belly. While the blow didn't knock the large vampire over, it seemed to free Elowyn from his grip, dropping her limp body to the grass. The large vampire turned his attention to Victus, grabbing him by the shoulders and plunging his large fangs into his neck. Jesus watched him feed until Victus' body went limp, dropping him to the grass. The large vampire went back to Elowyn, picking her up, her body slumped over in his large hands. The large vampire sniffed her briefly before dropping her back down beside Victus.

The large vampire next turned his attention to Jesus who was still sitting in the grass, watching the whole bloody scene. He walked over to him, picking Jesus up off the grass and pulling him to his face, sniffing the air around him. Just as Jesus was coming to terms with his death—again—the large vampire dropped him to the grass and walked away, disappearing back into the darkness. With the large vampire gone, Jesus looked at Victus and Elowyn, each of them lying completely still. While he knew he should run away before they regained consciousness, Jesus couldn't shake the feeling that something wasn't quite right.

He approached Victus and Elowyn, slowly at first, looking for any signs of stirring. He stood over their bodies, looking down at them, and saw they were completely still. He nudged Elowyn with his foot, but she didn't respond. Crouching down over their faces, fearing he'd regret his decision not to run away, it became clear to Jesus that they were both dead. He knew, however, that if they were dead, their bodies should've melted away. He ran over to a nearby tree, breaking off a thick branch.

Opening Victus' shirt and exposing his pale chest, Jesus held the branch over his head, bringing it down as hard as he could into Victus' heart. He watched and waited for what he knew was supposed to happen, but Victus remained in one piece with the branch sticking out of his chest. While he couldn't make sense of it, the truth seemed pretty clear to Jesus. Not only were Victus and Elowyn dead, they were also human.

PART THREE

THE IMPORTANCE OF MAINTAINING ORDER

CHAPTER THIRTY-FIVE

DARK FORCES

Jesus sat together with his father on the couch watching a lucha libre program on television. He was one night removed from near death, one night removed from watching Victus and Elowyn die as humans, one night removed from seeing a vampire who was unlike any he'd ever seen before in his life. For now, all he wanted to do was put it all out of his mind—for a little while, at least—and spend the day with his father. The previous night Jesus slept in fits, unable to fully rest, his mind racing with what almost was. He tried and tried to work it all out, but none of it made any sense.

He'd arrived at his father's house the following morning, surprising him since it wasn't Wednesday and he had no laundry with him. Juan Miguel was sitting at the kitchen table with a cup of coffee and a plate of huevos a la Mexicana, reading the newspaper as he ate his breakfast. The sight of his father in the midst of his usual mundane routine was so welcoming to Jesus, such a pleasant reprieve from the horror of the previous couple of nights. He watched his father for nearly a minute before Juan Miguel noticed him standing there. The smile on his father's face when he finally did see him nearly brought Jesus to tears. Juan Miguel got up from the table, setting his newspaper down, and gave his son a long, tight hug. Jesus couldn't remember the last time he felt so safe.

Juan Miguel sat Jesus down at the table and insisted he have breakfast. He cooked him a fresh serving of huevos a la Mexicana and warmed him a couple of flour tortillas. The two of them ate together in silence, while Juan Miguel continued to read the newspaper. To anybody who didn't know what they were looking at, they'd have no idea how happy Juan Miguel was to have his boy with him that morning. When they finished eating, Juan Miguel invited Jesus to take a walk with him around the block, which was a habit he'd picked up over the last few years.

Their walk, much like their breakfast, happened in almost complete silence. The only sounds were the birds chirping overhead and the wind rustling through the trees. Despite the sun shining down and the sky a clear blue, Jesus couldn't quite forget the reality that safety and security would expire just as soon as night fell. He'd gotten so used to being the hunter that he never imagined finding himself in the situation he was in the previous night, just another unsuspecting human on the verge of being killed.

Before he'd left for his father's house that morning, Jesus packed a few vital weapons in his car—including his silver knife, a stake, and a jar of garlic jelly. After his experience with Victus and Elowyn, he never wanted to find himself vulnerable to a vampire ever again. Following their walk, Jesus and his father sat on the couch where they spent the rest of the day watching television together. First, they watched a double feature of *The Godfather* and *The Godfather: Part II* on AMC. Juan Miguel loved the plight of the Corleone family and watched the movies every time they were on television.

Jesus also enjoyed the *Godfather* movies and had seen them before with his father, but he always felt like they were smarter than him, that there were too many important details he wasn't quite picking up on. Juan Miguel had once told him that part of what made *The Godfather* so wonderful was that you could watch it and re-watch and every time discover something new that you'd never noticed before.

Juan Miguel made lunch for him and Jesus during *The Godfather: Part II*. Jesus found himself getting confused when Michael Corleone was in Cuba for his meeting with Hyman Roth. There was a celebration and Hyman Roth had a birthday cake and later Michael kissed his brother Fredo and told him that he'd broken his heart because he knew he'd betrayed him. Jesus asked his father questions about the movie while he prepared their lunch and Juan Miguel happily engaged him. Hours later, when the movies were over, Juan Miguel found a lucha libre program for them to watch.

He made a fresh pot of coffee and brought out a box of pan dulce, which he'd gotten that morning while it was still dark out. As Jesus ate the sweet bread and drank coffee with his father, he made a promise to himself that they'd have more days together just like this one.

"Did I ever tell you about El Santo?" his father asked.

"The greatest luchador ever?"

"Yes," his father said, "he was a true warrior. Did you know he once took his mask off on national television?"

"I didn't know that," Jesus said. "I thought that was frowned upon."

"It is," his father said. "He did it on a Mexican program called *Contrapunto*. One week later, at the age of sixty-six, El Santo died of a heart attack."

"Really?"

"Yes," his father said, "only I don't believe it was a heart attack."

"No?"

"There are dark forces in this world, mijito," his father said. "Very dark forces that we are better off not knowing about. I believe these dark forces disapproved of El Santo showing his face to the world, and it was they who took him away from us."

Juan Miguel's eyes grew heavy and it was clear he was ready for sleep, so Jesus stood up to leave. Juan Miguel told him he could stay, but Jesus knew it was more of a gesture than a request and that his father would be sound asleep within minutes of saying goodbye. They gave each other a long hug at the front door and Jesus' father kissed him on the cheek, telling him to be safe and to come back soon.

During his short drive home, Jesus got a phone call from Nick.

"George wants to meet you."

"Really?" Jesus asked. "What for?"

"Well," Nick said, "I told him about how you'd been hunting vampires with kitchen appliances and whatnot and he was pretty impressed. I also told him about the strange shit that went down with the vampire we killed."

"What does he want with me?"

"I'm not sure exactly," Nick said. "He didn't give me many details. He just asked me to deliver you, so I'm going to drive back to Rancho Cucamonga in the morning to pick you up."

"For Las Vegas?"

"Yeah," Nick said. "You up for it?"

"Absolutely."

"Great," Nick said. "See you in the morning, buddy."

Nick hung up and Jesus realized he'd forgotten to tell him about the large vampire who killed Victus and Elowyn. It was just as well, he figured, as he'd be able to tell him all about it in person in the morning. Jesus drove by Memorial Park on his way home, not expecting to find any trouble, when he saw a young woman being chased by what appeared to be a vampire. He pulled his car into the parking lot and opened up his glove compartment, removing the jar of garlic jelly, spreading it on his neck and face. He strapped the stake around his ankle and took his silver knife in hand before running into the darkness of Memorial Park, hoping he wouldn't be too late.

Jesus couldn't see the woman or the vampire, but he could hear their footsteps as they ran through the grass. He followed the sound of their footsteps until they went away. Jesus stopped, closing his eyes and listening, hoping to hear another sound that would lead him in the right direction. The sound that came next was not footsteps but a deep and agonizing moaning. Jesus began running again, following the moaning until he discovered the woman pressed up against a large tree with her arms wrapped around the trunk. The vampire was behind her, pinning her to the tree with his body, his face buried in her neck. Jesus ran towards them, and as he got closer, he realized the woman wasn't just any woman.

It was Olivia.

Emboldened by a blinding will to protect her, Jesus charged forward, silver knife in hand. As he got closer, he could see Olivia's eyes were closed, not even putting up a struggle. He prayed to God this didn't mean she was already dead, that he wasn't too late. When he was just a few feet away, he could see blood trickling down her neck, disappearing into her blouse. And when he was right behind them, Jesus lunged forward and, with all his might, swung his silver knife down, stabbing it deep into the vampire's neck.

CHAPTER THIRTY-SIX

THE VAMPIRE, THE HUNTER, AND THE GIRL

dam was so excited about his *Dracula* date with Olivia that he couldn't sleep and wound up staying awake a full twenty-four hours, cooped up in his house from sunup to sundown. As soon as night fell, he went to the store to pick up some food and drinks, figuring that would be the appropriate thing to do. He'd never hosted anyone at his home before, let alone a human, so he wasn't exactly sure if he needed to provide dinner supplies or coffee table snacks. Or maybe he was supposed to order take-out of some sort—pizza or Chinese, perhaps—while also providing chips or something. By the time he got home, Adam had more snack food in his kitchen than had ever been in there before.

He bought Coca-Cola, potato chips, onion dip, corn chips, salsa, pita chips, hummus, M&M's, Skittles, Junior Mints, popcorn, licorice, frozen pizza, a Dutch apple pie, and a six-pack of beer. He didn't know if Olivia even liked any of those things, but he figured it was best to just load up. There was a working refrigerator in his kitchen, which he'd bought himself because Cherry—while she was still around—didn't have any use for one. He rarely kept food in there, so it was practically empty before he filled it up with all of the snack food. As simple as it was, the sight of the refrigerator filled with food was comforting, nostalgic even.

Adam also made a point of putting light bulbs in all of his open sockets. He even went so far as to buy a lamp for the living room, plugging it in beside the couch. He also had a series of candles on the coffee table and the mantle, just in case Olivia preferred candlelight. He bought a vacuum and feather duster at Target and, just in case it became necessary, he got a can of air freshener for the bathroom. He wanted so desperately for everything to go well that he couldn't help but feel he was forgetting something—but, really, it was just the opposite. When Olivia arrived, she showed up with a large cheese pizza and a two-liter bottle of Coke.

"I wasn't sure if dinner was part of the deal," she said.

"I picked up a few things, as well."

Adam invited Olivia in, taking the pizza and soda off her hands and setting them on the kitchen table. On the coffee table, he'd set up a variety of snacks.

"You have a lovely home."

"Thank you."

"It's so normal."

"I'll take that as a compliment."

"I think I might've been expecting something more gothic without realizing it," Olivia said. "It's very cozy. Nice neighborhood, too. What's that park you have across the street?"

"Memorial Park," Adam said. "It's been here for as long as I have."

"I see you've got quite the entertainment setup, too."

"When you're here for eternity," Adam said, "you may as well do it in style. Go ahead and serve yourself, and I'll get *Dracula* set up."

Olivia served herself a couple of slices of pizza and asked Adam if he was going to have any, but he told her that he only planned on having candy. They settled onto his couch, cozying up beside one another, as Adam started *Dracula*. During the movie, he built up some courage and placed his hand on Olivia's thigh and was relieved when she didn't remove it. Not only didn't she remove it but she even placed her hand on top of his. Soon enough, their fingers were interlaced. Olivia rested her head on Adam's shoulder and her legs over his lap.

He could hardly pay attention to *Dracula* anymore, though he tried—sort of. He caught most of the beginning where Renfield was on his way to Count Dracula's castle in Transylvania, and the local village people warned him to stay away because they're afraid that vampires lived there. The last scene he sort of paid attention to was still near the beginning, when Dracula was in disguise and driving Renfield by horse and carriage to his castle.

"The sets look so dated," Olivia said. "How old is this movie?"

"It came out in 1931."

"Were you alive when it came out?"

Adam laughed.

"I'm not *that* old," he said. "It came out before I was born."

"It's so weird to think of you as being older than me," Olivia said. "We look the same age."

"By the time you were born," Adam said, "I was already grown and married."

"You were married?"

"Yup."

"Is your wife alive?"

"She is, yeah."

"Does she know anything about you being a vampire?"

"No," Adam said. "She hasn't seen me in thirty years. All she knows is I went to work one night and never came home."

"Did you know you were going to become a vampire that night?"

"No," Adam said. "I had no idea."

"How did it happen?"

"My maker was a vampire named Cherry," Adam said. "She fed

on me in the alley of the bowling alley during my break."

"Which bowling alley?"

"The same one you work at."

"Really?"

"Yeah," Adam said. "Cherry had been drifting or something, and so she wasn't near a feeding post. Or maybe she was and didn't care. I don't know. Either way, she attacked me, drinking my blood until I was on the verge of dying. She gave me a choice to live, so I took it. I had no idea it would be as a vampire."

"Do you regret your choice?"

"Sometimes," Adam said. "But, not tonight."

Olivia smiled.

They continued watching *Dracula* and Olivia tried to act interested, but she found it sort of boring. The sets were old, the acting was silly, and she'd never really been a fan of black and white movies. She did, however, enjoy Bela Lugosi, whom she found to be both exotic and sexy. She didn't find herself really engaged with the movie, though, until Dracula met Lucy and snuck into her room in the middle of the night to feed on her. Olivia found the scene to be dangerous and seductive, setting off a tingle between her legs.

"Your skin is cool," Olivia said, squeezing Adam's hand. "Is it uncomfortable?"

"Not really," he said. "Is it strange for you to feel?"

"No," Olivia said, "not at all. Do you prefer to be warm?"

"Yes," Adam said. "I spend a lot of time reading by the fireplace. Hot showers are nice, too. The best way to get warm, however, is by feeding."

Olivia smiled, straddling Adam's lap.

"Is that a hint?" she asked.

Olivia hardly recognized this version of herself. She wrapped her arms around Adam's neck, whispering in his ear.

"Hungry?" she asked.

Adam took hold of Olivia's hips, guiding them as she rocked

back and forth on his lap, grinding herself against him. She slowly slithered backwards off his lap, pushing herself up and walking to the front door.

"It's so dark out there," she said, opening it. "So scary."

Adam stood from the couch and walked towards her. He reached his hands out to hold her waist, but Olivia stepped outside before he could touch her.

"I sure hope there are no big, bad monsters out tonight."

Olivia took off running into Memorial Park, giggling to herself and looking back to see if Adam was chasing her. So far as she could tell, she was all alone. She continued running, weaving about the trees and past the picnic tables, slowing down when her heart rate soared and her lungs burned, eventually stopping. Breathing heavily, Olivia looked around the park for him, realizing for the first time just how dark it was in the middle of the night. She called out to him, her voice sounding so small amidst the empty stretch of grass and trees.

There was a rustling in the leaves somewhere behind her, caus-ing Olivia to turn and look. She saw nothing. A snapping of twigs sounded behind her, so she turned back the other way but still saw nothing. She called out again for Adam, this time out of genuine fear. When he didn't answer her, she started walking back towards his house. Before she got far, however, she realized she was com-pletely turned around and had no idea how to get back.

A voice sounded behind her.

"Going somewhere?"

Olivia screamed and began running without looking back. Two powerful arms wrapped around her, lifting her off her feet. She rec-ognized Adam's embrace almost immediately. He set Olivia down in front of a large tree, pinning her against it with the weight of his body. Tilting her head to the left, Olivia let her raven curls fall off her neck, exposing her skin. She could feel Adam grow excited behind her as she anticipated the penetration of his fangs. He licked Olivia's skin from shoulder to earlobe, causing a pulse of moisture between her legs. As Adam pushed his fangs inside of her, Olivia guided his hand down her pants, prompting him to massage her most sensitive parts.

She closed her eyes, letting the passion build, feeling herself approaching a climax like she'd never before experienced—when, all at once, she heard a dull thud, followed by Adam falling to the grass, screaming. When she turned around she saw Adam writhing in pain as he pulled a large knife from out of his neck, blood spraying from the wound. Adam pressed his hands to his neck, still screaming as his blood pulsed through his fingers. Because it was all happening so fast, it hadn't yet occurred to Olivia to wonder who'd stabbed him— then a hand settled on her arm.

"Are you hurt?"

She turned and saw Jesus.

"What are you doing here?" Olivia asked.

"I know you're probably very scared and confused," Jesus said, "but—"

Adam tackled him before he could finish his sentence. They grappled on the grass, Adam's blood getting all over Jesus, covering his skin, soaking his clothes. Olivia screamed, begging for them to stop, but neither listened. Adam could feel himself getting weaker as he lost blood, so, instinctively, he sunk his fangs into Jesus' neck, burning his lips on the garlic jelly. He screamed again as he rolled off of Jesus, holding one hand over his burning lips and the other over his bleeding neck.

Jesus pulled the stake from his ankle strap and leapt atop Adam's chest, pinning his arms beneath his knees. He lifted the stake over his head, preparing to bring it down into Adam's heart, when Olivia grabbed his wrist.

"No!" she yelled.

"You don't understand," Jesus said. "He's a vampire!"

"He's my friend!"

Jesus looked at her, confused and, in that moment, Adam pushed him off. Olivia helped Adam up, while Jesus got himself back to his feet. When Jesus saw them together, he recognized Adam's face.

"You're the guy from Corky's," he said. "You're a *vampire*?"

"You're a vampire *hunter*?" Adam asked.

"Wait," Olivia said, "what's going on?"

Jesus looked at her, knowing it was too late to lie. Then it dawned on him that Olivia already knew Adam was a vampire—and yet, she was still with him.

"Are you two a couple?" Jesus asked.

"No," Olivia said, "not really. We're sort of on a date, I guess."

"Did he attack you?"

"Absolutely not."

"So, why was he feeding on you?"

Olivia didn't know what to say.

Adam shoved Jesus with his bloody palm.

"Maybe you should mind your own business," he said.

"Maybe *you* shouldn't touch me for the rest of your short life," Jesus said.

They stepped towards each other, prepared to resume their fight, when Olivia moved between them, pressing her hands against their chests. There in the middle of Memorial Park, the three of them looked at one another—the vampire, the hunter, and the girl—each of them coming to the rapid realization that they were in the midst of a seriously peculiar love triangle.

Jesus looked at her.

"Do you want to be with him?"

Olivia was quiet.

Adam looked at her next.

"Do you want to be with *him*?"

Olivia was quiet still.

Adam and Jesus pushed towards each other one more time before Olivia held them back. It was more of a gesture, as they were each much stronger than her. It was only out of respect for Olivia's wishes that they let her keep them apart.

"Knock it off," she said, "please."

"He started it," Jesus said.

"I'll finish it, too," Adam said.

"Nobody is finishing anything," Olivia said. "Not tonight, anyway."

She began walking away.

"Where are you going?" Adam asked.

"I can't even begin to wrap my head around any of this," Olivia said, turning to face them, "so I'm going home. And I swear to God, if you two try to kill each other when I'm gone, I'll never speak to either of you again."

She marched off, disappearing into the darkness.

Jesus looked at Adam.

"She's the only reason I haven't killed you yet."

Adam stepped face to face with him.

"I'd love to watch you try."

"Trust me," Jesus said, "you will."

Out in the darkness, Olivia screamed. It wasn't exactly clear to either of them which direction the scream came from, so Adam ran one way and Jesus ran another.

CHAPTER THIRTY-SEVEN

ADAM

Adam held his hand over his neck, the pain throbbing as blood continued to pulse out.

Jesus looked at him.

"She's the only reason I haven't killed you yet."

Adam stepped face to face with him.

"I'd love to watch you try."

Fear lifted from Jesus' pores.

"Trust me," he said, "you will."

Out in the distance, Olivia screamed. It wasn't exactly clear which direction the scream came from, so Adam just started running. He wondered what Olivia saw in that hunter anyway. If somebody tried to kill Olivia, Adam wouldn't ask *her* not to seek vengeance. He still liked her, though—he just felt like they'd need to talk a few things out before moving forward with whatever it was they were on the verge of becoming. Before they could talk, however, he'd have to find her and, despite his superior vampire senses, Adam wasn't having any luck with that. Olivia's screaming stopped just as suddenly as it began. Her silence made finding her far more challenging.

A pair of swift and quiet footsteps approached Adam from

behind, concealing his vision with a burlap sack. Two powerful arms wrapped around him, and before Adam had a chance to struggle, a needle pricked his neck. In a matter of seconds, the whole world went away.

CHAPTER THIRTY-EIGHT

JESUS

Jesus looked at Adam.

"She's the only reason I haven't killed you yet."

He stood his ground as Adam got into his face.

"I'd love to watch you try."

"Trust me," Jesus said, "you will."

Out in the darkness, Olivia screamed. Jesus ran as fast as he could in the direction of her voice—or at least the direction he thought her voice was coming from. Whatever betrayal he was feeling at seeing her with a vampire was nothing compared to his overwhelming instinct to protect her. Olivia, of course, would have some explaining to do, but in order to ensure she got that opportunity, Jesus needed to make sure she was all right. He wondered how long she'd been fooling around with Adam and, more importantly, what she got out of being with a vampire. It was clear to Jesus that if she had any idea how dangerous vampires were, Olivia wouldn't have stopped him from killing Adam.

Olivia's screaming stopped just as suddenly as it began. Jesus really had no idea where he should be looking now. He didn't exactly want Olivia to scream again, but he hoped she would make some sort of noise to help lead him in the right direction. As his legs tired, Jesus stopped running a moment to gather himself—and, in that moment, a set of swift and quiet footsteps approached him from behind, concealing his vision with a burlap sack. Jesus tried to struggle, but a pair of powerful arms wrapped around his torso, holding him steady. A needle pricked his neck, and in a matter of seconds, the whole world went away.

CHAPTER THIRTY-NINE

OLIVIA

"Knock it off," Olivia said, "please."

"He started it," Jesus said.

"I'll finish it, too," Adam said.

"Nobody is finishing anything," Olivia said. "Not tonight, anyway."

She began walking away.

"Where are you going?" Adam asked.

"I can't even begin to wrap my head around any of this," Olivia said, turning to face them, "so I'm going home. And I swear to God, if you two try to kill each other when I'm gone, I'll never speak to either of you again."

Olivia marched through Memorial Park, through the darkness and through the trees, scarcely able to concentrate on where she was going. She never wanted to hurt Adam or Jesus, but now they appeared primed to hurt each other more than she ever could. Olivia knew that any harm they might eventually bring upon each other was ultimately going to be her fault, and she hated herself for that. Having two guys fighting over you seemed so much better when it happened in the movies or in television, but, as Olivia was finding out, real life was nothing like those fictional worlds.

Olivia stopped walking when she realized she had no idea where she was going. She surveyed the park, trying to figure out which direction to move in next. She never heard the set of swift and quiet footsteps approach her from behind. A pair of powerful arms wrapped around her, causing Olivia to scream. A burlap sack was thrown over her head, concealing her vision. She continued screaming until a needle pricked her neck, and in a matter of seconds, the whole world went away.

CHAPTER FORTY

THE ANTAGONIST

Somewhere beneath the earth, through the dirt and below the sewers, past the roots and beyond the rocks, was an underground palace with tall marble walls and elegant paintings, fireplaces the size of bedrooms and tuxedoed servants who moved swiftly and quietly. Of the hundreds and thousands of rooms within this palace, there was one particularly big room with walls so high the light turned black before it reached the ceiling. Like every other room in the palace, it had a fireplace and elegant paintings, but, *unlike* every other room, it had three chairs lined up side by side at its center, each respectively occupied by Adam, Jesus, and Olivia.

The three of them had burlap sacks over their heads, concealing their vision. One of the palace's swift and quiet servants entered the marble room through its exceedingly tall doors, approaching Adam, Jesus, and Olivia, removing the burlap sacks from their heads. As the trio looked around, trying to figure out where they were, the servant made a swift and quiet exit. While they could now see their surroundings, they couldn't move to explore them, as their arms and legs were strapped to their respective chairs.

"What's going on?" asked Jesus.

"This feels like a dream," said Olivia.

"This is no dream," said Adam.

Their voices echoed up the tall marble walls, trailing off somewhere in the darkness. The tall doors opened again and another tuxedoed servant entered the room with such swift quietude that he seemed almost to float as he walked to the fireplace, which was burning logs the size of full-grown trees. The servant pushed a button on the marble wall beside the fireplace and, in an instant, the fire inside doubled in size, sending a wave of heat through the air.

"Excuse me," said Olivia to the servant, "what's going on?"

The servant, however, ignored Olivia and her question before exiting the tall marble room. Once again alone, Adam, Jesus, and Olivia sat silently, each of them equally confused as to where they were and, more importantly, why they were there together. The tall doors opened once again and a long red rug unrolled towards the trio, stopping at their feet. A couple dozen tuxedoed servants poured through the open doors, lining up shoulder to shoulder on either side of the red rug. From the darkness of the open doors, a methodical clicking of heels sounded, growing louder and louder, until a tall, handsome figure appeared in the doorway. The servants all dropped to one knee, bowing their heads as the handsome figure passed, walking down the long red rug.

This figure—who was, in fact, their captor—wore a dark suit with a red tie. His black hair was slick and shiny, combed tight over his scalp, displaying a pointed widow's peak. His skin was pale, his cheeks sharp. His lips were rosy and his teeth white, each of them perfectly straight, not a molar out of place. When the tall, handsome figure reached the end of the rug, four more of his servants entered the marble room with a large throne made of solid gold and red velvet, setting it down behind him. Without looking back, the handsome figure sat down. He looked over each of his guests—Adam, Jesus, and Olivia—smiling as he crossed his legs, setting his hands in his lap. All at once, the servants poured out of the tall marble room, shutting the doors behind them, leaving their master alone with his guests.

"Hello," he said. "Welcome to my home. I am Dracula."

Adam, Jesus, and Olivia were silent. They saw the tailored suit and the unblemished skin, the sharp nose and the deep, dark eyes, but they weren't sure if they believed what they'd just heard.

"I know," Dracula said, "you're not sure if you believe what you've just heard. But, sometimes, more often than you might imagine, fairytales are true. Not that I think of myself as a fairytale, mind you. I simply use it as an example to help the three of you process what I can only imagine has been a strange and wholly unfamiliar set of experiences."

Silence.

"You might've already figured out that I know exactly who the three of you are," Dracula said, "but, in the interest of breaking the ice, as well as general etiquette, I'd like for you all to introduce yourselves."

Adam, Jesus, and Olivia looked at each other, but none of them spoke.

"Names are fine for now. Best to start with you, my dear," Dracula told Olivia, "as you and I will be spending a bit of time together from this point forward."

This got Jesus' attention.

"What's that supposed to mean?"

"He speaks," Dracula said. "I'm happy to finally hear your voice, only you've spoken out of turn. I'll get to you soon enough, but for now I'd like to hear from the young lady. Dear?"

Olivia looked at Dracula, hesitating a moment before responding.

"My name is Olivia."

"Indeed it is," Dracula said. "It's a pleasure to meet you."

He turned his attention now to Adam.

"And you, my child," Dracula asked, "what's your name?"

"Adam."

"You're quite the youngster," Dracula said. "I can only hope that helps explain your actions as of late. But, I'm getting ahead of myself."

He turned his attention to Jesus.

"And you," Dracula said, "please introduce yourself."

"I'm Jesus."

"I could've sworn your name was longer than that."

"My full name is Jesus Hector Guerrero."

"No," Dracula said, "that's not it. You have a moniker, no? Sort of a professional nickname. I believe it's Jesus the Mexican Vampire Hunter."

Silence.

"No need to be modest on my account," Dracula said. "It's no secret to anybody in this room that you're a vampire hunter. I do have to say, though, it's a very specific name. Do you only hunt Mexican vampires?"

"No."

"So, you hunt vampires of all nationalities?"

"I guess so."

"Well then," Dracula said, "you might want to consider revising your title. You see, the word 'Mexican,' which is serving as the modifier in your moniker, is not close enough to the subject, which, in your case, is the name 'Jesus.' I'd go with Jesus the Vampire Hunter of Mexican Descent. It's much clearer and, I suspect, much closer to what you're going for."

Silence.

"It's just an idea," Dracula said. "I'm not married to it."

More silence.

"I'm sensing some tension in the air," Dracula said. "Is it the bindings? It's the bindings, isn't it?"

Dracula clapped his hands, prompting a set of tuxedoed servants to enter the tall marble room, stopping beside his throne. He whispered a brief order, at which point the servants moved behind Adam, Olivia, and Jesus, unfastening their wrists and ankles before exiting the room.

"So, here we are," Dracula said. "We've exchanged names and

general pleasantries, which was nice. But, there's still the looming question of what you're all doing here. The first thing I can tell you is that none of your lives will ever be the same from this moment forward. Intriguing, yes?"

Silence.

"I'll take that as a yes," Dracula said. "In the meantime, let me take a few moments to properly introduce myself. I've no doubt you've heard my name before, and I suspect you've seen representations of my likeness on film and television. Perhaps you've even read the book that bears my name. I can't say I bear *no* resemblance to the myth of Dracula you've come to know, but I can say I'm a bit more complex than the figure who's been romanticized in cinema and literature for so many years. I am, of course, a vampire. I am not the *first* vampire in the history of existence. There were many, many vampires before me, all through the beginning of time, evolving, not unlike humans, forming into the general species that you all have come to know. As such, I am the head vampire, the king, as it were—though I hesitate to use that title, as it's a little embarrassing. My role is to rule over the vampire population, making sure everything runs as it should, enforcing laws that have been in place for longer than any of us in this room have been alive. Which, not coincidentally, is why the three of you are here. Pardon me just a moment."

Dracula clapped his hands, and a single servant entered through the doors. He gave the servant a quiet order before turning to Adam, Jesus, and Olivia.

"Can I get you three anything?" Dracula asked. "A beverage? Some food perhaps?"

They all three shook their heads, no.

"Very well," Dracula said. "If any of you change your mind, just let me know."

The servant left the tall marble room, returning moments later with a silver platter holding a wine glass half-full with blood. Lifting the glass from the platter, Dracula nodded his appreciation to the servant before excusing him. He sipped from the glass before setting it down on the arm of his throne. A blood mustache formed over his lip, which he promptly licked away.

"The vampire community has recently entered a state of unrest," Dracula said. "Adam, as the only vampire amongst you, would be the only one who might know what I'm talking about. So, let me ask you, Adam, do you know what unrest I speak of?"

"No."

"That's good," Dracula said. "Adam's oblivion is a testament to my efforts to keep this unrest under control. Jesus, ironically enough, *does* know something about it—he just doesn't realize it yet. As for you, Olivia, you know as much as I would expect you or any other human to know, which is nothing. That's the way it should be, the way it's meant to be. One of the primary duties of any leader is to keep his followers ignorant of the truly scary threats that compromise their safety. Unfortunately, if the unrest I speak of continues to grow out of control, there will soon be little I can do to keep it quiet. And so, that is why the three of you are here."

Dracula sipped from his glass.

"There is a vampire currently roaming about the Inland Empire who is bigger and stronger than any vampire walking the planet. He is, quite literally, a freak of nature. We call him Frank. As it is with vampires, Frank feeds on blood. Unfortunately, he has a taste for *vampire* blood. And, if that weren't concerning enough, Frank has the effect of turning vampires into humans once he's fed from them. I don't pretend to know how or why it happens, so I can't give you any information on that, not that it would help matters much. By the time the vampires he's fed on become human, they're already dead, which is just as well, because, really, no vampire in their right mind would want to live a life shackled by the chains of mortality. Now, the three of you are probably wondering what any of this information has to do with you."

Silence.

"It's simple, really," Dracula said. "I need Frank to be taken care of, and I'm charging the two of you—Adam and Jesus—with the task of killing him. More on that in a moment."

Dracula clapped his hands and two tuxedoed servants entered the room, approaching Olivia. One of the servants reached for her hand, but Olivia snatched it away.

"Please," Dracula said, "don't be rude."

The servant again reached out for her hand and this time Olivia let him have it. He led her to Dracula's side, while the other servant set her chair beside the throne.

"Have a seat, my dear."

Olivia did as she was told.

"Jesus," Dracula said, "let me ask you a question. Between the two of us, you and I, who is the bad guy?"

Jesus said nothing.

"Don't be afraid to answer," Dracula said. "I'm not trying to trick you into saying something you'll regret. Just give me your most honest answer. Which of us, in your opinion, is the bad guy?"

"You are."

Dracula smiled.

"That's what I imagined you'd say. I, in turn, view *you* as the bad guy," he said. "Olivia, my dear, you're a writer, yes?"

"Sort of."

"What's the literary term for a bad guy?"

"The antagonist?"

"Yes, thank you," Dracula said. "The antagonist. So, in the world as *you* see it, Jesus, I am the antagonist, yes?"

Jesus nodded.

"But, not just me," Dracula said. "*All* vampires, in your worldview, are antagonists. Correct?"

"Yes."

"And why, Jesus, do you see vampires as antagonists?"

Silence.

"It's okay, really," Dracula said. "If it makes you feel better, you have my word that nothing you say will result in me or any of my servants inflicting any physical, mental, or emotional harm to you or anybody you love. Does that help?"

"I guess."

"Good," Dracula said. "Now, tell me, why do you see vampires as antagonists?"

"You're killers."

"That's precisely what I imagined you might say," Dracula said. "Of course, I can say the exact same thing about you."

"It's not the same."

"Before we agree to disagree," Dracula said, "I'd like to posit an argument to help illustrate why, with all due respect, you're wrong. It might surprise you to learn that I read comic books. I'm not a fanatic, mind you, but I enjoy them. My favorite comic book superhero has always been Superman. Did you know I once fought Superman? Not in real life, of course. He's make-believe. I fought him in the comics. I read all about it in February of 1980 in *Superman*, volume one, number three hundred forty-four, an issue titled 'The Monsters among Us,' with me and Frankenstein's monster on the cover—or, you know, what cover artist José Luis García-López imagined we looked like. We fought again in May of 2002 in *Superman*, volume two, number one hundred eighty in an issue titled 'The House of Dracula,' but, in that instance, cover artist Ed McGuinness didn't see fit to put me on the cover but rather a picture of Superman as a vampire, which is just a ludicrous idea. The fact that he gets his power from the yellow sun alone would make that a dubious proposition at best."

Silence.

"But, I digress. While it was flattering to see myself in the pages of *Superman*, my presence was never meant as anything more than a novelty. Superman, you see, already has an antagonist. A good one, too. Do you know who Superman's antagonist is?"

Jesus shrugged.

"Oh, come now," Dracula said. "Even if you don't read comic books, you surely know who Superman's archrival is, no?"

"Lex Luthor?"

"Very good," Dracula said. "And, as antagonists go, Lex Luthor is right up there with the very best. He's bright and articulate, charming in his own devious way, clever, and not without a sense of humor. But, more than anything else, he's human. Superman, on the other hand, despite any anatomical evidence to the contrary, is *not* human. His given name is Kal-El and he's an alien from the planet Krypton. Earth is merely his adopted home. Despite not being of this planet, Superman is charged with the duty of protecting humans. And, more times than not, he must protect humans from themselves."

Dracula paused, sipping from his glass.

"Superman," he continued, "on his planet of Krypton, lived briefly under the red sun, which made him no more powerful than any human here on Earth. On Earth, however, living under the yellow sun gives him amazing powers, such as super strength, flight, and x-ray vision. Because Lex Luthor is human, he must rely on his intellect and ingenuity in order to do battle with Superman. Several times along the way, Lex Luthor has created weapons and gadgets to counter Superman's super powers. Vampires, as you well know, have amazing powers, sort of like Superman. And you, Jesus, being human, cannot match a vampire's powers naturally, so, like Lex Luthor, you rely on your intellect, creating weapons and gadgets to counter our abilities. So, as you yourself acknowledged that Lex Luthor is Superman's antagonist, I claim that you are *my* antagonist. You, Jesus, are the bad guy."

"But, it's not the same," Jesus said. "I kill to protect people. Vampires kill because they're evil."

"A vampire killing a human is no more malicious than a human killing a cow," Dracula said. "It's simply how you survive. Of course, humans, if they so desired, could survive without killing other living beings. Vampires, unfortunately for your kind, are not afforded this same luxury. We *have* to feed on human blood or we'll die. When a great white shark eats a baby sea lion, it is not acting out of malice. Despite its robust frame and intimidating teeth, the great white shark is not a villain. It's just a fish surviving in its environment. It's the natural order of things."

Dracula paused, sipping from his glass.

"Anywho," he said, "I don't want to get too far away from my original point. You're a vampire hunter, Jesus. You kill my kind. And yet, here you are, sitting before me, healthy and unharmed. Why do you suppose that is?"

Jesus shrugged.

"Do you think it's because I'm incapable of killing you?"

Silence.

"Do you think I didn't know what you were doing before we met here tonight?"

More silence.

"Do you read books, Jesus?"

"Not really."

"So, you've probably never read the novel *Dracula*."

Jesus shook his head, no.

"In *Dracula*, there's a character named Renfield who acts as my dutiful servant. Renfield has a peculiar appetite for, amongst other things, spiders. Bram Stoker, the author of *Dracula*, wanted readers to find this creepy, which, by and large, they do. The reason he knew it would work is because humans, generally speaking, have a natural fear of spiders. Despite their comparatively minuscule size, most humans feel threatened by them. What the more enlightened of your kind know is that spiders serve a very practical purpose in the natural order. They eat insects, most notably flies. Flies, I'm sure I don't have to tell you, can be quite a nuisance, yes? Can you imagine how awful it would be to live in a world filled with flies? You don't have to worry about that, however, because you are fortunate enough to share your natural environment with spiders. So, while most humans don't like spiders, they might take comfort in the realization that spiders serve a purpose. You, Jesus, are a spider in my world."

Dracula paused, sipping from his glass.

"Most vampires," he said, "like Adam here, don't like you. But, the more enlightened vampires, like myself, understand that you serve a purpose. You see, Jesus, the only reason you kill vampires is because I let you do it. And do you know why?"

Jesus shook his head, no.

"There are so many people on this planet," Dracula said, "billions in fact. Vampires are turning humans every day—even now, as I speak, it's happening all throughout the world. And that's good, as I want the vampire population to exist in healthy numbers. Unlike humans, however, I actually worry about the overpopulation of my species. In fact, if it weren't for vampires, humans would have reached overcapacity here on Earth a long, long time ago. But, while billions of humans represent a seemingly infinite supply of blood, that supply shrinks dramatically if too many humans are turned into vampires. Left unchecked, this would eventually result in a world with too many vampires and not enough humans."

Dracula paused, sipping from his glass.

"Just as a spider unwittingly controls the population of flies," he said, "you, Jesus, and every other hunter in the world, unwittingly help to control the population of vampires. As it is with the spider, your actions actually make the world more comfortable to live in. So, thank you."

Silence.

"You must now be wondering why I have bothered to tell you any of this," Dracula said. "What's the point, right? Well, the point is this. You owe me. And today, Jesus, I've decided to collect on your debt."

"What debt?"

"Have you listened to nothing I've just said?" Dracula asked. "You kill vampires and, despite that, I let you live. While I might tolerate your existence, because you provide a menial service, the world as it exists will go on just fine with one less hunter. I can squash you beneath my heel anytime I choose, but, up until now, I've chosen not to. So, the debt you owe me is your life, and the time has come for you to pay me back."

Silence.

"The way you will pay your debt is by hunting and killing Frank," Dracula said, "or, more importantly, you must die trying."

"Absolutely not."

"I had a feeling you would say that," Dracula said. "And I have a feeling I know why, too, but go ahead and explain yourself. Tell me why you will absolutely not try to hunt and kill Frank—or die trying."

"I've seen him."

"And what did you see him do?"

"I watched him kill two vampires," Jesus said. "It was easy for him. They couldn't do anything to stop him. I know that vampires are stronger than me and faster than me, so if they couldn't stop him, then there's nothing I can do to stop him. What I think is you just want me dead and you want this monster to kill me. I'm not interested in playing your game. So, if you want me dead, you'll have to kill me yourself."

Dracula smiled.

"That was a very nice speech," he said. "But, let me be clear about something. I have no intention of killing you. There will, however, be consequences if you choose *not* to hunt and kill Frank—or die trying. But, I'm getting ahead of myself. We'll get to that soon enough."

Dracula turned his attention to Adam.

"How's your neck?"

Adam touched his fingers to where Jesus stabbed him.

"Better," he said.

"That's good," Dracula said. "Your clothes, however, were irredeemably ruined. I took the liberty of having my servants dispose of them and dress you in something more presentable."

Adam looked at his clothes for the first time since having the burlap sack removed from his head. He was indeed wearing completely different clothes than he'd had on earlier in the night.

"Thank you."

"No problem," Dracula said. "I take care of my own. How old are you?"

"Thirty."

"Practically a toddler," Dracula said, "still so close to your human life. It's no wonder, then, that you were so willing to break the laws of vampire society by engaging in extensive socializing with Olivia. When you spent time with Olivia, eating pie and revealing the secrets of our kind, you knew you were breaking the law, didn't you?"

Silence.

"Listen," Dracula said, "as I did with Jesus, I promise not to harm you for anything you say, so please feel obliged to speak openly and honestly with me. Did you know you were breaking the law by socializing with Olivia?"

"Yes."

"And, yet, you did so willingly?"

"Yes."

"Have you ever made a vampire, Adam?"

"No."

"Did you have any children in your human life?"

"I have a son."

"What do you remember about him as a child?"

"I've never met my son."

"Why not?"

"He was born after I was turned."

"Ironic, isn't it?" Dracula said. "For your human son, you won't break the law. But, for Olivia, a woman you've known only for a few weeks, you will. But, I digress. If you'd *had* the opportunity to raise your son, one very important lesson you would've learned is that it's very difficult to teach a child with words the importance of maintaining order. The only way a child can truly feel the gravity of order is to break the rules they've been told not to break, and following that, they must suffer the consequences. So long as the consequence is severe enough, the memory of it will be implanted in that child's mind for the rest of his or her life. As I am the ruler of all vampires, you, Adam, are like my child. And you've broken the rules. By your own admission, you knew the rules existed, but you broke them anyway. The only reason you would break the rules knowingly is because you have no fear of the consequences. Therefore, it is incumbent upon me to inflict a punishment on you that is so severe it will be implanted in your mind for the rest of your life."

Dracula paused, sipping from his glass.

"So," he said, "what do you think would be an appropriately severe punishment?"

Silence.

"Come on," Dracula said, "humor me."

"I don't know."

"Assume you were in my position," Dracula said, "and the vampire in question was *not* you, what would you do?"

"I truly don't know."

"No?"

"No."

"Well, you and I differ in that respect," Dracula said, "because I know exactly what I would do. I'm going to order you to hunt and kill Frank—or die trying."

Silence.

"But, don't worry," Dracula said, "you don't have to hunt for Frank alone. You will do so with Jesus. The two of you are going to work as a team, like Batman and Robin. What do you think about that?"

Silence.

"Please, don't get quiet on me again," Dracula said. "It's rude. Now, what do you think of what I've just told you?"

"I understand," Adam said.

"Good," Dracula said. "And you, Jesus? What do you think?"

"You know what I think," Jesus said. "If you want me dead, you'll have to kill me yourself."

"About that," Dracula said, "so far as I'm concerned, you are well within your rights to refuse. But, before you make your final decision, would you like to know the consequences of that choice?"

Jesus nodded.

"If you choose *not* to hunt and kill Frank—or die trying," Dracula said, "then I'm going to kill Olivia."

Olivia shrieked.

"It's nothing personal, my dear," Dracula said.

"She has nothing to do with this," Jesus said.

"Oh, but she has everything to do with this," Dracula said. "But, just so we're clear, as long as you boys hunt and kill Frank—or die trying—then Olivia lives. But, if you choose *not* to, then she dies. And, just for good measure, I'll make you both watch."

"You said we have to hunt and kill Frank or die trying," Jesus said. "What if we hunt him and try to kill him, but we don't die trying. Will you let us live?"

"In your hypothetical scenario," Dracula said, "does Frank survive?"

"Yes."

"In that case," Dracula said, "you will not have satisfied your obligation and Olivia will die."

"If all you want is for us to die," Jesus said, "why are you bothering with any of this?"

"Because," Dracula said, "I want to see that Frank is killed."

"If you want Frank killed," Jesus said, "why are you asking us to do it? You've got to have better options."

"Oh, of course I have better options," Dracula said. "You, Jesus, are neither my first nor my best recruit. Better hunters than you sat before me just like this, and we had a very similar discussion to the one you and I are having, and all of them died when they tried to kill Frank. So, with all due respect to your hypothetical scenario in which nobody dies, if and when you engage Frank in battle, I don't expect it'll result in a draw."

"So, I was right," Jesus said. "You just want me dead."

"No," Dracula said, "I want you to kill Frank. But, I'll settle for your death."

Silence.

"I've laid out the circumstances of your new reality," Dracula said. "Adam has already given me his answer, but now I wait for yours, Jesus. Either you both agree to work together in an effort to hunt and kill Frank or Olivia dies. So, what'll it be?"

Jesus looked at Olivia. She was shaking, on the verge of tears.

"You don't have to do this," she said.

Jesus nodded.

"Yes," he said. "I do."

Dracula smiled.

"So, you'll do it?"

"Yes."

"Splendid!"

"But," Jesus said, "only if you swear not to hurt Olivia."

"You have my word."

"How do I know I can trust you?"

"That's simple," Dracula said. "You're the antagonist, not me. I'm the good guy."

Dracula clapped his hands and several tuxedoed servants entered the tall marble room, two of whom stood behind Adam and Jesus, placing burlap sacks over their heads.

"Before I forget," Dracula said, "you only have seven days to hunt and kill Frank—or die trying. If in one week's time you've failed to do so, then I'll kill all three of you."

TO BE CONTINUED IN...

THE VAMPIRE AND THE HUNTER TRILOGY: BOOK TWO
THE VAMPIRE, THE HUNTER,
and the Witch
MARTIN LASTRAPES

NOW WHAT?!

Thanks so much for reading *The Vampire, the Hunter, and the Girl*. If you enjoyed your reading experience I hope you might leave a short review. Reader reviews from good folks like yourself are like gold for authors, so it'd mean a whole lot to me if you could.

Mailing List

Want to be the first to find out when *The Vampire, the Hunter, and the Witch* is released? Just sign up for my mailing list here:

MartinLastrapes.com/contact

I'll send you an email just as soon as *The Vampire, the Hunter, and the Witch* is published! You'll also receive news and updates regarding events, giveaways, and all of my upcoming books and projects!

Buy My Books

Looking for a fast and convenient spot to shop for all of my books? Well, all you have to do is go to the shop page of my official website here:

MartinLastrapes.com/shop

Podcast

Be sure to listen to *The Martin Lastrapes Show Podcast Hour* on iTunes or on the official website:

MartinLastrapesShow.com

The Martin Lastrapes Show Podcast Hour is the show that may or may not be an hour long, based on your perception of time and how much I've got to say! It's both a silly and earnest look into my mind as I talk about writing, publishing, and most anything else I find interesting.

Social Media

Keep in touch with me at any of the following outlets:

- **Twitter: @MartinLastrapes**
- **Facebook: Facebook.com/MartinLastrapes**
- **Goodreads: Goodreads.com/MartinLastrapes**
- **Instagram: Instagram.com/MartinLastrapes**

ABOUT THE AUTHOR

MARTIN LASTRAPES is a bestselling and award-winning novelist. He is also the host of *The Martin Lastrapes Show Podcast Hour.* He studied at Cal State San Bernardino, where he earned a Bachelor's Degree in English and a Master's Degree in Composition. This is his second novel.

9 780985 704322